KAY LANGDALE

The Comfort of Others

HODDER

First published in Great Britain in 2016 by Hodder & Stoughton
An Hachette UK company

First published in paperback in 2017

1

A CIP catalogue record for this title is available from the British
Library

Paperback ISBN 978 1 473 61842 8
Ebook ISBN 978 1 473 61839 8

Printed and bound by CPI Group (UK) Ltd, Croydon, CR0 4YY

Hodder & Stoughton policy is to use papers that are natural,
renewable and recyclable products and made from wood grown in
sustainable forests. The logging and manufacturing processes are
expected to conform to the environmental regulations of the country
of origin.

Hodder & Stoughton Ltd
Carmelite House
50 Victoria Embankment
London EC4Y 0DZ

www.hodder.co.uk

Praise for *Away From You*

'This haunting and beautifully written novel about love will linger in your mind long after you've turned the final, satisfying page' Lucy Dillon, author of *A Hundred Pieces of Me*

'Langdale's psychological intelligence informs every angle of a thoroughly contemporary tragedy' *The Times*

'A compelling exploration of the nature of grief . . . a moving tale of motherhood and morality' *Oxford Times*

'Langdale is a wonderful writer, plots beautifully and is brilliant at showing her characters' inner worlds' *Daily Mail*

Praise for *Her Giant Octopus Moment*

'Readable, poignant . . . the author's skill is to woo the reader into empathising with conflicting viewpoints' *The Sunday Times*

'Thought-provoking' ★★★★★ *Woman's Own*

'An endearing child-heroine and a controversial moral question make *Her Giant Octopus Moment* a must-read' *Good Housekeeping*

'Poignant novel about parenthood' *Woman & Home*

'A poignant, at times funny, at times saddening book about morals and motherhood' *Tatler Ireland*

'The sympathetic understanding of [Langdale's] characters, the even-handed exposition of different types of mothering and the b⎯⎯⎯⎯⎯⎯⎯⎯⎯⎯⎯⎯⎯ther

About the Author

Kay Langdale is the author of six novels: *The Comfort of Others*, *Away From You*, *Choose Me*, *Her Giant Octopus Moment*, *What the Heart Knows* (Rowohlt, Germany) and *Redemption* (Transita; published as *If Not Love* by Thomas Dunne Books). Visit Kay's website at www.kaylangdale.com and follow her on Twitter: @KayLangdale.

For Rachel, Simeon, Seb and Rosa, with love.

Simple, though not easy
this waiting without hunger in the near dark
for what you may be about to receive.

From *Grace*, by Esther Morgan

I

Max

An author came into school at the end of last term and he said everyone was a writer. 'E-ve-ry-one of you,' he said, with his finger pointing at us in turn as we sat in a semicircle on the mat around him. Mrs Winters didn't look convinced. She's been trying to get Johnny Parsons to write a full sentence for most of Year Six. The man was wearing a red neckerchief with black whirls on it, and a jacket the colour of rust. I'm telling you that because he said writers are noticers, and that was what I noticed; the whirls, like busy tadpoles, the bright red of the neckerchief, and the brown of his jacket. I'd clocked them before he said the noticing part, so it felt like a sign that what he was saying about being a writer might actually be true, if not for Johnny Parsons then for me.

The fly in the ointment is that I'm left-handed. Also not such a good speller, although I always give it my best shot. Most of the time I can hardly see what I'm writing. 'That's one long spidery trail of smudginess,' is what Mrs Winters said about my topic on Martin Luther King. I think she might have a dream in which she has a class of completely different children.

My final primary school report said I am not a confident speller. But I am a confident speaker. My school report didn't say that, but it's true. My mum says I'm a Chatty Cathy. I pointed out to her that I am a boy, so should be Chatty Charlie, but she said that Charlie's not my name either so one thing wrong is as good as another. I think there's quite a big difference, but if I said so my mum would just wave her hand, her polished nails all shiny like ice cubes, and my words would bounce right off them. Anyway, it's down to my mum that I'm writing this – although I'm not actually writing it. Here's the bang – I'm speaking it, into the little Dictaphone machine she used to keep in the Powder Room.

The Powder Room is next to the kitchen in our house where just the two of us live. It is her *place of work* (that's what she calls it) where people come and have treatments. Facials, waxing, manicures, pedicures, makeovers, fake tans. All kinds of stuff goes on in that room. She painted the walls lilac, which is *fresh*. *Fresh* is one of her favourite words, and also *cute*. And when she likes clothes she says 'oh that's such an easy piece'. I'm not sure whether a difficult piece is one that's hard to wear or hard to look at. She also says 'whaddyaknow' a lot, usually when I tell her something I've done at school. It doesn't actually make sense when she says it, because obviously what I know is what I've just told her.

She had the Dictaphone because she found it handy to help her keep a list of what she needed to get from the wholesalers. When she said I could have it, I played it back and there were long bits of silence and then her voice sounding a bit annoyed saying *wax strips,* then *shellac remover,* and *eyelash tint; brown.* She also said *smoky eyes palette,* but then, a few seconds later *no bother, found it.*

I know most of the words for the stuff she uses. That's because sometimes, when she has a client, the room gets a bit hot (even though it's meant to be *fresh* because of the lilac) and so she opens the door just a crack and calls me. ('Coo-eee,' she says, which apparently doesn't bother someone lying with cotton pads on their eyes waiting for an eyelash tint to take). I come in with the steps and very quietly flip them out, scoot up them and push the Velux open. 'Here's my little helper' is what she always says if the woman's eyes are open, like if they're having their nails done and are popping them under the UV light. Sometimes they smile at me, sometimes they just nod. Most of the time they're just looking at themselves in the magnifying mirror on the desk, and tugging at their wrinkles or smoothing their lips.

Mum said I could have the Dictaphone a little while ago. I hadn't thought of a use for it until now, the first week of the summer holidays. I don't actually have anything to order which isn't delivered with the Tesco shop on a Wednesday night, but then today I was thinking about the author telling us we were all writers, and I thought hey presto, I get to do all my noticing with none of the spelling or my left hand smudging everything. I'm just going to speak it as I see it. Even Mrs Winters couldn't find fault with that. And I might look like a bit of a secret agent as well. Maybe even an on-the-spot-reporter. That's cooler than being a regular writer.

Mum's calling me now – it's time for my supper. I just flicked the Dictaphone off for a moment and when I turned it back on it was her voice saying *emery boards*. I'm not sure what I should say when I come to the end of a chapter. I'm going to call it a chapter even if it's not written down. For our history topic on the First World War, Mrs Winters took us to a museum which had an exhibition of people's stuff from that time. Jam pots they'd opened the day war was declared, things you'd never think were history. There was a tape recorder with old people's wobbly voices telling their memories. 'These are oral histories,' the guide said, 'and just as important as anything written down.' Cheers to that. So this is *my* oral history, spoken into my mum's Dictaphone which she doesn't want anymore because now she does her ordering on an app on her iPhone.

Maybe when I finish a chapter I should say Roger, or Over and Out? Or perhaps you don't say that if you're just talking to yourself.

2

Max

'Bring all your intelligence to bear on your beginning.' The author said that, and then he said, 'That means using all your smarts at the start.' I think he knows what he's talking about. Mrs Winters had lined nine of his books up along the library table. That's a lot of beginnings.

My beginning is a bit misty; I think that's probably the best word for it. My mum went with some friends on a holiday to Kavos in Greece and she came back with me; not straight away but nine months later, obviously. She doesn't really talk about it; but once, when I was doing a topic on Greek Gods in Year Five, she said, 'Beware of Greeks bearing gifts.' I wasn't sure what she meant. 'Gifts' sound like a good thing, but not so much if you remember 'beware'. I only properly understood it when my teacher explained about the wooden horse and the siege of Troy. Then, when I thought about it some more, I wondered whether it was me or my dad who jumped out and gave her a shock. Maybe she was a little bit beware of us both. Either way, she's never said anything else about it so I've no idea whether my dad is actually a surprising Greek or whether she met another English person in Kavos. My only clue is that my grandad, who's dead now, referred to him once as 'bloody Zorba', but he always had a roundabout way of talking so I shouldn't bank on that. When he was dying he took my hand, his face all purply-blue, and said,

'I am a busted flush.' I found out on Google that that's actually a term from playing poker, so you can see why I'm not properly going with Zorba. After he died, my grandma moved to Florida and met a different man at a golf club. Mum says she's become addicted to plastic surgery. When she Skypes, her face hardly moves at all, and her top lip looks as if it reaches right back to her ears. When she leans forward and says 'Say hi to Grandma', it's quite spooky and I feel a little bit sick. Mum says that that's not really beauty, and she should know, what with spending her entire working life on it: *She'd have been better with some serum, and some tinted moisturiser applied with a brush. Setting powder to finish.*

I have very pale skin, and my hair is what Mum calls dishwater blonde. She says I might have to address that one day. Dishwater blonde's not very Greek is it? If he was Greek I think I might be a little darker. Sometimes, when there's an unexpected knock on the door, I think I'm going to open it and he'll be standing there, all tanned and dark-haired like the man who fries and scoops the chips in the Mediterranean Fish Bar and he'll say *yassou* – which I also Googled and is hello in Greek – and boom, I'll know who my dad is. So far there's no *yassou* in sight.

I don't think she's completely given up on the man front, although she's going through a quiet period now. She says a glass of Pinot Grigio and watching *Downton Abbey* is a better bet. A while ago she did something called speed dating. She said the best thing about it was that she wasn't out for long so the baby-sitting was cheap. Also, apparently it's cheaper if you go to the sitter's house rather than have them come to yours. So she used to walk me round the corner to Mrs Philips' house which was also by the bus stop making it a *win–win*. Mrs Philips' husband died of a stroke suddenly and she says she'll be non-stop grieving now. I don't think she's planning on a new man and some plastic surgery. When I used to go round, she mostly sat in her armchair with the TV turned off and said 'dearie me' and sighed over and over and it felt like all the dearie mes were flumping onto the carpet like soft, wet tissues. The only thing that made her happy was buttered brazils. She'd crunch them between her teeth, little splinters of caramel spraying out, and she'd rustle the box at me – which was lined with red tissue paper – and say 'help yourself chum, help yourself', but I never did. I think it was also because of the budgie. She had a budgie, Horace, whose cage was next to her armchair, and while she was eating buttered brazils he'd be nibbling away like crazy on a bit of cuttlefish or some seeds and the whole room contained so much crunching I felt one of us should be sitting with a perfectly still mouth. When my mum came back – not necessarily as speedily as she might have thought – Mrs Philips would say 'hasn't the time flown?' and it would have been rude to say 'not particularly'. The smell of buttered brazils and cuttlefish in your nose takes a surprisingly long time to go. On the upside, I'll be twelve in November so I won't need to go to her house anymore. If Mum starts speed dating again, I can sit here in my room and report my story.

I think I'll describe what's around me a little bit, just to give the picture. Drawing's not my strong suit either (that's another word from card games which I learned after I looked up busted flush) so it's easier for me to speak what I can see. Mum and I live on an estate and in the middle of it is a massive, very old house. Not long after the Second World War, the man who owned the house sold all the land around it and they built houses so people would have new places to live. The big old house sits like an island in the middle of them all. Two old ladies live in it; I think they must be sisters. One goes out and does the shopping and the other one doesn't. She stands or sits by the big front window and looks out quietly. Her window is opposite my window. If we wanted to do signals to each other we could; like the flags sailors wave on the decks of ships. We've not done any signals yet. I've lived here for two years, but maybe we might start one day soon.

Their house looks crumbly, that's my best word for it. When I pull back my curtains in the morning I always do a quick check and see if anything has fallen off in the night, like a bit of window-sill or some of the swirls which run along the top. You can see the wood where the paint used to be. It has a grand old gate which is very tall. One of the hinges is broken and so it dangles rather than swings. I saw the one who goes shopping looking at it once. She poked it with her stick, shook her head and then got going.

We have other neighbours as well. There's a woman called Martine who has a sofa outside her house and she sits on it sometimes with her daughter and they chat to everyone who goes past. Apparently *she could make more of herself, beginning with an eyebrow shape and a full leg wax*. There's a man who does his garden a lot. Once he was carrying a huge armful of flowers. They were a really dark purply colour. I said, 'Excuse me mister, but what flowers are they?' And he said, 'Dahlia,' which sounded a bit like Delilah, which was kind of funny because his head is all bald like an egg and we'd just been doing Samson and Delilah in RE. His arms were a bit trembly because he's quite old, and he was wearing the kind of sandals that I used to have when I was about six which have a buckle and gaps cut out so your feet don't get hot. It made me think of Samson, all weak after Delilah had cut off his hair. 'Perhaps you'd like a couple for your mum,' he said, all proud, and he reached over and gave me three. The colour still looked brilliant, and the petals were really shiny, but they smelt terrible. It reminded me of when a cat ran in through the open front door and weed in the corner. 'I can't abide the smell of cat pee,' Mum had said. We sprayed no end of stuff to get rid of it. Then she left bowls of bicarbonate of soda and cut-up onions next to the skirting board because she said they would absorb the smell. It took longer than you'd think.

I didn't think she'd like the dahlias because of that but it would have been rude to say no, what with him looking so pleased. So I said thank you, gave him a little bow which I think was a bit of a surprise to both of us, scooted upstairs to my room and stuffed them under my bed so that neither of them would be put out. It worked. Putting things under the bed always does. I hid under it myself once, when she was whirling round the house like one of those dust tornados. She blew right past me.

3

Max

Old people worry me. Just thinking about Samson and his dahlias again has made me feel sad. When you look at an old person's face, there's something so pale and rimmy about their eyes, and you can mostly see their scalp even if they still have hair. The corners of their mouths tremble like a diving board when you've just jumped off it. Not Grandma's, her mouth hardly moves at all. She's started wearing a white sun visor, so her scalp's a bit of a mystery too.

Little children upset me as well. I hate it when they cry and it sounds as if they are dragging all their tears up from the bottom of their stomachs not their eyes, and they can't get their words out for big sobby breaths. At the bus stop on the way home from school a man was shouting at his little girl. 'Just be silent,' he said, 'SILENT!' and when she took a step over to her mum he said, 'And you will not hold Mummy's hand.' That seemed pretty mean to me. Had Zorba rocked up, I'm hoping he'd never have said anything like that. One of the good things about him not being here is that at least I can make him kind in my mind.

People are very quick to judge. I read that somewhere. Case proved by the question of school bags too, which was a surprise to me. I'm going to secondary school in September. There's a boy called Jay who lives round the corner who's two years older than me. My new school chose him as my meet-and-greet buddy.

That meant on Induction day I got to sit with him for fifteen minutes while he gave me his top tips on how to be happy at Wellbrook. This is what he said: 'Mate, I have two pieces of advice. One, don't be a wanker. Two, don't get one of those rucksacks which have wheels. Only tossers and nerds have those.'

I didn't really know where to start with that. After he said it he got up and went, even though we were only three minutes into our session. I'd been going to ask him about library access after school and whether you needed a passport photo for your card. His comments on rucksacks with wheels were a blow. Firstly because I'd seen a nice one in Mr Kipling in Bicester Village Outlet Mall when we went one Sunday because Mum wanted a pair of ballet flats to work in, and also because how can a bag tell you anything really important about anyone? Who decides that?

The old lady across the road – the one who goes and does the shopping – has a trolley that's on wheels. It's patterned in red and black squares. Laid flat, you could use it for a board game, not that she looks like she'd be up for that. She has a very stern face. She looks straight ahead of her, although she steers the trolley very carefully where the pavement is uneven. The one who watches from the window stretches her neck to catch sight of her as she comes back around the corner. She doesn't wave or anything; she just watches.

The shopping lady has a stick. She *tap tap tap*s the tip of it as she goes along the kerb. I don't think she's blind or anything. I think she just likes to tap it as she walks, like some kind of Morse code. Maybe it's to tell the ground ahead that she's coming. Maybe she doesn't like being a surprise.

Mum's not like that. She likes to make people look at her. She went through a phase last summer of dying her hair what she called *iced blonde*. She said that with a tan she'd look like a Starbucks frappe. I thought her hair looked like a big stick of candy floss. Each time I looked at her it was a shock.

That's another thing I've learned – along with the part about people being quick to judge. Sometimes, when someone asks you what you think, like she did when she came out of the bathroom with her new hair, and you think that your answer is not what the person wants to hear, it's better to do something which doesn't give the game away. A good old thumbs up is often the answer. That way nobody gets upset.

4

Minnie

Clara will be rounding the corner soon. I could set my wristwatch by her. *Tap tap tap* goes her stick on the pavement, but I can't actually hear it so I am embellishing that part. The shopping trolley looks particularly full. Likely she will have bought curly kale, swedes, turnips; floor wax, too. Tomorrow I will polish the hall floor. The colour of the wax is Bishop's Cardinal Red.

Clara's posture is impressive. 'Did you ever ballet dance, m'dear?' a market stallholder asked her once. She told me she shook her head and said, 'No, never.' She is not stand-offish, but she can be mistaken for being so. I am less likely to be misunderstood, mostly because I hardly go out and I speak as little as possible. It has crossed my mind that all my unsaid words might be stacked up somewhere, waiting, like a wick, to be set alight. If it ever happens, I wonder if I will find myself torched by a hot flame of words.

The marmalade cat which belongs to a house down the road is looping itself around the gatepost. It lifts its tail like an ensign. Clara will shoo it away with her stick. She can't abide cats, their scratching and scraping. Sometimes, I think it would be companionable; a soft tabby in the parlour, mewing when it is hungry. Instead, there is mostly silence, always order, myself and Clara moving around Rosemount.

There are rooms I have not been in for years: small attics, the billiards room where the green baize table gathers dust. Clara steps purposefully in there sometimes, the ostrich-feather duster held upright in her hands. I'm not sure it does much good. Dust re-gathers, re-groups, re-falls anyway; rooms become softly shrouded in greyness.

However one tries to avoid it, matter settles and ossifies.

Clara is getting closer. A boy cycles past her, and it looks like he is singing or shouting. She doesn't flinch. The woman in the post office asked her if she considered herself a target, what with her fixed routines. 'I'd be worried,' the woman said. Clara replied that she didn't see why anyone would target her. She's probably right. There is something in the way she wields her stick, some kind of peculiar authority and untouchability, which means it would take no small measure of courage to mug Clara.

A mug used to be something one might drink from; now it also means a kind of assault. There is no denying it; words scamper forth and make new meanings for themselves. You can look out of a window for the best part of fifty years, and the whole world can label itself differently.

My label changed. I began as Hermione, my baptismal name. It was rapidly truncated to Minnie; sometimes Min, my father's pet name for me. Hermione, Minnie, Min. Smaller and smaller, as if I were shrinking.

Clara always insists on unpacking the groceries herself. She says I am undisciplined about what goes where in the refrigerator, which is not entirely fair. Also that I do not always replace the newspaper which lines the vegetable basket before laying out the fresh potatoes and onions. It is not worth a squabble. I am usually relegated to watching as Clara takes out carrots, cauliflower and a small block of cheddar. Perhaps she will have treated us to a custard slice each. Or it might be a jam tart, red and smooth as wax.

As I sit now by the bay window again the late afternoon sun casts long, angular shadows and the gate is picked out by the light. Rosemount Park, written on slate, retains its purchase on the ornate ironwork. The lowest hinge is broken. Clara has noted it in the Repairs book, which is no longer necessarily a step to it being repaired.

Our house stood, previously, in a hundred acres of its own parkland. There was a tennis court, a croquet lawn, a walled garden fragrant with pleached fruit trees and soft, blowsy roses. There is an ancient photo of myself and Clara, dressed in white sprigged muslin dresses, obediently holding hands in front of the neat vegetable garden. The butcher delivered meat tied in waxed-paper parcels, and the fishmonger, on Fridays, a fillet of cod or haddock laid out on granules of ice. I remember the gardeners, their tools, barrows, clippers; a man who pruned the trees, harnessing himself to the branches, and who with particular skill trimmed the wisteria, encouraging it to thread its way along the length of the glasshouse. The apples from the orchard were stacked in trays in an outhouse. 'Apples from the garden,' our mother used to say, 'right through until February.' It was Father who, after the war, in the mid-1950s, sold off all the land to the council to build a new estate. The houses now lap practically to the front door. The child who lives opposite is physically closer to me than Clara making tea in the kitchen. 'People need homes,' my father had said firmly, 'the time for all this is gone.' When I close my eyes, I can still see the lake, the parkland, the feathery asparagus beds, the row of delicate aspen trees. The planners tried to commemorate the original context. Lake Street. The Long Walk. Wisteria Avenue. It's all a nod to Rosemount's vanished space.

The money gained is perhaps now almost gone. Clara has not said – the accounts are her business – but last November she burned our stack of accumulated Yellow Pages in the woodstove, cutting them up with her old pinking shears. The flames danced green.

What plays out now in front of me are other people's lives with all their business and colour. I watch the hurry and scurry of their routines; women on their way to nurseries with pushchairs, stooping to pick up things their toddlers hurl; schoolchildren bumping up the kerb on their bikes and wheeling with no hands on the handlebars down the middle of the road; teenagers smoking and laughing by the row of garages; grocery deliveries arriving in supermarket vans; young women in high heels teetering out on Friday night; a man in a yellow sou'wester walking his dachshund at precisely the same time, twice daily. I can measure my day by it all.

I am not alone in watching, in taking it all in. The child opposite does so too. I would guess him to be ten, possibly eleven if he is small and slight for his age. He sits on the low brick wall which runs in front of his house, and watches the comings and goings. He swings his legs as he sits there. He waves to other children as they go by, and sometimes he walks to the park but is not gone long. I think that he does not have a father; there is no sign of a man. He has the air of a child who has been brought up by women and the elderly. I don't know why I am so sure of that, but I am. He is considered in his movements, and there is about him a gentleness which is the opposite of the boisterousness I see in some of the other children of his age. When he first moved in, an old couple used to visit, and he would walk very slowly around the block with an elderly man who wheeled an oxygen tank. I imagine it was his grandfather. I would watch him talking intently to him, and there was a sweetness about him which I found heart-warming.

The boy looks across at me sometimes. We catch each other's eye and hold our gaze for a second. Sometimes he stands by the window ledge of his sitting room, or at his bedroom window, scanning the length of the street. In the last day or so I think he has a new project. He seems to be talking to himself, his lips moving quickly, animatedly. He is holding something constantly in his hand. It is a machine of sorts; perhaps a phone, or maybe a tape recorder of some kind. Perhaps he is telling himself a story.

Would I be telling myself a story? Perhaps. I have a sudden, overwhelming desire to write what happened. It is different from a story. In doing so, I wonder if at last I will be able to let it go. As I look up at his window, the boy is talking into his machine again. We would be twinned in our endeavour. This is how I will think of it.

The paving slabs, the parked cars, the differing perspectives make it difficult to remember for certain where things once were. The thing I would most like to know is exactly where the indigo hydrangea bush stood. It troubles me whether it was closest to where the third or fourth lamp post stands now. The diggers, the heaps of rubble, the twisted tree roots made it so difficult, at the time, to be sure. The not knowing nags at me.

Tomorrow I must polish the quarry tiles. My nails will carry a small blood-red crescent of wax. Looking at my hands has never ceased to bother me. They remain culpable. Sometimes, when I sit at my dressing table, I look at myself, and try to locate the vestiges of my younger self, wondering if she is tucked somewhere beneath the soft, faded, slackness of my skin. I am tempted to tap on my cheek, to ask *Are you there?* It is hard to believe so. The face which looks back at me is frequently a study in disquietude.

My mother used to say 'There is not enough stillness in your expression'. She would find enough stillness now. When I pinch the apple of my cheek the bones feel all too imminent beneath.

Clara and I have spent the evening in the parlour as is our habit. Clara worked on her needlepoint and I looked at an old book of Father's on maritime history. Our television no longer works. Apparently the world has digitally switched over, it no longer speaks the same language as the transmission mast. There were leaflets pushed through the door which Clara had disposed of. 'It will save us the licence fee,' she said. 'Most of what's on is rubbish; we're better off without it.'

I did not disagree. I miss, however, the wildlife programmes: lions brazenly stalking the Serengeti, and, more mundanely, *Autumn* and *Spring Watch* – robins on a bird feeder, badgers at play. A crow, once, clever enough to extract a key from a puzzle box.

We have not removed the set. It watches us, from the corner of the parlour, with a dispassionate eye. I like to imagine the lions and the robins digitally happening elsewhere.

In their absence I have transferred my attention to the child. He has drawn his curtains; his light is off. Perhaps he is lying in bed and talking to his machine. I think it is not unusual for children to talk to themselves; I think it is probably a particular comfort, a telling either of how it is, or how we'd like it to be.

They are rarely the same thing.

5

Minnie

My father's fountain pen is newly in my hand. My fingers are sensitive to the unfamiliar weight of it. Who am I writing for? Absolutely only myself. Why am I writing? That is harder to answer. A feeling descends; the desire to see it all in sequence. A life less lived. My life less lived.

Before I retired, I sat beside many people as they contemplated the span of their years. I think it is my turn to do so now, but not pale-lipped, motionless, frail beneath a counterpane; instead in reasonably good health, and concentrating on mostly the first part, written down here in this diary, in royal blue ink.

I will begin with my beginnings; with what I see as where it all began.

How old was I – fourteen, fifteen – when I used to go with my mother to visit people who lived in the village? She took linctus for sick infants, old sweaters for impoverished farmhands. It was plain to see, even then, that she was not a compassionate angel of mercy. There was something about the visits which carried an unspoken reprimand; they should have rather provided for themselves whatever it was she bestowed.

There was a small farmhouse on the green, with wooden shutters and a pear tree adjacent to the gate. It was lived in by a stockman, who died suddenly, messily (gored by a bull – was that it?). There were whispers, lowered voices. His wife went to live with her sister on the other side of the village and did not set foot in the house for three years. It was said the thought was unbearable to her. I watched the pear tree repeatedly bloom, fruit, and weep leaves whilst the shutters remain closed. One day, walking past, my mother pulled up short, and said enough was enough.

Another woman, Mary, let us in. We stood by the fireplace in the kitchen, the stockman's armchair as it had been on the day that he died, his winter coat still on the peg, and a pack of cards, well-thumbed, on the table. I stood with my hands on the back of the chair, touching a dark, oiled patch which was the trace of his living head. I rubbed my fingertips together and wondered if they now carried motes of him, the knowledge, dawning upon me for the first time, that absence could be as strong, as physical, as presence.

'Something must be done,' my mother said, a tureen of soup held under her arm, intended for another, but which now implied that a mouthful, cradled in a wide-bowled spoon, might bring the widow to her senses and set in motion a flurry of scrubbing and wiping which would bring the house swiftly to order. Behind her, yellow wallpaper curled in loops from the plaster.

Mary nodded impassively, before saying, 'That's an enormous spider in the sink,' her arm outstretched as if she might suddenly lace it between her fingers. She hobbled off down the hallway. I looked up and saw the widow standing on the village green, staring at us through the open door, the pear tree shimmering beside her. I took my hand from the chair, feeling as if touching it was rude. It was as if the house was disintegrating with its own sorrows.

Rosemount is falling softly down around us. It is an unspoken understanding we have. We try and disguise the fact. I buff the quarry tiles in long smooth arcs. Clara bleaches the Belfast sink in the laundry. We take it in turns to polish the range, small huffs of our breath misting the steel lids.

Clara has written a list of who is responsible for what. It is propped on the kitchen table beneath a brass weight shaped like a bell. It is a manifesto of resistance, achieved by our knees, elbows, arms, knuckles and fingertips. Neither of us acknowledges the futility to the other. Someone likely will come, one day soon, and tear out frayed wires, old lead pipes, the wheezing boiler. Someone will make new, but until then we will continue to move around Rosemount, measured and disciplined, trying to keep dissolution at bay.

The boy is sitting on his wall opposite, looking to the left and right, holding whatever it is in his hand, and talking rapidly into it. I cannot hear him but I can see it is a tumble of words. The front length of his hair is long, and it swings as he moves his head.

Clara and I do not speak in a tumble of words. We use them frugally, parsimoniously; each sentence landing on the Persian rug between us like an object we might consider, carefully, protractedly, at length.

Shall you start to peel the vegetables in a little while?

The candlesticks need polishing; I will begin them tomorrow.

There is a piece of guttering worked loose above the scullery window.

And, woven through our sentences and the pauses, the delicate clinking of our bone china cups on their saucers, and the sound of Clara, neatly, precisely, eating a lemon shortbread biscuit. What would it be like to suddenly throw out a whoop; to watch it rocket across the room and land in the hearth? It is inconceivable.

It is twilight now. He is not yet at his bedroom window. A couple have walked past on the street, holding hands, the man reaching across to kiss the woman swiftly, decisively. A courting couple. They are not called that anymore.

If I had a machine like the boy's, what would I tell it, where would I begin? Would it be easier than trying to write it all down?

I was wrong-footed so long ago it is difficult to unpick my way back to it all; to when I stood in that old farmhouse, my mother clutching soup, and realised that everything came at a cost.

The sound of the wireless is trickling through from the parlour. Clara will be listening intently, a shawl pulled around her shoulders. After the Shipping Forecast she will go to bed. Each night she listens to it gravely as if she might be called upon to muster a lifeboat, even though we live far inland. I think she is soothed by the voice threading its way fastidiously around the shoreline. I think that it reassures her that someone will continue to be on watch while she sleeps. My sister is vigilant. Responsible. This is also probably my fault.

In the beginning – see how I can write the words – *In my beginning*. As the darkness steeps around me, my mind opens wide like a jawbone, and there is a memory – intact, freshly lit, luminous.

I am crouched in a flower bed, a velvet-soft, emerald green caterpillar curled in the palm of my hand, its body thrumming against the curve of my skin. My mother's voice, imperious, comes from an open window. 'Hermione, get up. You are muddying your knees and spoiling your frock.' I look up, the house pale in comparison to the vivid green of the caterpillar, and Mother closes the window and pulls the blind half down to preserve the bedroom furniture from the sun. She then appears, briefly, hazily, again, carrying a large bowl of wilted roses from another sill. Beyond me, Clara stands as if to attention by an easel, a bee buzzing fatly around her so that she shoos it away with her brush. She pauses to consider what she has painted, her head on one side.

I know if I put the caterpillar back on the Lady's Mantle where I found it, and sidle up to the easel to see what Clara is water-colouring, I will find a stiff little image painted on the creamy-smooth expanse of the paper, most likely the lichened urn that stands before her, but shorn of its wild shock of scarlet geraniums. She will have made it neat and tame. And so instead, I tilt myself back in the sunshine, lifting my knees clean from the soil to pay lip service to my mother's scolding, and look up through my lashes, up through the trembling leaves of the hornbeam, and the world seems to shimmer with latent warmth, and a feeling, unexpected, suddenly showers me, the sensation fountaining through my lips. *I am alive. I am so very alive.*

6

Max

The day started well. She's *on a health kick*, and she's bought a blender. She made a smoothie and topped it with chia seeds, which I think looked like little curled-up grubs but which she says are *fabulous* for you. At least they are not compulsory. As it's the summer holidays she ordered Frosties from Tesco as well, so I was allowed to have a bowl of those while she drank the chia seed topped smoothie. That's a win–win.

After that I wasn't sure what to do. We don't go away in the school summer holidays and I am mostly responsible for amusing myself (her words). This is because these six weeks are *PEAK BUSINESS* time in the beauty world. Mum says there is a four hundred per cent increase in the number of clients who want their toenails painted. Also an upsurge in waxing, and interest in a particular makeover she offers which is called *Summer Glow* and involves *bronzer swept in figures of three along the brow, cheek-bone and chin*. This is called contouring and *needs a steady hand*. She says that she tells me these things so that if she ever fell down in a faint I could technically step right up and carry on. Practice doesn't seem to come into it.

So, in the summer holidays she's in the Powder Room all hours – some clients come at night after work or when their toddlers are in bed. She says she truly doesn't know how half the area would cope with their beauty requirements if she wasn't prepared to work very long days to make everybody their best self.

She does her own face first thing, at the dressing table in her bedroom, not in the Powder Room. It's very important that she gets her look right, *both seasonally and on-trend*, to set a good example. You can't be in the beauty business and go around looking *a little bit frayed at the edges*. Those are her words for someone who is not making the best of themselves. Therefore, she always looks whatever the opposite of a bit frayed is. Her make-up is spot-on.

There's a little blue suede pouffe to the right of the dressing table and I sit there and talk to her while she applies it. She bought the pouffe when I was a toddler, and she says she used to plonk me on it, right in the middle like someone in a life raft, and that way she knew where I was while she put her face on. It's my favourite place to sit. There's a loop on the side of it which I have almost worn through with thumbing.

I always watch her very carefully. I know all of the different things she does; the way she uses wax to give the arch of her eyebrow a little curve that stays in place through the day, and the way she holds her wrist – the exact angle – to put on her kohl. She switches lipstick colours through the seasons. I know it's May when the coral comes out, and a frosty November morning gets matched with a carefully outlined bright red. She likes a charcoal grey polo neck to go with that look. When she puts away her brushes, she blows herself a kiss in the mirror and says, 'My, am I looking fly.'

I would say that we chat while she's doing it, but in truth it's mainly me doing the talking. She says *hmmm* as she tilts her chin to the left to get the base colour on her eye sockets even, or she says *uh-huh* while she's blending her foundation into her neckline. Apparently not blending is the most common mistake she sees. *A line round the jaw as if drawn with a compass. Rookie error.* Apparently, you can never over-blend.

I still sit there, each morning, on the pouffe, even though it's a bit small for me. We start the day like that, even on school mornings. In the winter, I make myself porridge in a cup and eat it with a teaspoon. I am not allowed Coco Pops in case they spill and stain her pale carpet. Whatever I eat, if the day starts like that it means that even if she's busy all day we've still had our dressing-table time.

Today she was giving herself the *Summer Glow* facial. 'Do I or do I not look as if I've been on the beach in St Tropez all day?' she asked, slipping on her sparkly flip-flops. I gave her a big thumbs up.

After finishing my Frosties (I tipped the last soggy bits down the sink and saw a few chia seeds nestling in the plughole so I wonder if maybe they don't taste that fabulous after all) I walked down to the Rec. I was hoping there might be some people from my old class kicking a ball around or playing on the seesaw. There were two boys from Year Five with a ball and they said I could join in. They made me be goalie the whole time. I hardly saved any (the goal mouth is full-size) and when it was my turn to be striker, they said they had to go home. I just shrugged rather than point out that it wasn't fair. I gave them a thumbs up too as they walked away and I wondered if it was going to be that sort of a morning.

I stayed out until almost lunchtime, because I'd sat on the seesaw for a bit and watched some little kids playing with their mums, and an old man throwing a ball for a dog. He threw it over and over to the exact same place and the dog ran to and fro, to and fro, each time with the same expectant dopey look on its face, and it made me feel sad because if you thought that was what life was like, over and over the same thing, always hoping that something would turn out a little bit differently the next time, you might just want to lie down in your basket, and not put your snout out at all.

Then, when I came home I learned two things. Number one: that it's cheaper to have your boiler serviced during the peak season of the beauty business, because that is exactly the quiet time for the boiler servicing business. Apparently, no one thinks about having their boiler done until the first time they turn the heating on in October and then it doesn't work. So if you're smart, you get it done in July for a discount. That way, when you turn the heating on in October, it works right away and you can sit toasty-warm knowing you've saved money too. I learned this while Mum stood – actually mostly half-leant – against the airing-cupboard door, where the boiler is, with the toes of her right foot slipping in and out of her sparkly flip-flop, and she was laughing and fanning her face with her hand and she was all of a summer glow, extra to that which she'd applied this morning when I was sitting on the pouffe.

The second thing I learned was that she's obviously moved on from the glass of Pinot Grigio and *Downton Abbey* phase, because when I heard him ask her if maybe she'd like to go out for a bite to eat tonight, she explained that she had clients until 8.45, but that if he wanted to pop back later she could rustle up supper. 'No Michelin stars,' she said, 'my last one's a back wax and a facial extraction and that often over-runs.' (I haven't mentioned that some of her clients are men; they are, and she says that's a good thing because not only does it *grow market share*, it allows everyone to be their best self.) I'm guessing that's where her plan for my dishwater blonde hair will eventually come in.

So he said yes. Just like that. Putting a wrench or something back in his tool box, and wiping his forearm on his forehead and I swear the width of it almost matched the size of his head, and the hairs on it were so thick they looked like they were made of wire. If she tried to wax those it would be a job and a half.

He has a large tattoo on his bicep; it says something in a foreign language. She leaned on the airing-cupboard door, and the tip of her tongue was on her lip for a moment, and she said 'What does that mean?', her fingernail almost touching the tattoo – which, had it done so, would not have been the best thing as he was sweaty from all the boiler servicing and she'd be touching someone's face within minutes of the doorbell ringing for the next appointment. (Hygiene is extremely important in the beauty business). He said, 'It means strength through deference.' First of all, I thought he said strength through *deafness*, which made no sense, and then I cocked my head so I could read it properly for myself. I've just Googled 'deference', it means polite respect. I'm not sure whether it's him who's paying it, or whether it's being paid to him. Either way, if the tattooist *had* put *Strength Through Deafness* on his arm it would have been accurate as he certainly didn't want to listen to a word I had to say even though I asked him lots of questions about the boiler servicing industry.

7

Max

All afternoon she kept popping out of the Powder Room and into the kitchen. She opened a tin of olives with pimentos in them, and speared them on cocktail sticks. She started arranging them on a small white saucer, and when her next client arrived early, she asked me to take over, which I did, and very neatly if I say so myself. I did a Jenga grid: left to right, and then right to left. The pimentos came out of it looking good. She squeezed a lemon and pulped some garlic and mixed it with olive oil and spooned it over some chicken breasts. She stood by the fridge door, the dish in her hand, her head on one side and said to me, 'In or out? I don't want to give him salmonella by marinating at room temperature on a warm afternoon in July.' I shrugged, firstly because I thought it would take a lot more than salmonella to take him down, and secondly because I don't believe in pretending to know things that I don't. If I knew about food hygiene I could have a summer job in it and not be arranging olives in Jenga grids on saucers for free.

She nipped out between the next two clients and said to me, 'Do you think he looks the kind of bloke who would enjoy couscous? He's been to Indonesia – that suggests he's not a meat and potato kind of guy.' I struggled for an answer to this too. Sometimes I think people go on holiday to places just because Easyjet fly there, and sometimes, whatever airline they've flown,

I think they come home and complain about the food they've had to eat. There isn't necessarily a connection. I sat next to a man on a bus once and he said to me, 'You have no idea how much I've been dying to have this pasty,' and then he took a huge bite out of it. He didn't have a sun tan or anything, so there was no clue where he'd been or what he'd been doing. I told her I think everybody likes couscous.

When the client came out, I noticed the fake tan on her calves looked a bit streaky, which almost never happens. She either hadn't noticed, or didn't mind. She winked at Mum and said, 'Enjoy tonight – look forward to hearing all about it.'

Mum says everybody spills out all their news in the Powder Room. She thinks that it's something do with lying with a nice white towel under your head and a blanket over your legs and feet. She says everybody feels like a child tucked up safely in bed, mostly because when she raises them up their feet can't touch the floor anymore and they are warm and safe and so they sing like canaries. They tell her all manner of very personal things. Her way to describe this is *womb talk*. Some nights she'll pour herself a glass of wine and say, 'oh my goodness I've had so much womb talk tonight if someone else says menopause or hysterectomy to me I'll start mixing HRT with the Fakebake.' This didn't use to make sense to me; firstly because when she said womb I misheard it as room, and thought they were chatting about the lilac paint so couldn't understand why that would be anything other than a pleasure for her, and secondly because when I Googled 'menopause' I wasn't much clearer. I don't think it's something I need to bother my head with. But today, as ol' streaky legs stood by the door, it was the first time it had occurred to me that maybe Mum did some chatting back; some telling of stuff. Maybe you didn't need to be under the blanket to sing like a canary, and maybe discussing episodes of *Downton Abbey* wasn't completely enough.

When he arrived at 8.45pm he looked a whole lot cleaner. That was the first thing I noticed. His fingernails were as white as a sliver of new moon which must have taken some doing as when he left our house earlier he looked like he'd been down a pit. There was no oily grease still on him, and when I got to the door, I could smell his aftershave before it was open even a crack. He was carrying a bottle of rosé wine. That was a smart move. I knew straight away she would like it. It would match with her menu. *Summer Mediterranean food is best complemented by a light, dry rosé.* She read it in one of her magazines. He didn't mess about on the doorstep. He walked right on in, like I was a butler or something. I'm not kidding. I think he should have said thank you when I invited him in, and then followed me slowly down the hallway into the kitchen to find Mum standing all casually, shaking her hair back a little, leaning on the kitchen worktop, not giving the smallest clue that she'd been refreshing her lip gloss a split second earlier. Instead of that happening, he just barged right past me so in fact I followed him down the hallway, making it look like it was me who was the visitor. Clearly I'm not.

I was a bit surprised to see that Mum had laid the table while I'd been combing my hair and putting a clean t-shirt on. Even more surprised to see that she'd laid out only two empty plates. On the kitchen side there was a plate of crackers with some cheese and an apple sliced like a fan all nicely. I thought at first it was maybe a Mediterranean dessert, until she said, clocking that I was looking at it, 'That's for you darling, I thought you might like to eat it in front of the television. Special treat!' I did a double take, and she nodded towards the chicken pieces which were all marinated and laid out on the grill pan, and I realised – what with the Tesco delivery coming last night – she'd have only ordered a pack of two as she wouldn't have known he'd be here. Two into three doesn't go; it wouldn't have looked right to cut the two breasts into strips. *FHB* is what my grandma used to say if we went for tea at her house and there were other guests. *Family Hold Back.* Even if you were starving.

Mum offered him the olives on the saucer, and when he took one the whole stack fell down. I'd call that a little bit careless but they seemed to think it was funny. I picked up my plate and stepped past him as he opened the wine.

While I was eating the cheese, crackers and fan-tailed apple in front of the telly I could hear them chatting. 'You see, sweetie,' he kept saying, and then, 'Well, what a beautiful woman like you has never had to learn is . . .' When I went in to put my plate in the dishwasher, she was laughing her head off at some story about him trying to ride a camel. She'd tilted her chin right back and he was looking at her throat, his big meaty hands all over the table, and his tattoo shivering when he flexed his arms.

They had ice cream for pudding, and she did a big bowl for me. While she scooped it out of the tub, he asked me what sport I played. I was glad I do play one, or that would have been a bit embarrassing. Sometimes, I think people don't think properly about how they phrase their questions. *Do you play any sport?* would have been better. Anyway, I answered football, and he asked 'which club?' and I don't play for a club so that was a bit awkward. Then he asked me what position I played, which varies because I mostly don't get to choose at school, and while I was thinking about that, he'd gone on to another question about the new England formation, and I just ducked that because I'm not an expert on football tactics, so I stayed silent for a bit because I think it's better not to shoot your mouth off if you don't know what you are talking about. While I was reflecting on that, he leaned right forward so that his chest was practically flat on the kitchen table. I could see the dark hair on the inside of his nostrils. He said, 'Cat got your tongue laddie? Your ma says you're usually quite the talker.' I was tempted to poke my tongue right out, to show it was still absolutely mine. Lying here, I'm thinking it's probably a bit lame that when I feel awkward I think it's a good idea to poke out my tongue. I managed to resist and I just stood there looking at his nostrils, until Mum nudged me with the ice-cream bowl which she'd been holding out to me the whole time. I pulled out a chair (our table seats four which is hardly ever necessary but tonight was one of those nights) and went to sit down, but he put his big meaty hand on the chair-back, asked what I'd been watching on the television and said if I hung around much longer I'd miss the best part of it. Here's the thing; he didn't even know what I was watching; and it doesn't count as hanging around if you are standing in your own kitchen.

I'm in bed now. I can hear them downstairs in the hallway. I think he's leaving, although he's taking his time about it.

My conclusion to the evening is this. If I were to bother to say it to him, I'd tell him these four things:

1. She's not my ma, she's my mum.
2. I'm not called 'laddie'.
3. I've Googled it and the England formation is apparently a work in progress. Even the experts haven't decided.
4. I may be unsure about what the rules are when you let someone into your house so he can have the benefit of the doubt on that one, but I'm certain it's not good manners to shut the kitchen door right on one of your hosts, after pretty much telling them to go away and watch television.

She's coming upstairs now. Singing to herself. Actually it's more like humming. I can hear her taking her jangly bracelets off. She must be extra-tired, because she's gone straight to her room instead of coming in to check I'm asleep like she usually does. Clearly I'm not.

8

Minnie

Until I fetch my diary, I haven't been in the nursery for years. Clara cleans it, telling me that the old nursing chair is leaking its horsehair innards, that the lashes of a china doll on the shelf seem, inexplicably, suddenly to be moulting, and that a small pane of glass in the window has cracked.

When I open the door, it is as I remember it; the dappled rocking horse, the figure of a porcelain girl in the branch of a cherry tree, and an almost bald teddy bear with eyes made of tweed buttons. In the drawer, I find a sheaf of Clara's water-colours held by a primrose ribbon, and a Bluebird toffee tin, which, when opened, contains a threepenny bit and a hair slide in the shape of a star. Are they my treasures or Clara's? I cannot remember. They were evidently precious once.

The curtains in the nursery are still the colour of lemon drops. That was how I used to think of them, kneeling on my bed impatiently when I was supposed to be having my afternoon rest, looking out into the garden, watching Hooper mow the lawn in broad, contrasting stripes. Everything I looked out onto then has gone. It belongs to a vanished world, a world upended, bitten into, by the vast jaws of diggers and ground-breakers.

I find the diary in the third drawer. Across the cover, mis-spaced on two lines, *HERMIONE SUMMERS, WORLD EXPLO-RER*.

On the first page I have written, in precisely-joined italic script:

I will learn to speak Italian. I will walk in very remote places and wear stout boots which cleverly dry almost as quickly as they get wet. I will have a pet monkey which will walk alongside me wearing a turquoise collar and lead.

I have misspelt turquoise.

On the next page, I rail about having to sit quietly next to Clara, methodically sewing our alphabet samplers. Clara's is neat, with beautifully spaced letters, and mine is apparently a hotchpotch, the thread tangled in clumps at the back. I have pressed my fingertip to the page to show where I have pricked it. The blood has faded to brown.

I intend to travel. There are long lists of the places I will visit, an itinerary mostly informed by an old encyclopedia in the library. I decide that I will have a suitcase entirely covered in stickers which tell where I have travelled. I will drink lime sherbets on terraces, eat small cones of roasted pistachios by hot springs, and watch fireflies in the twilight over a humid paddy field. I will wear, on separate occasions, a crimson sari, a white broad-brimmed hat, and supple, black buttoned shoes appropriate for the tango.

I have not done any of these things. I continue reading.

Father asked if I am planning to run away and join the circus, which now that I think about it could be travelling of the very best kind. I would like my own caravan, painted claret and blue, and a costume that is entirely covered in sparkles. He asked me because in the hallway I cartwheeled, right across the quarry tiles over and over. He saw me from the drawing room and clapped hard so that I could hear him through the open door. Mother came in from the garden, carrying a wicker basket of mulberries. 'Hermione,' she said, 'you are too old for that. It is not proper to hurl yourself about in that way. If you want to be so lively, I will think of other, more suitable accomplishments, ones that may be more useful than your skirt falling over your head.'

Beside the account I have drawn myself cartwheeling. My tartan skirt is inverted so that my hands look like my feet. The basket my mother is carrying spills over with mulberries that I have crayoned so deeply purple the page is almost worn through. I have included the drawing-room door beyond her, and in now faint pencil is the outline of my father's clapping hands. They are not attached to his wrists, so appear to be floating beyond my flying feet.

I read my mother's words again. *More suitable accomplishments.* I can hear the inflections of her voice. I have recorded her words accurately.

'What are you doing?' Clara calls as I return from the nursery, the diary held pressed to my chest. She puts down her knitting.

'Nothing in particular,' I say with a small shake of my head, as if to avert suspicion landing and taking root in my hair.

'Did you go to the second floor? I thought I heard you go up the second stairwell?'

'I thought I heard a bird and that it may have been inside, that perhaps it had flown down one of the attic chimneys. Remember when a starling came down and flew around in a panic for days?'

'Did you check carefully?'

'Yes. I think it must have been beating its wings against the outside of the pane.'

'Do you remember the bees which made a nest up there?'

'Yes. The noise was not like that at all.'

Clara and I listen, always, to the sound of the house breathing and moving around us. Vast timbers creaking, pipes gurgling, the plaster on the cornices cracking. One morning in the late summer several years ago, climbing the second staircase, my ear suddenly attuned to the softest of buzzings. I placed my palm flat to the wall and felt it tremble within, the soft skein of a bee nest making the plaster pulse softly.

Now Clara is in the drawing room, playing Patience on the walnut table. When I finish writing this first entry, I will nod to her as I pass by the open doorway, the smooth, familiar shape of the afternoon settling softly upon us. Beyond us, other lives unspool. Adventures take place. Lifting my eyes now, I see the boiler engineer arriving at the boy's house again. He gets out holding – a little awkwardly – a rather stiff bunch of rosebuds. This is unexpected. One would expect spanners and wrenches, not flowers. He raps on the door and the boy answers, holding himself straight like a sentry. His expression seems wary even from where I stand.

Five minutes later, the man comes back down the pathway. The woman is standing on the step, holding the roses and waving goodbye with her fingertips. The boy has moved to the low curve of the brick wall next to his gate. The three of them exist in relation to each other like a geometry problem. The boy catches my eye before we are both distracted by the sound of the van door closing. The man dips slightly towards him and the child looks perplexed. His mother welcomes a woman who is hurrying up the path. She has transferred the flowers to the crook of her arm, like an actress taking a protracted curtain call.

I turn to a fresh page after where my childish handwriting stops, and ask myself where to begin – beginnings, unlike endings, being so much harder to detect. And yet, one beginning is likely as good as another. They all migrate to the same place, make their way inexorably towards the end. Suspended above it all, a girl merrily turns cartwheels across polished quarry tiles, drunk on the fragrance of mulberries and clapped by ghostly hands. In a life lived otherwise, perhaps she might actually have gone on to have a hundred adventures, and a monkey which walked in a turquoise collar and lead.

Instead I am an elderly woman finally deciding to give an account of myself.

And here is what I write, the tense chosen as if my family exists in a continuous present, which – to my surprise – appears to be something that I find increasingly to be true. The fountain pen makes its way placidly across the page.

My mother and father enjoy going to the races.

9

Max

You'd think she'd never been given a bunch of flowers in her life. She stood in the hallway, half laughing in an embarrassed way, and swish-swatting her hand in front of her mouth. She'd had time to put some lip gloss on; she applied it while she made me run to the window and confirm it was his van pulling up on the kerb. 'Oh you shouldn't have,' she said to him, and then, 'you really didn't need to do that,' and 'I never get flowers – they're lovely, really lovely, pink is my favourite colour.' It isn't. Red is. Scarlet red. Once, when we went to the garden centre, it was the only colour she would look at.

He stood there, holding on to the roses, with a big cheesy grin on his face. 'Max,' she said, 'go and put some water in a vase,' (which frankly proves that she *has* had flowers before, quite regularly from one ex-boyfriend in fact; there's a choice of three vases). 'Would you like a cup of tea?' she said. 'I've got a quick ten minutes before my next client, and she's always late.'

She took him into the Powder Room. She says that room expresses her best; the circle of pebbles she has on a shelf, the orchid in a chrome pot, the way the nail varnishes are lined up very neatly in graded colour shades. I might have guessed she would want to show him it all. I came in shortly afterwards with the tea on a tray (she'd mouthed to me 'on a tray, the blue one', out of the corner of her mouth). I put the sugar in a bowl because

I knew she wouldn't want the bag just plonked there next to the mugs. He was standing underneath the Velux. 'Very primitive,' he was saying, 'I can fit you a blind onto that in a jiffy, with a nice little remote that you just point to close it, and also a new hinge action – remote too – so you can open the whole thing on a warm afternoon without any bother.'

'That would be fantastic,' she said. In fact she didn't say it, she cooed it, like the pigeon that sits outside my window sometimes. And then she added, 'It's always been such a pain, such a hassle. It'll be brilliant if it's all automatic.'

And I stood there holding the tray, a little bit bothered because actually who had it been a hassle for? Who was always in the sitting room, the door a little bit open, ear cocked, watching Wimbledon even though I don't particularly like tennis but just making myself available in case she needed me to scoot in with the ladder, ready to *let in a little ventilation*? I could have been outside riding my bike. Meanwhile he put two heaped spoons of sugar in his mug and stirred it roughly so that tea splashed on the tray. I started dabbing at the spill with one of her neutral-shade tissues from the box on her desk, while he went right on and asked her to go to the cinema.

She jumped at it.

And then there's this. When he was leaving, she stood on the step, keeping the door open with her foot, holding the bunch of roses and waving with just the top part of her fingers. I moved to the brick wall which runs next to our gate. I was just sitting there, and he came past me, and just as he went to open the van door, he ducked down and spoke to me out of the side of his mouth. He looked a bit like a ventriloquist, but a rubbish one because his lips were clearly moving, and his voice had a slightly different tone, none of that cheery *I'll fix your Velux in a jiffy*. Instead, it was like he slapped the words right down on the ground like something I could trip over. What he said was, 'Do you ever stop staring? It's bloody easy to take exception to', and I didn't answer because I didn't know what 'take exception' meant. I've just Googled it. It means *to take offence at or disagree with something*. Just for good measure, I Googled 'offence' as well.

I've no idea how you can take offence to someone who guesses you take sugar in your tea and bothers to put it in a bowl instead of making you dig about in the packet. Or someone who had no chicken for dinner because of FHB.

When he drove off, he didn't look best pleased, but he'd probably clocked that I was still looking at him from where I sat on the wall, which must have counted as even more staring so extra exception and offence taken.

After he'd gone I stayed sitting there for a bit. Mum had taken her next client in. If the room got too hot I decided she'd have to come and find me. She could *cooee* her heart out to the empty living room. It's just occurring to me that keeping yourself always in earshot could be easily taken for granted.

While I was there, the old woman opposite got up and was gone for a while, and then she came back and picked up some sort of book from beside her. It was on one of those trays on a frame that you can easily put over a bed. My grandad had one in hospital. I used to take him puzzle books and he'd lean on it to write out the answers. His tray had *Property of St Xaviers* painted in red letters on the side. Mrs Winters would have been pleased that I'd noticed there was no apostrophe. The author probably would be too. It's all in the noticing. The tray opposite was the same thing but different. When I stood up and really peered, I could see that it was very smooth, polished wood. She opened the book, but she didn't write straight away, she stared into the distance for a long time. It felt like she was looking right through me, as if I was made of glass. I guess I'm sort of standing in her garden. I've never thought of it like that before. I must look like a trespasser, sitting on what used to be her lawn. She wrote for a while and then she put down her pen and lifted her head up, and I don't know what came over me to do it, but I gave her a wave. Not one of the fingers-only waves like Mum had given to him, but the sort of one you do across the playground, when you spot a new person who maybe doesn't know how to join in. She looked surprised at first, and I wasn't sure what she'd do, and then she lifted her hand, quite slowly, and gave me a wave back. Hers was more like when you see the Queen do it on TV, but she gave me a sort-of smile as she did it, as if waving didn't happen very often and she wasn't sure what face to make to go with it.

Maybe she's writing a diary. That's just occurred to me now, sitting here in my bedroom, talking into the Dictaphone. Perhaps we're doing the same thing.

Mum's gone to the cinema. She tried on three different outfits before she went. I had to sit on the pouffe while she turned round three hundred and sixty degrees, and tell her she looked good from every angle. It felt mean to remind her that in the cinema you are mostly in the dark. She twirled round and round in front of me in each of the outfits, and I remembered a music box of Grandma's, which had a little ballet dancer who popped up and pirouetted when you opened the lid. Her skirt was made of white netting which had gone all yellowy, and I think a moth might have eaten some of it so she looked a bit sad and tatty. Mum didn't look tatty. She finally plumped for the bright orange skirt and some espadrille wedges. She kept smoothing the skirt over her bum and I didn't want to point out to her that he'd hardly see it anyway, since she'd be sitting on it for the whole entire movie.

She went to the corner shop and bought me a can of Coke and a Mars bar. She said it was because she's saving on baby-sitting money. She made me lock the door when she left and then she stood on the step and made sure I'd put the chain on correctly. I had to open the door twice so she could check it was working. When she comes back, she's going to let the landline ring three times to tell me she's waiting outside, and I mustn't pick up, because when it stops after three, I'll know it's her and then I can open the door confidently. *Confidently*'s her word. The fly in the ointment which I don't think she had time to think about (she decided last minute to give herself some shellac nails) was that it means I have to stay awake until she gets back. I'm hoping her sense of the time is better than when she was caught up speed dating, otherwise I'll not be confident at the door, more half asleep.

The old lady across the road is in her bedroom now. It's got dark really quickly and started to thunder and I feel a little bit less alone looking across at her. She's sitting at a little dressing table with the book in front of her. I just held up the Dictaphone to her and she looked a bit perplexed, but then I mimed speaking with my hand, like a quacking duck, and I pointed to it and I think she understood. She started to nod, and she held up the book and her pen, and that made me smile, because I think we are joined in being secret agents or reporters. Now I think about it, maybe I'm more of a reporter than a storyteller. I'm not making anything up. I don't know whether she is. It doesn't matter that she's old and looks quite different from me. One time, my grandad and I were both laughing at the same thing on the TV, although by that time whenever he laughed he ended up coughing like mad and having to spit into a tissue. 'Inside every old person,' he said, 'there's their young self just wanting to jump right out, jump out like a frog and leave their old bones, slow muscles and aching joints behind.' He might have added wheezy lungs, but that didn't need saying.

When I look at old people, I often think of what he said, mostly because it's nicer to remember his words rather than the spitty tissues, and I'm looking at her now, trying to imagine her younger self taking a smooth, flying leap through the air.

I hope the film's good and I hope it's not long. Almost twelve may be old enough to be left alone in your house, but even with the chain on the door it doesn't feel as safe as you might like. The thunder storm's not helping. Lightning can strike a house right out of the blue. Grandma used to make me switch off everything electric and take the plugs out of the sockets. I don't know if my Dictaphone counts because it's battery operated, but to be on the safe side I think I'll stop talking. Over and out.

IO

Minnie

My mother and father enjoy going to the races – the Cheltenham Gold Cup, the Derby. My mother wears a jaunty hat with a feather, which I stroke between my finger and thumb. I think it is from a jay bird, but I have no real idea. I hope it is; it has a dapperness to the sound of it. When she is not wearing it, it sits on a shelf in her dressing room, alongside hats she wears for Ascot, for weddings, for the Christmas Eve crib service in church. Sometimes, when she is out visiting, or in the sewing room, I go into her dressing room and stand before the armoire and try them all on one by one. If it's a summer hat, I pretend to hold a tea cup. That happens at Henley; they have tea in vast, flapping white marquees. 'This heat!' I say to the mirror, 'I've never known such a June.' If it is a hat for the races, I also lift down her fox-fur muff and push my hands in deep. I nod my head to myself, with a considered tilt to the right. 'Dee-lighted to meet you,' I say, and, 'Heavens, there wasn't a cigarette paper between them.' I stand on my tiptoes to assume the appearance of heels and criss-cross the dressing room. There is something in my gait which reminds me of the Tamworths in the piggery, their neat little trotters planted carefully across the cobbles of the yard. I am confident this won't be the case when I am allowed real heels of my own.

My parents have gatherings, drinks parties for which my mother hires additional help – women who stand at the door wearing black dresses and frilled aprons. They take coats, or hold trays with rows of crystal glasses of gin and tonic or Pimms, or sometimes cocktails with colours deep as rubies. They nudge each other and whisper as people go past. My grandmother says that whatever they are saying will be the talk of the village. The Hunt Ball takes place at Rosemount each year. The gardeners string lanterns along the length of the driveway, and there are flares – great plumes of flame – alight on the terrace. There are urns of roses the length of the dining table, and the silver is polished for two whole days before. I am forbidden to attend, and am shooed from the kitchen by a maid with a candlestick. I crouch at the top of the stairs with Clara and watch the guests drinking in the hallway below. There are men with bright waistcoats, and moustaches, and ruddy cheeks, and their voices boom up to me. 'I took a hell of a tumble,' they say, or, talking of a horse, 'you cannot question that one's spirit.' The women have dresses made of silks that shimmer like sunlight on water, and necklaces that sit at their throats like plums in a pie. When the double doors for the dining room open for dinner, they move in unison like a ripple of flame and I scoot downstairs to steal a flute of champagne and then some canapés, held carefully in the bowl of my nightgown. I offer the glass to Clara. 'Champagne modom?' I say, 'perhaps a pinwheel?' Clara shakes her head, so only I drink it. The bubbles burst against the roof of my mouth. I tell her I am going to drink champagne in Paris and in Berlin. I know these places because of the photographs in the encyclopedia; I like the Eiffel Tower and the way it looks like a building undressed. Clara does not want to drink champagne in Paris or Berlin. She doesn't even want to drink it crouched in our own stairwell. She could even have been at the dinner; she is thirteen and old enough to stay at the table until dessert. I have stamped my foot and said there is so little difference between nine and thirteen. Clara brokered the peace by saying she would not go. She is keeping me company instead, although she is reluctant to sit with me in the stairwell and would prefer to be doing her threadwork in her room. Again I offer her a slightly squashed pinwheel. She shakes her head. I am a mystery to her.

When my parents came back from the races a few days ago, it was with a tale of a horse that had won, a horse which belonged to one of their party. 'We went into the winners' enclosure,' my father said, 'to congratulate the jockey. The sweat on the horse was like the spume on a wave. My glove was white with it,' he added, holding his bare hand out above his dinner plate.

The next day I find his gloves in the scullery, where they are waiting with his shoes for polishing and his hat for brushing. I pick one up, press it to my face and inhale deeply, curious to see how endeavour might smell, and wondering if the foamy sweat has steeped into the pores of the leather. As I stand there, I hear someone behind me and think that it will be one of the maids. I turn to face them, the glove still pressed to my face. But it is Clara, who is searching to see if her galoshes have been cleaned, and she looks at me aghast and says quietly, 'How could you?'. I realise when I am a little older that it wasn't intended as an expression of disgust, but, rather, bafflement and incomprehension. She turns away from me, and I am still holding the glove when the maid comes in.

My mother usually regards me with an exquisitely pained expression. 'Sit up, Hermione,' she says at table because my posture is not good. 'Sit down, Hermione,' in the drawing room because I insist on walking the length of the fender as if it is a tight-rope. 'Stand up, Hermione,' because I forget to do so when my grandparents enter the room, and, most often, 'Hermione, that's enough,' because my chattering drives her to distraction. I am not neat, I am not tidy, I am not precise in my movements. I ask if I can have lessons in tap dancing and she says I will end up a showgirl; I ask for a silver dress for my birthday and she buys me a brown mackintosh. When she helps with my hair she always chooses to plait it. She weaves it so close to my scalp that it makes my eyes water. I understand later that she is attempting to contain me; that *for now, aged nine, the most she can do is try to tame the unruly curl of my hair.*

My father's world moves beyond us, like a shoal of camouflaged fish. He goes to London in the morning for business at the bank. His comings and goings are marked by what I see as a separate, masculine version of time, marked by the strike of the grandfather clock in the drawing room rather than the tick of the one in the parlour. He catches trains, drives cars, carries briefcases, speaks on the telephone. He does not talk to butchers, or fishmongers, or most of our staff, though he stands by my mother when she gives them their envelopes after Christmas. He gives the beaters their brace of pheasants after a day's shooting. He smells of cigar smoke, and shaving cream, and polished shoes and newspaper ink. His suits hang in his dressing room on broad wooden coat hangers. I stand and part them, and it feels as if I might step through them and beyond into a world where so much more is allowed. I hover on the threshold of his study when he is busy with his papers. I can be there for many minutes and he seems not to know I am there. Then, he will lift his glance from his papers, and look over his glasses at me, or fold down his newspaper so that I can see him fully, and he will say 'So, will-o-the-wisp, what are you doing now?' or, 'Miss Min, what brings you here?' and I don't have an answer, because the truth is I just like to look; at his pen stand, at his cherry-wood blotter, at the strict functionality of the companion set by the fireplace, at his volumes of books, at his leather and walnut desk. I would like to look at it more closely, but no doubt I would do something clumsy. Once, I am touching the brass stopper of his crystal inkwell with just the tip of my finger, and his voice comes suddenly behind me: 'I think that's not going to end well.'

There are vast areas of Rosemount – our parts – which he never steps into; the nursery, our bedrooms, the music room where we are supposed to practise piano, the sewing room where we are required to stand on a stool while my mother's seamstress takes our measurements for a new dress. Once, I chalk numbers on the black and white parquet tiles which run from the scullery to the housemaid's pantry, and play hopscotch, throwing a button for the stone. Behind me, by the stairwell, I hear a soft chuckle, but by the time I turn he is already almost out of sight.

I am fourteen and have rolled myself into the curtain in the drawing room when he comes in with my mother one morning. He asks her to sit on the pale-blue silk chair and she asks him, 'What is this about?' Through the gap in my cylinder of grosgrain, I see him gesture to beyond the French windows. 'The time for maintaining all this is gone,' he says, with a sweep of his arm which I imagine takes in the asparagus beds, the poplars, the herbaceous borders, the stream. 'People need homes, people want change, simpler times are coming.' My mother sits forward on her chair and her pearls swing softly at her throat. 'What can you possibly mean?' she asks and he says, 'I've sold the grounds and the parkland to developers. They will build houses, a whole estate,' and my mother puts her hand to her mouth, which I am sure is a perfect round 'o', and excuses herself from the room. My father sits there for a while, his foot upon the fender, and he swats at a fly which is irritating him, and he mutters something to himself which I cannot discern and I am becoming hotter and more uncomfortable, and I feel like the tobacco rolled in one of his cigars.

When he walks out, I unfurl myself and flop onto the carpet. I look out of the window and understand that my life as I know it will alter. The maid comes in and begins to sweep the grate, and I see her for the first time as being one of the people who need homes and want change.

Clara has just tapped on my bedroom door. She asks if I am still awake, and wants to know what it is that I am doing.

'What have you been busying yourself with?' she asks. 'You came up hours ago.'

I tell her I am doing nothing of note, which is true.

She says 'I'll say goodnight then.'

How formal we remain with each other. I listen to her footsteps recede along the landing and to the sounds of the house cooling down around us, the great joists and timbers shrugging off the heat of the day. A sudden gust of warm wind causes the scullery guttering to rattle. I think it will bring rain. I imagine it drenching the gardens of old: the lupins with their blooms like birds' throats, swallowing the rain. Beneath the foundations of all the houses, might scraps of them remain? Nubbles of roots, bulbs, corms, seeds beneath the vast slabs of concrete? Perhaps a tangle of knotweed, waiting to pounce.

The wind is soughing around the window and bringing the first drops of rain, pattering softly on the glass and gathering in sweeps. Low on the horizon, sheet lightning flashes. The boy has opened his curtain and is standing at his window. He looks out into the street, and sees me here at mine. His face looks tense, his expression alert. Is he afraid? The wind increases to a gust, and brings a swirl of fully formed raindrops. He continues to look at me while the brief storm flurries itself out, the rain stopping suddenly, the lightning fading to a sullen gleam on the horizon.

A car pulls up and the boy's mother gets out, and also the man who arrived earlier in the van. She stands on the doorstep and takes out her mobile, and the child darts from the window, and reappears to open the front door. He comes back to the window a short while later, as the last soft throb of thunder fades. The breeze shifts again, bringing a lick of coolness. I lift my left hand to the glass in an unexpected gesture of affinity.

The tarmac of the road shines with a smooth slick of rain. Through my window, which is ajar, the outside world smells impossibly sweet.

II

Max

He stayed all night. When I let her in after the movies he came in too. He just stepped right in, his hand steering the back of her as if she might not know where she was going. 'Shall I put some coffee on?' she said. 'Or maybe you'd prefer a nightcap?' I guessed that would be the cue for the bottle of Grand Marnier to appear. It was given to her by a customer one Christmas. I don't think she actually likes it. She experimented with adding it to chocolate mousse once and that wasn't a hit either. He said yes to the Grand Marnier and she stood right on her tiptoes to reach the special glasses you're supposed to pour it in. I'd have offered to stand on the stool and reach them for her like I usually do but she didn't even give me a glance. Instead, he turned towards me and said, 'It's late, you should be in your bed,' and the way he said it was what Mrs Winters would have called in key stage two comprehension practice 'less of an observation, more an actual instruction'. I waited to see if Mum would disagree, or if she would start telling me about the film, which would normally be what she would do, but she just poured the Grand Marnier, and went through to the sitting room couch, tucking one leg up underneath her when she sat down. The storm was rumbling away. I went up to my room and looked across at the old lady. She put her hand flat on her window pane and I thought if I did the same on mine it would feel like we were pressing palms, and so I did that and then stood there for a little while longer until it was too dark to see.

It's weird but when it's dark you can hear things better. Maybe your eyes distract your ears from their business. My bedroom is over the sitting room so I could hear her laughing, the lowness of his voice, and then both of them laughing together. That's nice, I thought, that's good that she's having a fun time. Sometimes the beauty business isn't much fun. She says people mostly look in the mirror and wish they saw something else. She says there are only so many ills you can cure with a tinted moisturiser applied with a brush.

When I woke up I made straight for her room. I knew she had early appointments so our blue pouffe chat time might be a bit quick. I thought maybe now she'd tell me about the film while she straightened her hair, or put on her mascara.

Instead when I walked in, I saw his hairy back. He was lying in the bed, propped on one elbow, his shoulder turned towards me like one of those cement bollards that block your way in the street. As well as being hairy, his back is white and shiny like lard. My grandma used lard to cook her roast potatoes and I'd watch her slice through a block of it and it looked just like his skin. Mum wasn't in bed; she was up and sort of dressed in matching coloured underwear, which is usually only for special occasions and going out. She had a hairgrip in her mouth and was trying to pin up her hair. It was tumbling all down her neck and she kept reaching for it and missing. She was flushed rosy-pink, although she hadn't put on any blusher, and she was laughing and saying, 'You've made me late, I'll be on the back foot all day.' Her voice didn't sound cross though. She turned to pick up her uniform and he reached across and gave her a slap on the bum. Not a slap that would hurt, just as if her bum was *his*. That's the best way I can describe it, like when explorers reach the North Pole and stick a great big flag on it. His hand was almost as large as the part of her bum covered by her pants. That was when he saw me standing in the doorway. 'Where did you appear from matey, what are you doing here?' he said, as if I had no right to be there, and as if it isn't the way we begin every day. His voice wasn't what I'd call friendly, it was a bit like a policeman's when they're moving you along in a traffic jam and they expect you to do just what they say. I looked over to Mum to see if she'd explain, but she just said, 'Morning Max!' in a tone that was oddly jolly. It's the one she uses when she talks to the window cleaner before she suggests he changes the water in his buckets.

He sat fully up in the bed, his chest practically as wide as the pillow, and looked me straight in the eye. 'You're too old to be coming into your mother's bedroom of a morning. And if you did think it was a bright idea, you should at least give a good knock.' That was me told.

I stood there for a bit, waiting for her to say something, but instead the bedroom was just busy with silence. She stooped at the mirror to put on her lipstick. She didn't bother with doing the lip-liner first, or any primer before her tinted moisturiser. That'll mean it's not looking so tidy by elevenses. *If you take short cuts in beauty, you don't get the same finish.*

I shrugged, went downstairs and poured myself some Frosties. My heart was beating quite fast and I sat at the table and stared hard at the kitchen wall to calm me down a bit. He came in whistling, wearing just a t-shirt and his boxer shorts. She was behind him, buttoning up her white overall. He helped himself to bacon and eggs from the fridge, and cooked it standing at the stove like he was the captain at the wheel of a ship. He had the gas turned on too high so all the fat spat everywhere and normally she would mind but she didn't even seem to notice. He rubbed his chin with his hand and said, 'I look like Desperate Dan in the morning if I don't shave; it's not a good look for business.' She told him he could borrow her razor from the bathroom cabinet. She only waxes anyway so it never gets used. She carried on gulping down coffee *so hot it's scalding* and snapping her bracelets on, and hopping round the table looking for her other flip-flop. When the doorbell rang with her first customer I think I was the only person listening for it. He was sitting at the table by then, using the knife and fork like shovels to get it all into his mouth. I looked down at the floor because it wasn't a pretty sight. And then, on his feet, on his toes, were thick, dark tufts of gorilla hair. I wondered if she'd noticed. She might think of adding toe-waxing as a summer treatment option. If there's a *four hundred per cent increase* in women wanting their toenails painted, there might be as many men wanting their feet not to look like King Kong's.

He waited until the customer had gone into the Powder Room before he went back upstairs to get dressed. He left me his plate to clear. He came downstairs smelling of aftershave and let himself out. He didn't say goodbye to me, although I was putting stuff in the dishwasher so he might have waved from the hallway and I just didn't see.

When I went upstairs, there were two things I noticed, noticing being my skill. First, mum's pink razor by the tap and his dark bristles in the basin which he'd not made a very good effort of swooshing away. I finished the job for him. And then, second, something different in the spare bedroom. We call it that but there isn't a bed in it, and you could probably only fit a cot in it anyway, not a proper-sized bed. Mum has a wardrobe where she keeps clothes that it's the wrong season for wearing. There's also a box of shoes which she labelled *Oh God what was I thinking*. There are some lime green suede loafers which she takes in and out because she can't quite make up her mind.

And now, there, in the middle of the carpet, is the blue pouffe. Just right there, instead of in its usual place by her dressing table. My first thought was that it had been some kind of mistake. Maybe she'd stood on it to reach something she wanted to show him. But there's nothing out of reach in the spare room, you don't even need to stand on tiptoe. The pouffe was just plonked right there.

I picked it up and held it in front of me, like a shield for a battle. Then, I walked back into her bedroom and went over to the dressing table. That had also been moved a little bit, so that it was centred to the wall. I couldn't really put the pouffe back in its proper place without it being squidged up against the laundry basket. Sitting next to the dirty clothes wouldn't be the nicest of things. The bed had been moved too, so that it lined up a little more with the full length mirror. They must have done that last night when I was sleeping or I'd have heard. She'd moved some of her shoes so that they didn't look all of a clutter. I stood there with the pouffe for a minute and heard her say goodbye to her client, and then straight away call the next one in from the sitting room. The smell of slightly burned bacon was drifting up the stairs. I took the pouffe back to the spare room and put it neatly right in the middle.

What I'm thinking now is that she might have said something. Not so much as a by your leave (that's another of Grandad's expressions) but we could have had a little discussion. When someone's started their day in the same place for as long as they are able to remember, the least you could do is have some kind of final ceremony; one last chat while all the make-up goes on. I looked at the little Moroccan glass she keeps all her brushes in and ran my finger over the top of all the different bristles. They felt a whole lot nicer than what he left in the sink.

12

Minnie

*When my mother's parents visit from India – it is the first time I
meet them – she does not tell them that Father has sold the parkland. They stay for a whole week and it is not once mentioned.
There will not be a swarm of men measuring, drawing, planning
for some time, so my grandmother sits in a high-backed chair in
the walled garden, and Hooper, who is the plants man, talks to her
about roses. I hear her talking to him about the jacaranda that
grows on their terrace and I hold the word in my mouth like a
bright, hard jewel. She tells of the peacocks on their lawn, and how
they shriek, and that the pink of the bougainvillea has to be seen
to be believed. I watch her, restored to solitude after Hooper has
continued with his work. She dabs at her mouth with an embroidered lace handkerchief, and her back is as straight as a ruler.
Sitting there in the shade of the pergola, she already looks like a
photograph of something in the past. My grandfather walks with
a cane that is cut from the tree in their peacock-shriek-filled garden.
He insists on it being taken from the highest branch as he says it
will have absorbed more sunlight and will be good for his rheumatics.
I am taken with the idea of a cane that is jam-packed with sunshine.
I am curious to touch it, to see if it transmits a warmth to my
palm. On the one occasion I am bold enough to do so, it is propped
against the breakfast table while he is eating the kedgeree my mother
has asked Cook to prepare especially. When I reach out to hold it,*

*I accidentally cause it to clatter to the floor. I am sent from the
table. It did not feel warm.*

*Father decides that I will transfer to the grammar school. It has
recently opened in town and even though I am fourteen he says I will
benefit. I don't take Common Entrance as Clara had done, or go to
Elizabeth Hall, where the boarders are allowed to bring their ponies
and where on Commemoration Day there is a picnic on the school
lawn and the mothers wear vast-brimmed hats and kitten-heeled shoes.
I go instead to the grammar school which is filled with girls I have
never encountered before – daughters of shopkeepers, of seamstresses,
even someone whose father works in a factory. My father thinks this
is good and that it is time to 'mix it all up'. My mother purses her
lips and says, 'I fear you will become a Socialist,' which in their circles
is a word which carries fear like polio and scarlet fever. It will, they
say, take away everything they have. 'I think I already am,' he says,
'the arguments are convincing,' and my mother leaves the drawing
room as if she can't bear to look at him.*

*I love my school. There is so much of an appetite for learning, it
is as if some of the girls would like to actually eat their books. We
read* Wuthering Heights *and* Jane Eyre *in English class, and talk
of who we would like to marry most. I choose Heathcliff because I
think he would love me to my very bones. We have science overalls
with our names embroidered on them, and stand before Bunsen burners
learning the periodic table. I come home and chant Latin declensions
for homework, and French irregular verbs. We do not have sewing
lessons, which is a source of joy for me, but we have lessons in Home
Economics because we are told it is important to know how to feed
our families properly. It is assumed we will have husbands and children, but a woman comes to talk to us from Oxford, and she tells us
that we should also aspire to make great contributions. After she visits,
the headmistress has some polished oak boards nailed up in the entrance
hall, and she tells us in assembly that the names of the girls who
achieve places at Oxbridge will be painted upon them in italicised*

gold lettering. I pause before them when the first names are being added, and the names of the colleges become my own kind of rosary. Somerville, Lady Margaret Hall, St Hilda's, Girton . . . *I repeat them in time to the pedal-turn of my bicycle.*

I am standing by the boards one day and there is a girl I don't know beside me. When I ask her name, I discover she is Hooper's granddaughter. I like it that she wants her name on the board too. I tell my parents at dinner time and my mother says, 'I don't know what will become of you,' which seems a new level of potential disapproval. Her focus has moved on from my posture to my outlook, but anyway she will know soon enough.

Clara is calling me. 'Are you ready, Minnie? What on earth are you doing in there? It is time for our walk to the churchyard.' She adds for good measure, 'We shall miss the best of the afternoon.' She has cut ruby pelargoniums from the pots by the kitchen door. 'They will tolerate the heat best,' she calls, and then tells me to bring the small watering can in case the communal one is missing.

I do as I am told. I stop writing and go and find the small watering can. We are trapped in a pattern of familiar behaviour. She is in charge and I am the one who is to do as I am told. My mother made this clear, and even now neither of us disobeys.

The light in the churchyard always feels darker, greener, than anywhere else. There are yew trees and a vast flat-leaf holly tree which stands to the left of my parents' grave. It is hard when I stand before it not to be reminded of the discrepancy in their life span. I can't help but feel that my father, who we buried aged fifty-five, shares his final resting place with a very old woman. My mother lived to ninety-three, and would have been unrecognisable to him.

The pelargoniums in the urn are a blaze of colour against the lichen on the headstone. Clara busies herself tugging at a weed, and brushing away a scattering of beech leaves with her palm. We only speak occasionally, to reminisce. *Remember the milk pudding she would give us when the nights began to draw in?* We behave like good children in front of our parents' grave. We are both wearing straw hats against the sunshine, just as Mother would wish of us.

It strikes me as I kneel down and touch the weathered stone that even though my mother found out all too soon what became of me, it is still a cause of quiet, profound gratitude to me that my father did not.

The old school building has been knocked down recently to make way for a smart new Academy. I wonder what become of the oak boards in the entrance hall. All those clever young women and their gold-lettered futures. I like to hold onto the thought that they made their great contributions, and that Elizabeth Hooper's name was painted up in the absence of my own.

13

Max

I wouldn't have called it 'in a jiffy'. Not when he spent most of today (which is a Sunday, the day when the Powder Room is closed for business and we usually go out for a burger or go to a movie or go shopping) making me watch him do DIY and then help him clear up. There was lots of sawing, hacking and crashing and then some plastering. The Velux opens all by itself now; you just have to press a remote control. The blind that is attached to it also slides down, all quick and smooth. You just point at it with a different remote and hey presto. She's labelled the remotes with Dymo tape – one says *window*, the other says *blind*. She's propped the two of them up against the bowl which contains exactly a hundred glass pebbles. When he did the first demonstration she clapped her hands as if she'd never seen anything like it. We all stood there, him grinning with his hands on his hips, and me with the dustpan and brush in mine because he'd told me to sweep up. Another thing Grandad once said to me is that if the people who make the mess are also the ones who'll have to clear it up, you generally find that they work a bit tidier. He knew about that because he was a painter and decorator. He said plasterers mix more neatly than a woman icing a cake if it's their hoover that's going to be sucking round the skirting boards. Sweeping up made me sneeze, not that she noticed. She was too busy saying,

'Sayonara step ladders, hoorah, I shall never need you again.'
It didn't seem the moment to point out that it was actually me
who'd always been fetching and carrying them, and climbing
up and down them, with the added stress of trying to be very
quiet because of the client. 'They come here to escape noise
and fuss, not to have more of it,' is what she always says.
If anybody should have been applauding the remote controls, it
was me, not that clapping would have been possible with a full
dustpan in my hand.

It was gone four o' clock by the time he was finished. Tomorrow
night he's going to paint over the new plaster when it's had time
to dry out. When I emptied out the dustpan I felt sick with
longing for our usual Sunday, although now that I think about
it I might just have been sick with actual hunger.

When I said that we go out for a burger or to a movie or
shopping, I should say that it's actually mostly shopping.
Sometimes a burger is tacked on at the end. Mum needs to spend
time in the shops because she *needs to be on top of seasonal colour
palettes. Spotting key trends* is important for her work. I joined a
hockey club not last spring but the one before, and it meant she
had to take me on the bus to practices mid-week and to matches
every Sunday morning. The tournaments actually went on until
the middle of the afternoon. She reckons because of that *the neon
trend completely blindsided her*. Since then, she's *always on high
alert for the next pop of colour*.

While he put his tools back in his box she sat on her desk,
swinging her legs. She looked at her watch and said, 'Is it too
early for a glass of wine or a cold beer?'

'Almost five o'clock,' he said, 'I'd say that makes us practically
Methodists.' I've just Googled that; apparently Methodists drink
hardly anything at all. Sometimes, *a schooner of sherry is permitted
on very special occasions*. There's no sign of sherry in our kitchen,
although I was surprised to see the six-pack of beer in the

fridge. She must have added that to this week's Tesco delivery. I didn't spot her unpack it and it was stashed right at the back of the top shelf. She never orders beer, not since she decided wheat makes her bloated – although not the wheat in pasta which is weird. It's also weird because I thought beer was made from hops not wheat. I only know this because Mrs Winters hung hop vines round the classroom for Harvest Festival. Her brother-in-law is a hop farmer in Herefordshire.

He went and had a shower and came down wearing a clean shirt, although it was a bit stuck to him because he ~~was~~ wasn't properly dry. He sat on the couch with his feet up on the chair opposite, and he swigged the beer from the bottle without even thinking about a glass. Mum sat on the arm of the couch with a glass of white wine, and she was flipping her hair from her neck and smoothing her lips together and he said, 'I know, perfect end to the day, let's order a Chinese.' He said he had a favourite restaurant where he was an absolute regular, and where he only had to call and they recognised his voice straight away, and then always prepared for him the meal they were actually planning to eat later themselves.

'Whatever's the best bit,' he said, 'that the old man has got at the market.' Mum licked her lips and said yum, and he got out his mobile and pressed the number on speed dial, which I guess was proof of him being a regular.

Twenty minutes later I went to answer the door to a man who had just got off a moped. He stood on the step and didn't take off his helmet so his words were a bit muffled, and his accent was a little bit tricky, but I heard it right the first time, even though I asked him to repeat it to check. 'Meal for two,' he said, swiftly passing me the bag. And it was, and they're downstairs, eating it right now. The smell of noodles is wafting up the stairs. He got two plates out of the cupboard, as if he'd lived here all his life, and it was only then Mum realised that he'd ordered for two not three and she looked at me, her mouth a bit wonky on one side, and he caught her look and laughed, lifted one hand in the air, his fingers spread wide and said, 'Trust me, babes, he wouldn't enjoy this anyway. There's squid, lots of chilli, ginger. I know what kids like to eat.' She finished snapping open the chopsticks. She'd blushed when he said babes, but it didn't look like with embarrassment, more like she liked him saying it. She hesitated for a moment, and took out a third plate and gestured as if I could share hers if I'd like to. I caught the look on his face, directed right at me, and I thought it was probably better not. I offered to make myself some cheese on toast instead. She told him I'm a Michelin-starred chef at making it: 'Aren't you darling?'. Her face looked relieved, like she'd been let off the hook.

I've eaten it here at my bedroom window. My room's a bit hot. It's almost six o'clock and the woman down the road is still sitting outside on her sofa. Just now an ice-cream van came by. Some of the little kids chased down the pavement to catch it up. I don't think the song it plays is very cheerful. When it drives away, it always leaves me feeling a bit sad. The old lady opposite lifted her head when she heard it and she watched the kids all cluster round for whippy ice cream. She looked up at my window and she looked again at the van. I think she was wondering why I wasn't queuing for some too. She tilted her head. She looked a bit like a bird. Sometimes what people are saying doesn't need words. I lifted up my cheese on toast, which I'd dotted and dabbed with some tomato ketchup. She smiled and nodded.

They haven't turned the television on downstairs. That's what normally happens on Sunday night, but not tonight. It feels like everything that is usual is becoming the past. Their voices have gone a bit murmury. I can't hear what they're saying. He's properly closed the door again, which is most likely why. I'm thinking the best bet is for me to stay up here in my bedroom. I haven't had a chance to look at *The Way Things Work* for a while. It's my fattest and most interesting book and I keep it on the shelf by my bed. The last time I read it, I learned a lot about the mechanics of movement. Inclined planes, cams and cranks – I was a total expert. Maybe tonight I'll move on to 'Harnessing the Elements', or 'Electricity and Automation'. That's what the Velux is now an example of.

I'm guessing ol' hairy arms will probably be staying the night again. He'll be in her bed in the morning, all white and lardy. It's probably a good job the blue pouffe has stayed in its new place in the spare room.

14

Minnie

The last summer that the parkland and gardens belong to Rosemount, my mother develops a sudden liking for tennis. She does not play herself, but she organises tournaments, and Saturday afternoons are filled with doubles pairings, and racquets in heaps on the lawn, and a large chalkboard propped up by the lupin border where my mother sits and writes out the scores in uniform, italic script. She wears a broad-brimmed straw hat which keeps her face entirely in shade.

Clara and I play with the adults sometimes but mostly we help. We carry trays of drinks to the ladies who sit fanning themselves beneath the purple beech. 'Would you care for some orange barley water?' we say, with a little bob that is almost a curtsey. The ice in the glass chinks as we reach down. My hands are sticky with the sweetness of orange. My mother says manners maketh man but that it's true for girls too. We move between the trees, our voices soft and low.

Clara is almost nineteen, has left school, and is doing a Pitman's typing course. She sits daily in the parlour and types the quick brown fox jumps over the lazy dog. *She stands by the telephone in the hallway and lifts her arm to an imaginary switchboard. 'I have a call for you, Mr Jennings,' she says in a voice which is not entirely her own. I think she hates the tennis afternoons with a passion, not that she would ever own up. Not about that, or the Pitman's course, or the young man, James, who recently came calling. She sits next to* him on a bench by the delphiniums, her legs neatly crossed at the ankle. I am sitting above them, wedged in the crook of a branch of a tree. The boy shows her a small drawing he's done of a lacewing on a leaf. Its wings are green and gauzy. I have learned from my encyclopedia that lacewings sing courting songs to each other and cause the leaf beneath them to tremble. I appraise him from my branch and wonder if he has chosen to draw a lacewing as a subtle, delicate, courtship song to Clara. 'Hmm,' she says, studying it intently, as if she is an entomologist checking for absolute accuracy, and then she says nothing further, folding her hands in her lap and the boy says nothing at all but blushes a little and folds up the drawing and puts it back in his pocket. If I could have whispered to her from my nest I would have told her that she should have said 'Why, how beautiful!' and asked if she might keep it; to have understood that it was meant as some sort of token. His visits dwindle after that, and then stop altogether. My mother is disappointed because she says she would have liked a wedding while there was still lawn enough to pitch a marquee.

Clara for her part is becoming so quiet, so stiff, that I think if someone were to touch her she would either crackle with static or bloom blue with a bruise.

My father loves the tennis. He shouts 'Shot!' with vigour and careers across the court. He does not play in the mixed doubles because my mother doesn't; he plays in the men's four, where they slap each other's shoulders when one of them has served an ace. I stand, my tray empty of glasses, my shoes kicked off so that I can feel the softness of the grass (something I know will provoke a reprimand when my mother catches sight of me) and I watch the men playing tennis together, laughing and bantering and then serving with force, a whup! as the racquet strings strike the ball. Even though I am not yet fifteen, I am sure I will like men when I am older. I will like kissing, and being held in arms more muscled than my own. I want to lie on a man's chest and hear his laugh rumble inside his ribs, and also the beat of *his heart through a freshly laundered white shirt. I will wear an over-sized sweater which will belong to the man I marry. It will swaddle me in softness, and with the smell of his skin and his soap. Cigarette smoke will spiral up from where he lies beside me on the pillow. We will drive up to Scotland in a Volkswagen Beetle, and catch fish in lochs in the Outer Hebrides. He will kiss me in a blue hurl of rain, and my hair will be drenched and I will be soaked to the skin. I will rub myself dry with a tartan blanket from the car, and we will return to our cottage and lie naked before a fire on a thick paisley eiderdown. He will read me poetry and I will feed him honey from a spoon. I decide all these things holding my tray of empty glasses, the grass soft to my feet, the low murmur of women's talk beyond me. They talk in whispers of wombs, of a baby with too much fluid in its skull, of a recipe for Bakewell tart, of hosiery, of knitting patterns, of something on the wireless. I decide then and there I will never in my life sit down with a knitting pattern. My mother's voice is sharp from beside the raspberry lupins. 'Stop daydreaming, Hermione,' she says, 'attend to the glasses and put your shoes back on your feet.'*

I am grateful in retrospect for my tender, naïve imaginings. I may not actually have been loved, but I have conjured it up fully.

The idea for the tennis lessons comes from my mother. She is less convinced than my father that my route to accomplishment is through Chemistry, Latin and Mathematics. She says eligible men are put off by too much learning and that it is generally more fruitful to be able to walk well in heels and play a decent game of tennis. She arranges for a tennis coach to come, but Clara is so miserable at the prospect my mother quickly relents. Clara says playing tennis makes the bones of her wrist hurt, and that being out in the sun gives her a headache. It is agreed that she will read in the glasshouse instead, or practise the piano. I am quick to hope that the prospect of the lessons might allow a little bartering. I say I am happy to start them, but please may I have white frilly knickers like Gussie Moran. The answer is no. Predictably, absolutely, flatly no. I am to wear my school regulation navy gym ones, with my name clearly sewn on a label in the back.

When it happened, if I'd been wearing knickers like Gussie Moran's, would I have blamed it on that? Would I have thought it my fault for wearing something so obviously enticing: a pair of white lace knickers, my legs below them lean and tanned? But I was not. I was wearing a pair of thick navy blue pants, with additional elastic around the thighs.

The tennis coach is about forty. His hair is parted to the side and slicked with a little Brylcreem. He wears tennis shoes with a green arrow on the sides and pungent aftershave – Old Spice. I know this because I see it in his sports bag.

Brylcreem, Old Spice. The beginnings of fresh sweat. A litany of scents which can still send me, in free fall, down through the years.

15

Max

Turns out he's got a daughter. She's two years older than me, quite a lot taller, and she's called Jasmine. She lives miles away in Wetherby with his ex-wife. 'Fragrant by name and fragrant by nature' is what he said when he introduced us. I doubt it's the first time he's said it. It's also a tricky line; when you open a conversation with something like that, it's understandable if the listener gives a big old sniff. I was tempted to recite the poem 'Whether the weather be fine', which was one of my grandad's favourites. He'd usually recite it after the one about if the cows be lying, the weather be dying. He loved a rhyme about weather. I thought Jasmine might get a kick out of hearing it, what with her coming from Wetherby, but I think I missed the moment. My mouth was half open to say it and she was already texting.

He wasn't expecting her to come down. Her mum got an offer to go away for the weekend with some of her friends, and Jasmine was 'right out of alternatives'. I don't know whether that means she likes visiting him or not. It certainly put him right out of alternatives other than bringing her along for brunch.

I'm going to say a little bit about brunch before I say more about Jasmine. It's the first time mum's invited anybody for brunch. It's a new thing for her. It *requires advance preparation but can then unfold in a relaxed and informal way, and leave the whole afternoon wide open for something spontaneous.* She made

American pancakes (batter whipped up in advance), which she served with blueberries, bacon, and maple syrup, and a lemon almond cake to follow. She made a berry smoothie in the blender which she decorated with some seeds, and she put yogurt in small bowls with a swirly drizzle of honey. She was going to do initials, but decided that would look like trying too hard, which she says as *TTH*. Jasmine said it was all 'super-pretty'. He mostly just ate the bacon. My Frosties weren't allowed on the table because Mum said it would spoil the look. She had a point. She'd spent ages preparing it, which wasn't that relaxing, and arranging it all very carefully on the table to *give the impression of delicious plenty* just like her magazine described.

She clapped her hands when he introduced her to Jasmine. 'It's so lovely to have a teenage girl in the house,' she said. 'Why don't you pick a treatment after brunch and we can have some girly time in the Powder Room?' Jasmine looked almost interested. But then when we were eating she was spearing blueberries with her fork in a way that I thought was a little bit spiteful. She was already wearing make-up and I wondered if mum was itching to get it off. When you know how to apply it, it's very frustrating to look at a bad job. Her eyeliner started all at the wrong part on her lid, and she had a big smudge of blusher that was not in the apple of her cheek. You notice stuff like that when you have *a trained eye*. I think I have it too, mostly from listening rather than doing it, obviously.

Mum did her a two-tone manicure. It went from plum to indigo, which is a tricky combo; when you get to halfway it has to look like a mix of the two colours. She also whipped off the eyeliner and blusher and replaced it with nude eyes and a pop of candy gloss on her lips. Jasmine looked a lot less sulky although I wouldn't exactly say pretty. Mum came out of the Powder Room, clapping her hands again and saying, 'Look! Look! How beautiful is your girl?'

He seemed more interested in looking at Mum's top. I was surprised she was wearing it, because when she bought it at River Island I was with her in the changing room and she said, 'This is too see-through for wearing anywhere but on the beach, but it's one of those pieces I could wear on holiday year in year out. It'll be a perfect little lunch cover-up over a bikini.' She'd obviously had a speedy re-think on that one, and decided it was also okay for a brunch. She went and stood with her hands on Jasmine's shoulders and stroked Jasmine's hair, and made a pouty sad face and said, 'Oh you've made me wish I had a daughter now,' which I think was a bit insensitive and hurtful. I can understand how she wanted to make Jasmine feel welcome and special, but it's a bit of a poke in the eye with a stick if you're her unexpected, Trojan-horse son. I also thought it showed that she wasn't really using her memory again. When she was training for the Powder Room and getting all her certificates at college, she used to come home every night and practise what she'd learned on me. She said it was cheaper than paying for models, and also she could just do one eye which they'd never settle for, so she could use less product and save money too. She used to make me lie on the couch under the blue Aertex blanket, and she'd tint my eyelashes, and practise pulling the thickest hairs of my eyebrow out with her tweezers so that it was *swift and painless* (which actually, it mostly wasn't). She took ages to master painting a thumbnail without making me twist my wrist right round on the table. I bet Jasmine wouldn't have lain there silently without ever complaining. Also, after practising, Mum was never that interested in getting it all off. She preferred putting her feet up with a glass of Pinot Grigio and saying things like 'I'm totally bushed' or 'Standing all day is a bugger'.

One eye with tinted lashes is more noticeable than you'd think, and a flannel dipped in water and rubbed over it until your eye fizzes doesn't touch it. And a Raspberry Sherbet thumbnail when she's run out of remover stays put even when you scratch at it with a corner of your ruler until you make the cuticle bleed.

When Jasmine had finished fluttering her two-tone nails around, he said, 'Why don't you two go for a walk? Max, give Jasmine the neighbourhood tour.' She didn't look that interested, but he raised his eyebrows at her so she started pushing her feet into her Converse so that the heel was all trodden down at the back. 'Make it lively,' he said, dipping his head at me as if it was an order. I think that makes what happened next partly his fault. I think he planted the seed, even if he didn't realise he did. I think that happens a lot; people set things in motion with no idea of the consequence. If you suggest something should be lively, mostly it turns out to be.

We came out of the front door and I hadn't even had time to pull it to when I could see he was shooing Mum up the stairs. He was walking behind her with his palms flat to the cheeks of her bottom. He was sort of squidging and patting it, and she was laughing and sort of tipped forwards a little, and he put his teeth to her back to where her bra does up, and I wondered if, when she was making brunch, this was what she had in mind when leaving the afternoon free for *something spontaneous*.

Jasmine wasn't that chatty. We sat on the wall for a bit because she didn't want to *challenge her nails by doing up her laces*. She had her toes tipped up so her Converse didn't fall off. The old lady was sitting in her chair opposite writing in her book. 'She looks like a right old bat,' Jasmine said, which isn't true. Her face is soft, that's the best way to describe it, and then sometimes soft and sad which I don't really want to think about. When Jasmine put her head down to finally do up her laces, I gave the lady a little wave. She gave me one in return and raised her eyebrow a bit quizzically at Jasmine. Jasmine had sat back up and popped some gum in her mouth now and was chewing with big, wide, figure of eight lips. The candy gloss Mum put on didn't look like it would last a second.

I tried making conversation as we set off round the block. I told her the estate was once the massive garden of the big house with lakes and a tennis court and massive flower beds. I'm not sure if it's actually true – Mum told me it was – but anyway sometimes you have to exaggerate to make a story better. It didn't impress her much anyway; she mostly kept checking her phone for texts. I asked her what her mum did and she told me she was an estate agent. 'It would be much cooler for me,' she said, 'if she worked in the beauty business. When I go to college, I think I might like to do that.' I thought I wouldn't point out that it mostly meant you stayed home all summer holiday doing bikini waxes. If she's thinking of a career in beauty, it would be mean to say anything which might put her off.

Then, out of the blue, she said, 'I bet my mum isn't going away with her friends. She'll be going to a hotel with some bloke she's met showing a house.'

She looked at me, and yawned (I could see all of the chewing gum) and she tugged at a little bit of the skin at the side of her nail, and she said 'Dontcha think sometimes that they don't behave like grown-ups at all?' I nodded but didn't say anything else as I'm not really qualified. Some of my friends at school have divorced parents who don't get out of the car when they hand them over after the weekend. One of the dads drives off giving the 'v' sign out of the window, over and over. If I look hard enough there are advantages to be found in Zorba not being around.

Jasmine was taking a bit more interest in her surroundings now. She clocked Martine and her daughter, and took a selfie next to the lamp post with *WILD CHILD* sprayed on it. She looked a bit further along the road and then something caught her eye. She suddenly looked like one of those sphinx cats which set puzzles for Egyptian travellers, her chin tilted upwards and the corners of her mouth turned up. 'How about a game of dare?'

My first feeling was that it wasn't going to end well. I hate playing dare because I don't like asking anyone to do something that either might upset them, go badly wrong, or just not be a sensible thing to do. That's probably enough reasons. I also don't like going first at setting the dare as you might mis-judge the tone. For some people a game of dare might just be whirling round in a nice, safe, open space till you're dizzy, whereas others (and I know this) want you to play chicken with a car.

I nodded, although if she'd actually looked at my face, she'd have seen that I was uncomfortable, but she wasn't looking in my direction at all, she was bug-eyed, focused on whatever it was up the street.

'See that ladder,' she said, not missing a beat and pointing to a house further up which was being re-painted, 'I dare you to go and shake that and then run away. If you don't there's a forfeit. My choice what the forfeit is.'

I don't quite know where to begin. The thing about being someone whose grandad was a chatty painter and decorator is firstly that you know many words relevant to house painting and secondly quite a lot about Health and Safety as it applies to ladders. I know why it's harder leaning on roofs which have dormer windows (you need scaffolding or you might crack the tiles) and how to secure a ladder the most safely when it is fully extended. Also the importance of having someone at the bottom – ideally all of the time – but certainly when the person up it is at a stretch reaching for a window sill or the soffit or fascia.

As we got closer to the ladder, I could see that the person up it was very slapdash as far as Health and Safety was concerned. There was no one at the foot of it, and the only thing to stop it moving was a stack of three bricks pushed against the bottom.

Also, he had paint tins, a tray, and two rollers just higgledy-piggledy close to where he would step off the bottom rung. That's a trip hazard right there, and before you know it you've brought the whole lot clattering down.

I looked up as we approached and all I could see was his paint-splattered overalls. It was difficult to tell whether he was an old guy or someone young. If he was young he'd be less to blame, because unless someone has taught you best practice, how would you know? I'm lucky because even though I don't want to be a painter and decorator when I grow up, if I ever did I'd have Health and Safety totally nailed.

I stood there looking up at him, and she stood right by my elbow saying, 'Go on then, divvy, give it a shake,' and I knew that I wouldn't, knew I wouldn't for all kinds of reasons, but mostly because he wasn't even holding on with one hand (*rookie error*, Grandad said in my head) so was likely to come tumbling right down on the pavement. I had to close my eyes and swallow just at the thought of his body hitting the pavement with a *whump!* The paint would spatter everywhere.

I put my hands in my jeans pockets, and pushed them down really deep. She raised her eyebrow at me and gave the gum a flick with her tongue from one side of her mouth to another. 'Chicken?' she said, turning it into a question. I told her it was a stupid idea and that somebody would get hurt. That bounced right off her. She just said 'Chicken' again, but with no trace of doubt in her voice this time. Then she said, 'Time for your forfeit; let's walk back to your house.' I swear she hadn't looked as pleased or as happy all day.

She told me to sit on the wall and she went into the house. Mum and her Dad must still have been upstairs in the bedroom. I'm guessing they didn't even clock her coming back in. She went into the Powder Room without so much as a by your leave, and she helped herself to the sharp steel scissors that Mum uses to cut the waxing-cloth strips to size. She must have spotted them when she was having her nails painted. She came back and sat beside me on the wall. 'I'm going to cut a chunk out of the front of your hair,' she said. 'Uneven Stephen, this is your forfeit.'

I'm going to say what I think in a numbered way now, because it helps organise my thoughts:

1. I haven't mentioned it before, but I'm growing the front of my hair. I like it short at the sides and quite long on top. It's a little bit floppy but I've even been thinking I might grow it long enough to go in a top knot, like the waiter who served us when we went to Gourmet Burger Kitchen.

2. You've got to wonder, if you think about it carefully, whether she hadn't planned the whole thing: the dare, the scissors, the lot. When my mouth was half open thinking about saying 'Whether the weather be fine', she was perhaps imagining how I'd look with the front of my hair cut totally short.

3. It's not OK to run away from a forfeit, which actually I could have done as she was coming back down the path with the scissors snip-snipping in her hand. I think if you agree to a forfeit, which I sort of did, you can't do a bunk, even if you don't want your hair cut and you've been growing it carefully since Easter.

4. Jasmine is bigger than me and taller than me but she is still a girl, and so even when someone comes towards you waving a pair of scissors that by rights should not have been taken from the Powder Room without even asking, even though you might feel like pushing her away really hard, you are likely to get in more trouble for doing that than for having your hair cut. Also you must look at yourself in the mirror that night and accept that

you did not behave properly because you used your strength against a girl which is never a good idea.

So I just sat there. She bit down on her chewing gum really hard, held a bunch of the front of my hair in her fist like a horse's tail and hacked it off with the scissors. She held it up above her head like a trophy and laughed and said, 'Next time Maxy boy, better to just go on and shake the ladder.' She wiggled her bottom as she said it.

It was at that point my Mum came out of the front door, with him behind her. He was bare-chested which I didn't expect. He has another tattoo like a vine which snakes up from his pants across his stomach. I was distracted by it while they all had a good look at me. Jasmine dissolved into giggles, suddenly acting much younger, and said, 'It was a forfeit . . . Can you believe it?' She held up the clump of my hair, which looked like a hamster. Its dishwater colour was the least of my problems now.

'You big girl's blouse, whaddya let her do that for?' he said, but he was laughing too, as if looking at me with a chunk of hair gone was the best way to round off a delicious brunch.

Mum had put her hand over her mouth to hide that she was trying not to laugh as well. 'I thought you were growing it,' she said, which was even weirder as it sounded like she was blaming me for changing my mind, rather than having the change bapped right at me by Jasmine.

If she'd asked me later, I'd have told her what happened: the careless man up the ladder who would have hit the pavement if I'd done the dare, Jasmine getting the scissors without even asking permission, and the problem of pushing a girl. But there was no opportunity to say any of it because they turned round and went back inside and Jasmine took a quick Snapchat of me when she thought I wasn't looking.

He stayed on and they watched a Netflix movie. Jasmine spent the evening on Facebook and Instagram and he suggested I go up to bed at nine-thirty. I'm lying here now feeling the soft fuzzy bit at the front of my hair. The bits either side of it are swinging like theatre curtains. He says in the morning he'll use his clippers to trim the rest of it to a number two to match.

The only good thing about it was the lady opposite. She saw the whole thing: me sitting waiting on the wall while Jasmine fetched the scissors, and the clump of my hair held up in her hand.

She stood up and looked across at me and I looked right back at her. Sometimes, with some people, you don't need to say anything at all.

16

Minnie

When first he arrives for lessons he marches briskly onto the court, a large holdall full of racquets in his hand. Father is playing golf; my mother, Clara and I are at home, and also the Saturday maid who my mother refers to as 'a slip of a girl'. I catch her rolling her eyes when my mother walks past and I am impressed with her insolence, although ashamed of my disloyalty.

He is called Mr Lucas. He extends his hand to shake my mother's when he introduces himself, but he also gives a bow which is comically deep, and ends with a flourish. I feel he should be waving a large hat as if he is a musketeer. I can see my mother likes his manners; she nods her head approvingly and gives an almost-smile. She reaches over to where I stand, puts her hands on my shoulders to adjust me to my full height and says, 'This is Hermione. It is my hope that you will make of her an accomplished tennis player. I am hoping that whatever she may lack in aptitude will be made up for by her particular spirit.' She enunciates particular *as if it leaves a tinny taste in her mouth.*

Mr Lucas turns to me and smiles, and his gaze sweeps from my plimsolls to my scalp, and I feel myself prickling red. I am conscious of his teeth, which are smooth and gleaming but a little crowded in his mouth, and a gold signet ring on his smallest finger which catches in the light. Beyond me, in the glasshouse, I can see Clara, seated in a wicker chair, reading a novel. She fans her hand in the heat, and moves to another chair in the shade by the grapevine. Mr Lucas is taking my hand and wrapping it around the handle of a tennis racquet.

'Shake it with a firm grip, your arm tense,' he says, 'and then I will know the correct size of racquet for you to play with. That is the best way to make a good start.'

My mother says she will fetch us some refreshments. She comes back with a tray with two glasses of orange barley water. The ice cubes bob and chink as she places them on the tray by the court.

'Four and a half,' he is saying to me, 'that should do it.'

The afternoon is hot. The grass of the court has been flattened by weeks of heat and dryness. He strikes a ball to me and it lifts a soft pouf! of dust. My racquet feels as if it is slicing through solid warmth. My mother has retreated to the house. The leaves on the purple beech barely move.

'So Hermione,' he says, with a smile that is a little lopsided, 'I am to make a tennis player of you. Good girl.' He passes me a ball and tells me to go to the service line. I notice, as he passes it to me, that his fingernails are long and he has a scattering of dark hair on the back of his hand.

Beyond him, Clara begins to walk from the glasshouse across the lawn. She does not raise her eyes. She seems to move slowly, her skirt lilting with her gait. She does not turn to look at me even though I am willing her to do so. I raise my arm to serve and am aware of him watching me intently. He comes and stands beside me, and bounces his hand once, twice, against the racquet strings.

'Commonly mistaken as cat gut,' he says, 'which is wrong twice over. Cat gut is used for the strings of musical instruments and has nothing to do with cats. It's short for cattlegut, and made from cows' and sheeps' intestines. Tennis strings are made from natural gut which comes from the part of a cow's intestine called the serosa. It's washed and cut into ribbons, and then dyed and polished to the right dimension.' He taps the strings again. 'Natural gut; nothing beats it.'

I prepare to serve again and lift my eyes to see where the racquet will strike the ball, and the sunlight dazzles me so that I squint against it, and I grip the racquet tighter and think of what he has said, and the afternoon suddenly smells of blood and guts and my mind is full of the image of sheets of cows' intestine being washed and be-ribboned like suet, and as he tells me to arch more, to lift my chest, to plant my feet wider, I am slow to notice that his thumb nail has traced down the length of my outer thigh.

'Mr Lucas seems very affable,' my mother says to my father as we are having dinner later that evening.

'Mr Lucas?' he queries.

'The tennis coach that Hugh Carpenter recommended. He taught Minnie for the first time today.'

He looks at me over his wine glass. 'So, Min, are we to prepare to watch you at Wimbledon?'

My mother dabs primly at her lips with her napkin. I shake my head. With my fingertips I trace the faint red scratch on my leg.

The next week he comes again. The heat has held, the roses are wilting and the court is scorched brown. My mother has a headache and tells the Saturday girl to give him her apologies when she opens the door to him. I wait for him by the net. There is no sign of Clara.

'Today we will focus on the forehand,' he says, standing beside me, and placing one hand over my right hand, the other taking hold of my wrist. 'Strike with this hand and follow through with the other. Lift it up, raise it,' he says, 'to counterbalance the action of the racquet.' He lifts my left arm straight up in the air, and now I look as if I am keen to answer a question in class. His left hand moves quickly to my breast, and cups it completely. With his finger and thumb he strokes at my nipple. I blush scarlet.

'There's a good girl,' he says, 'I think you will be a quick learner.'

★   ★   ★

The third week, when teaching the volley, he has me bend close to the net. And then his fingers, so quickly, so deftly, pushing inside my knickers which are not white or lacy or anything like Gussie Moran's; my eyes widening, a small, soft 'ohh' as his nails catch the soft, unknown part of my skin.

'That's my girl,' he says, 'much better. We can concentrate on your serve now.'

On the baseline I can see my mother opening her curtains. Her afternoon rest is finished. She comes out to the court to speak to him. She has brushed her hair and put on fresh lipstick. As he tells her of my progress, she fingers the pearls at her throat.

At dinner, my father asks about the lessons and I say I would prefer not to continue to have them. 'It is too hot to play tennis,' I say, 'It makes me feel unwell.'

My father shrugs and looks at my mother. 'If she's not enjoying it,' he says mildly.

She raises her wine glass to her lipsticked mouth and takes a considered sip. When she puts the glass back down on the table it bears the perfect imprint of her lips. 'The trouble with you, Minnie, is you lack persistence and application. You must persevere in order to achieve. Mr Lucas says you are making steady improvement.'

In the bath after supper I wash three times the part where he has touched me.

The fourth week the barometer has risen again; the blueness of the sky is stretched taut like a sheet. The heat thrums in the air. My mother brings the barley water and says she is going to retreat to the drawing room. 'This heat is a demon,' she says. Clara, she tells him, has gone out for tea. She says she hopes that she has remembered her sun hat, because the Saturday girl cannot follow after her with it. 'She is not here today,' she adds, 'people are not all as reliable and trustworthy as you are, Mr Lucas.'

He doffs an imaginary cap to her, and she smiles at him and makes her way back up to the house. A few moments later, I am by the practice wall, obediently bending to retrieve a ball. He turns me quickly, swiftly, noiselessly, and manoeuvres my back against the cement. He takes part of himself from his shorts, hard and stiff as a tennis racquet handle, and pushes it inside of me, his feet planted either side of my own.

This is what I know. A skylark sings throughout. It wheels above me in the sky and it does not stop singing. Over his shoulder I can see the ice cubes in the barley water melting. The glasses on the satin walnut tray drip a ring around themselves. Such pain. Such ramming. My shoulder blades chafe against the practice-wall cement, as does a small part of my hip, which will sport a bruise like a blackberry. Such an absence of all the wonderfulness I have imagined on the paisley quilt: my head like a rag-doll's, buffeted with his thrusting. The double green stripe on his tennis shoes is clear in my peripheral vision; the whiteness of them dazzling. On the right shoulder of my Aertex top a smear of Brylcreem where he has bowed his head. In my ear, his breath, thick, fast and hot.

Afterwards, he tucks in his shirt with crisp precision. 'Good girl,' he says, smoothing his hair back from his forehead, 'let's look at your forehand now shall we?'

After the lesson is over, I go to my bedroom and lie stunned on my rose-sprigged counterpane. In my knickers there is a silver slug-trail trace of him, and my own blood, vivid and scarlet. Clara complains that she has to call me three times for dinner. 'Listen up!' she says.

It hurts to sit fully on my chair at the table. I try to inch forward so that I am balanced on the edge of my seat.

'Sit properly, can't you?' Mother says sharply.

The fifth week I feign a stomach upset; I lie on my bed from ten in the morning, and ask Mother for a stainless steel bowl lest I be sick. The heat still hasn't broken. Mr Lucas arrives; she hasn't been able to reach him by telephone. I watch from my bedroom window. I cannot catch what she says to him but he laughs, and salutes her as he walks away. His tennis shoes are still pristine; I think he must whiten them each night.

I don't get up until supper time to make sure the coast is fully clear, and when I come down to the drawing room Mother says, 'Well, you've cooked your goose. He said he sensed you were beginning to tire of your lessons. He said girls your age are mostly fickle. He's been offered a job teaching three boys on a Saturday afternoon and he thinks they will be much more committed.'

I nod. We go into the dining room and eat cod in parsley sauce. The sauce has a thin skein of skin which ripples and snags with the light tug of the knife.

The weather breaks the next day; huge sheets of rain bounce up from the parched grass and then run in snaking rivulets across to the herbaceous border. Mother says, 'I doubt Mr Lucas will be teaching in this.' Apparently the rain is to set in for weeks.

I sit in my bedroom and watch the fat silvery raindrops race down the window pane. On my arms, where the skin has been deep brown, it is beginning to flake. I brush at the dry whiteness with my flattened palm, and watch it drift to my lap.

In the act of filling me, jamming me, stopping me right up, he has also winnowed me out. I become, overnight, a girl who walks along the street and looks at any man and shivers at the thought that he could, and might, decide to do that.

My father watches me walk noiselessly across the hallway. 'No tap-dancing or cartwheels today, Min?' he asks. I shake my head.

17

Max

I knocked on her door. Not out of the blue, obviously. I sat on my wall for a bit until she was in her chair, and then I caught her eye and pointed to her front door – which is massive, I swear you could ride a horse right through it – and I put on my best questioning face (it's quite hard to pull together an expression which says 'would that be okay, would you like that?'). She got up, smoothed her skirt down (that's one of her things, she always does it when she stands up), paused, and then nodded. I crossed the street, which is maybe fifteen big steps, and then the huge door swung open and she was standing there, her hands held together in front of her as if she might be all set to say a prayer.

'Hello,' I said, and she smiled with slightly tight lips and said hello back. 'I just thought it would be nice to meet you properly,' I said, 'since we've been waving quite a lot.'

'Come in,' she replied. 'We are not used to visitors, so you must take us as you find us.'

I put my hand out to shake hers, because I wanted do something properly formal, especially now that I look like a skinhead. She'd have plenty of good reasons to think I had no manners at all. When she stretched her hand out, it was shaking a little. I don't know if that's because she might have a disease that comes when you are old, or because she was shy and nervous. I think maybe the second. I said, 'I'm called Max,' and she said,

'I'm Minnie.' And I told her – which looking back on it may have seemed a bit crackers – that our names went together.

'Maximum and minimum,' I said, 'in key stage two science papers they're two of the terms you have to know.' She thought about that for a moment and we stood there in the great big hallway which even has a fireplace, and then a door from another room opened, and the other lady walked out, the one who goes to the shops. It was harder to judge her expression. I wasn't sure if she was frowning or shocked. She was carrying a cup and saucer.

'This young gentleman is Max,' Minnie said, changing the position of her hands so that her fingers tucked neatly into a ball. 'He's come for a cup of tea – with perfect timing – and to make my acquaintance.'

I liked the words that she chose. *Making her acquaintance* seemed the right way of putting it. The other woman looked at me as if I actually was a skinhead, nodded to me once and made her way carefully past me and up the wide stairway, her cup rattling a bit in the saucer.

At the top of the stairs I could see a big round window made from coloured daisy-petals of glass divided by stone. It was like something you might see in a church. The sun suddenly came out and poured right down through it. It meant Minnie was standing in a puddle of ruby and emerald light and she looked like a painting of someone religious, someone getting told something by God or an angel, standing there all meekly and accepting each word.

'Would you actually like a cup of tea too, Max?' she asked, and I nodded and followed her through to the kitchen. It had a big black cooker, and a rack all along the ceiling. It had huge copper pans hanging off it, some so big I'm sure she couldn't lift them. She poured me some tea from a pot into a china cup which had a pattern of rosebuds on it, and we went back into the room she called the morning room, and sat looking out in the street. My house is really close. It was surprising, seeing it from there. Watching us come and go must be like watching something on the television. My bedroom window looks very small. Compared to the size of her window, everything does. I put my tea carefully down on the little table beside my chair, then picked it straight back up and had a quick sip. It made a tiny chinking noise when the cup touched the saucer. I've always wondered if bone china has bone in it, or else where did the term come from? Now I wasn't holding the cup, I smoothed my hand over my head. It's a new habit I'm getting, partly because I'm so surprised by how it feels. Each time I touch it, it's a surprise all over again, especially just above my ears where it's rough like the side of a matchbox.

'I see you've had your hair cut some more,' she said.

'Yes, my mum's friend did it to even it up, after Jasmine his daughter – I think you saw her do it – chopped off the front bit.'

'Did you *want* him to even it up?' she asked carefully, which struck me afterwards was the first time anyone had asked. And then, unexpectedly, it all came tumbling out. Not a question about bone china and whether there was actual bone in it, or a question about how a stonemason might have managed to make the circular window and set the glass into the stone (those things had been buzzing in my head while I was sipping my tea) but instead I looked straight at the curtains, and I told her that he'd come into my room before Mum was out of bed, and in his hand were his clippers, which he said *do the business*, and he laughed and told me to sit up, man up, and get ready for your new look. He held the back of my neck between his meaty finger and thumb, and he went *zoop, zoop, zoop* up the side of my head. I looked at the tattoo on his stomach until I had to shut my eyes because of all the falling hair.

So here's the thing. I'm pretty sure that installing windows, servicing boilers and choosing your GCSEs don't train you for hairdressing. He and Jasmine might both want to think about that. He nicked the top of one of my ears, and when I touched it, my fingertip smudged red. He was whistling as he did it. When he'd run over my whole head in one final *voosh* he said, 'There's your new summer look; that'll be far cooler than what you had before.' I didn't think it was worth pointing out that what I had before was:

a) what I wanted
b) perfectly fine if you're not actually going somewhere hot on holiday – in fact not going anywhere much at all
c) cooler (not temperature-wise) because my almost-topknot was much better than looking like a skinhead.

Instead, I just stared down at my pyjamas which were covered in tufts of my hair. When I touched my fuzzy head for the first time, it was hard to stop my lip from wobbling, and even more when I looked in my mirror and saw what he'd done. I looked mean. Definitely mean. And that seemed doubly unfair when it was him who had been.

I told her all that – whoosh – out in one breath. I hadn't been planning on saying it so I think it was probably a surprise to us both. My voice shook a little bit and at the end of it I stared some more at the curtain just to make sure of myself.

She listened very quietly and she didn't interrupt, and when I'd finished, she said, 'That does sound a horrible thing to wake up to, and not at all kind.' And I felt very grateful because I'd expected Mum to say that, but she'd just said, 'What are you like?!' to him, and zipped her finger along the tattoo on his belly. I'd swept up the hair in my bedroom and I could hear her laughing downstairs in the kitchen, and whilst I don't think she was laughing about my hair, she was certainly cheery about something which was a bit unexpected.

Minnie had gone quiet and I suddenly thought that perhaps it wasn't good manners to just sit there and talk about myself. She writes a lot in her diary, so there must be all kinds of things that have happened to her. She might have had far worse things than being forced to have her hair cut. Then I heard the sister – she's called Clara – clear her throat in the hallway outside. I don't think she was eavesdropping, but I don't think she was pleased I was there. I think just the two of them there is fine and dandy by her. When she looked at Minnie from the hallway she looked a bit worried, as if Minnie was a bomb that might unexpectedly go off. She needn't have been concerned. Minnie didn't say anything personal. She speaks very carefully, as if conversation is something she hasn't quite got the hang of.

The house feels very private. Not private in that it has signs splashed up everywhere saying Keep Out or No Entry, but it feels as if that's what's happened; that people have kept away, not entered, for years and years. It's sort of miserable; that's the best way I can describe it. It matches how I felt sitting with all my hair in my pyjama lap.

To stop talking about my hair, I plumped for asking about the china. I thought that would be interesting and not at all personal. There were two identical things on the sideboard and I couldn't work out what they were for. She got up and fetched one and put it in my lap. She spoke without stopping as if she were giving a small speech.

'They're for standing pineapples on, to look splendid on a dining table, and they were made by Spode who were a very famous manufacturer in the early nineteenth century. This part is called the tazza; it's shallow and circular and has a central rounded support which holds the pineapple upright. See how it's painted with a border of sprays and flowers and fruit. These are gilded paterae.' She pointed at each thing with her finger.

I took a big calm breath and listened to what she was saying.

It was peaceful, sitting there, learning about the china. It was nice to have some details, some new words which weren't to do with cosmetics, or painting or decorating. It was like *Antiques Roadshow* but without the travelling and the crowds.

18

Minnie

Clara is hovering beyond the parlour door. She is perturbed with me, I can tell. I can hear her traversing the hall, tutting under her breath. We do not invite people in. We have not invited people in for years. The last visitor, I think, was a rather melancholy rector who used to call upon Mother when she was laid up one winter with bronchitis. Mother would sit propped up in the drawing room on the day bed, and he would sit by the fire which we stoked up especially, and she was always a little tight-lipped, and he would lay his Bible on his knee as if to signify that it was ready for the off should any salvation be required. Clara would sit straight-backed by the tea tray and I would mostly be banished upstairs out of sight. I'd stand underneath the rose window and feel myself to be showered with ruby light, and wonder if that was how it felt to receive some kind of blessing.

I think blessings are in short supply in this world, and the best that can be hoped for is a little mutual kindness. That was why I invited Max in; his expression was so plaintive, his humiliation so evident, his sorrows held close to him like a small, soft-boned fledgling. I have an instinct for sorrow, for sadness. It is not an accomplishment I would have hoped to achieve. Given a moment, he sang forth his grievances. This is usually the case when someone offers to listen and sits quietly enough to show their intent.

* * *

Clara comes in, and I stop writing. She glances at my diary, and places her fingertips on her lips. She will bring herself to ask me about it soon, but I imagine decides to prioritise one thing at a time.

'I have to say I am at a loss as to why you invited the boy in. Who knows where that will lead?'

I tell her I thought he looked as if he needed someone to talk to.

'But why to you; what could you possibly have to offer a young boy?'

I have no answer to give her; she is probably right to wonder, although he seemed to enjoy my explanation of the pineapple dishes. He has a mind like a magnet for detail, for information. His lips echoed the shape of the particular words I said to him – *paterae, tazza*.

'What can be the harm?' I say to her. 'I am showing him some of the china; telling him stories of things, not people.'

She furrows her brow and gives me a pointed look. I pick up my pen and begin writing again. It is the least combative way I can think of to signal that our conversation is over. Clara leaves the room.

I look across the road, and Max is standing at his bedroom window. He smiles across at me, which is surprisingly fortifying.

19

Max

She finished late in the Powder Room tonight and there was no sign of him turning up. I took that to mean that the coast might be clear. She came into the kitchen where I was eating cereal, and made herself some ginger tea which is *very settling at the end of the day*. She sat at the kitchen table and tucked up her knees, and the little upside-down watch she wears pinned to her chest flip-flapped over her legs. For a minute I occupied myself with trying to read the time upside down and across from me, and then I thought it was as good a time as any to bring him up and to tell her that from my point of view he isn't very kind.

I put my cereal bowl down and paddled the spoon a little bit in the leftover milk. 'Mum,' I said, 'you know your new friend, I just wanted to say, just wanted to . . .' My words trailed off. She was looking at me all bright-eyed over the top of her ginger tea, and the steam from it had made her cheeks go pink and I had a picture of how she might have looked when she was about my age.

'Yes,' she said, with a big smile starting, 'do you like him? We haven't really had a chance to have a talk about him. I really like how he takes an interest in you and includes you.'

That stopped me in my tracks a bit, and made me wonder if we'd been in the same room. I doubled the speed of twirling the spoon in my bowl while I caught up with that thought. It made quite a noise, and she screwed her nose up and said, 'That's really irritating, do you mind stopping it?'

I stopped. The last thing I wanted to do was annoy her.

'It's just . . .' I said again, and then I just blurted it all out like I had with Minnie. 'The pouffe was moved without you saying anything, and then the Chinese wasn't for me as well, and then he didn't really give me a choice about my haircut and he might have just asked and . . .'

She put the mug down, and I could see the start of her disappointed face, which begins at the sides of her mouth and spreads up to her eyebrows. I can still remember it from when I ripped my brand-new school jumper playing *carelessly* on the monkey bars in Year Four.

'Are you serious, is this for real?' she said, with one eyebrow right up. 'Oh goodness Max, you do surprise me.' She got up, came over and put her arm around me and kissed my forehead. 'Sometimes I don't know what goes on in that head of yours; you cook things up and over-stew them and before you know it there's a problem where none exists.'

So that's where she was coming from. She stooped and looked me right in the eyes. 'OK, the pouffe. We were re-arranging my bedroom which I was really keen to do because it's been bugging me for ages. Putting the pouffe in the spare room meant we could move the dressing table over a bit. He pointed out that you'd probably outgrown it anyway, and that you might be teased at big school if anybody knew that's how your day started. It was lovely to have a strong hand with it all.'

She sat back down and pushed at her tea mug with her index finger. She bit at her lip for a moment and then she carried on. 'As for the Chinese, he was sort of right about that too. It would have been far too spicy for you, you'd have hated it, and all he was trying to do was share his favourite menu with me. That was sweet. It would have been wrong of me to interfere and ask him to add on some chicken noodles or something – especially as he was paying. You can't presume on things like that early in a relationship. Thing is, Max,' and when she got to this part she leaned across the table and stroked my nose lightly with her finger, 'I know it's a hard thing to learn but as you grow older sometimes you have to step back and see that everything doesn't have to include you. As for your haircut, I think it looks better than it did after Jasmine cut it. If you hadn't got yourself in such a pickle with her, he wouldn't have had to ride to the rescue with his clippers. At least it's all one length now. I'd have thought you'd have appreciated that. He certainly tried his best.'

She took her mug over to the sink, and then came back and ruffled what passes for my hair. I was still having difficulty swallowing the sentence about getting myself *into a pickle* with Jasmine. She looked at me and scrunched her mouth up really small.

'I have to say I'm just a li-tt-le bit disappointed in your attitude. It's ages – actually two *years* – since I've had a boyfriend and he's being really good and kind and considerate to me, what with the Velux and the blind, and he didn't even charge me for the boiler service. He says he likes taking care of me, and that's nice when I've been on my own for so long, and even more so since Grandad died. I have to say I'm disappointed you're not a little bit happy for me. You're usually brilliant at seeing the bigger picture, which is why this conversation is a bit of a surprise.'

I took the cereal bowl to the sink and tipped the milk down the plughole.

I'm in bed now, feeling like that wasn't exactly a successful talk. I was trying to get her to see it from my point of view, and instead I'm lying here wondering about whether my thoughts actually *are* disappointing, whether I've been mean and whether I've failed to see the bigger picture. That's not a good hat-trick. She's right that I haven't thought about how it was for her with

Grandad. When you miss someone yourself, it's hard to make space for the thought that someone else misses them too.

I didn't really answer her when she'd finished. I thought about apologising but she sort of bustled out of the kitchen, leaving me standing there holding the cereal bowl by the sink like an idiot. When I went into the front room to say goodnight, she turned her cheek to me for a kiss but didn't look at me or say anything. I can fix that. I'll make her breakfast in the morning and put it on a tray and take it up to her in her room. She usually smiles at that when I do it on Mother's Day. If we had a pineapple I'd try and make it stand up in a saucer. I'd tell her it's properly called a *tazza*. I'll save that idea for if she ever buys a pineapple. The way things are changing around here, who knows if that won't happen soon.

Here's the thing though, whatever she says and however disappointing I might have been:

1) She's accepted his version of everything without even asking me. Who says I'd have been laughed at at big school for sitting on the pouffe – who'd have known? And, who says it isn't good to start trying spicy food when you're nearly twelve? And anyway, she could have offered to pay for mine. I don't know much about dates and relationships but that seems pretty fair to me. I might have told her that it's quite disappointing to sit eating cheese on toast when you can smell noodles.

2) How am I supposed to know how it feels when your dad dies, when I've never known what it feels like to even have one that's alive?

3) I didn't know the furniture arrangement in her bedroom had been bugging her for ages. If she'd said so, I'd have given it my best shot. My hands are stronger than she thinks.

4) Everything isn't always about me. I'd have thought she knew that better than anyone.

20

Minnie

All of August and early September is, my mother says, like a monsoon. She says the word with relish, as if it carries within it the timbre of her childhood. I wonder if she closes her eyes as she hears the rain and expects to open them on jacarandas and peacocks. Water streams down the windows in sheets, and I can smell its sharpness from the drawing room when the front door is opened. Hooper stands in the herbaceous borders looking glum in a mackintosh and sou'wester. The grass on the tennis court re-greens and grows lush and thick. I close my eyes and try not to see Mr Lucas walking briskly onto the base line. The apple tree throws a smudge of darkness by the practice wall which rearranges itself into his shape. I take to turning the pages when Clara practises the piano in the music room. Previously, she considered me too fidgety to do so; now she tells me, with a nod of approval, that I have suddenly learned to stand still. I toy with standing motionless outside on the lawn; allowing myself to be drenched, utterly drenched, in the hope of being washed clean. Beyond Rosemount, the lanes are sodden.

The platform that my father has stood on to catch the train to the City for almost twenty years is similarly wet when he falls down dead upon it, his heart crushing to a halt, briefcase still held in his hand. I know this detail because I overhear Cook tell the maid. He dies instantly, patiently waiting for the 7.17. It is of particular pain to me that it was raining; that his face, foamed with a brush which fascinates me because it is made of actual badger and so fastidiously shaved each morning, might lie in a puddle, his eyes still open, watching for the train to arrive.

One of his friends, a fellow commuter, comes to tell my mother. We are called into the drawing room where she is sitting, her hands in her lap, her gaze turned to fall upon Mr Kirkpatrick who is thumbing the rim of his hat as he speaks. Mr Kirkpatrick is one of the men who plays tennis. As he speaks he seems perplexed because rather than patting his friend on the back after an ace served, he has tried to help him up from where he lies senseless on the platform macadam.

My mother touches the corners of her mouth with her index finger and thumb. She pokes at the fire which has been lit earlier because the morning is unseasonably cold and which now feels prescient. I watch the flames dance. She has told me, previously, that in India the dead are burned on pyres. Birds wheel above them as they turn to ash. I look outside to the leaves of the Lady's Mantle which hold the raindrops like polished spheres and imagine my father buried instead in the deep, damp emerald coolness of the herbaceous border. I press my knuckles to my eye sockets and the world pulses green.

My mother is speaking to Mr Kirkpatrick. To look at her I cannot tell whether she is in shock or just mildly inconvenienced. Her skin is pale at her temples, but her voice is calm and even. Her mind turns to practicalities – not just the funeral, but the ongoing negotiations with the town planners to whom he has sold the parkland. Clara is sobbing softly beside me. Outside in the hallway I can hear Cook and the maid and Hooper murmuring. When I am sent to beckon them in because my mother wishes to speak to them, Hooper's galoshes have made a puddle of their own. He is holding his yellow sou'wester as if it might be a trilby for Church. Death and hats remain inextricably linked in my mind.

When they have gone into the drawing room I stand on the parquet and look up as if to see Father again with his newspaper in the armchair by the umbrella stand, asking me if I am to run away and *join the circus. I realise what I have lost is his tolerance, his particular benign bemusement and the opinion that I am not someone who requires straightening out, making good.*

I go upstairs and stand at the threshold of his study. Most of what is in it has defined angles and corners: the newspaper rack with the Financial Times *and* The Times, *the onyx pen stand, the cigar box, his rectangular binocular-case, the vast Queen Anne walnut cabinet. There is a jar of humbugs on his desk, whorled black and white, and round and smooth as marbles. I take one and place it between my palms and roll it to and fro. I cross the carpet to his taut ruby-red leather armchair and touch where his head leaned, as I did two summers previously in the stockman's farmhouse. I turn to find my mother behind me. 'Wash your hands,' she says, 'look how they will be sticky.'*

I return to school and my form mistress tells me she is sorry for my loss. Her words take anchor in my skin like a burr, and trouble me. She thinks I have lost something, which seems to suggest I am culpable, or at best careless. I want to tell her that I did not lose my father, rather that death has taken him from me.

The other girls side-step me for a day or so, but then resume their usual manner. The world of our fathers is one that is mostly invisible to us anyway: offices, clubs, pubs, racecourses. To have a father who has become permanently absent is mostly a question of degree.

A stream of advisors comes to Rosemount. They talk to my mother of investments, of policies, of stock portfolios. When they leave, she re-reads the papers they have given her and writes numbers in blue columns in a feint-line notebook. She snaps at the maid. She tells the rector that perhaps his ministrations are needed more elsewhere. A new, clipped coldness descends upon the house to chime with the first frost in October. She lipsticks her mouth with grim purpose, tells Hooper and Cook that she cannot keep them on, and tells Clara and myself that none of it is her fault. She learns to cook, and stands in the kitchen with an apron knotted around her, beating and chopping and shredding as if cutlassing her way somewhere else.

Father's things evaporate. They are folded, boxed, neatly labelled, stored. I go into my parents' bedroom which has become resolutely, solely hers. Her hairbrush has moved to centre position on the glass-topped dressing table. She has removed two pillows from the bed and placed the remaining two centrally. On his bedside table she has put her hot water bottle.

I study her carefully and expect to catch her unawares; to find her weeping, or folded, bereft, in an armchair. I do not. I can't ascertain whether widowhood is socially awkward or perversely liberating. 'What's more the tragedy,' I overhear her saying, 'is that it's my decision now and I'd have never sold it.' And then, once, to her cousin, crisply on the telephone, 'He was soft; that's actually what did for him.'

I understand the connotations that the word 'soft' carries for her. I watch her write her columns of blue ink, and her pen fizzes with a discernible fury. She says 'soft' in the same way other people say 'wicked'.

My stomach is no longer soft. From low down, very low down, it is becoming hard, compacted, just like a tennis ball. I place my hand on the scoop of it and sense its autonomy. It is not soft. It is most likely wicked. Perhaps, in my case, they are one and the same. I am not sure what it signifies but I know it cannot be good.

21

Max

She's definitely said something to him, which is a bit surprising because one of the things she's always said to me is, 'You can tell me anything, I'll always keep it a secret.' He came up the path wearing a t-shirt which said *All The Fun of the Fair* and said he'd booked a table at Sticky Ribs, which I've never been to until today. He says it's one of his favourites and the ribs are marinated for a whole day before being barbecued. The walls are painted bright red and every ten minutes the sound system plays 'Happy Birthday' to someone. The waiter was blowing a whistle as he led us to our table like a procession. I felt like I should have had a drum to bang along with him.

I sat opposite him, and Mum sat next to him, and I could tell she was trying very hard for everything to be warm and friendly because she ended every sentence by saying my name or *sweetheart*, and she was looking at me all the time and nodding a lot every time I said anything at all. He had his arm over the back of the red leather seat behind her, but it was actually mostly around her which didn't seem to get in her way when she was eating. She'd put on quite a lot of mascara. He'd ordered her a cocktail which came with a spotty pink paper umbrella, and each time she sipped it the little prongs of the umbrella nearly got caught in her eyelashes. It reminded me of a Venus Fly Trap. He kept taking a sip of his beer and smacking his lips together and all it would have needed was me to start flaring my nostrils and we'd have covered all the openings and closings it's possible for a face to do.

When the rack of ribs arrived it was enormous. I was about to take my first bite when he turned to me and said, 'Here's a funny story; the fact that it's true makes it even funnier.'

This is what he told us. When he was growing up he had three brothers and they played lots of games together. They were always getting up to mischief. One day, when they were playing on their bicycles and pedalling very fast, a neighbour's cat darted from behind a wall in front of him and he had no chance of avoiding it. He ran right over it and killed it. Time, he said, for some quick thinking. He picked up the dead cat and laid it by the back wheel of his parents' car, got in, took off the handbrake, and let it roll back onto the cat a bit so it looked like his parents had reversed over the cat without knowing it when parking their car. They went in and told them – the four of them standing in a line and trying to get the words out first. His mother said, 'Oh my goodness that's awful of us,' and went straight outside. His dad put the car up on a jack so that the cat could be lifted away without any further damage. None of the brothers ever told, although it's just occurred to me that he's pretty free and easy with telling it now, and you practically have to shout to be heard in Sticky Ribs, so if his parents are still alive who knows, they might finally get to know the whole truth.

When he finished the story, it was very hard to think about eating ribs. All the twenty-four-hour barbecue sauce in the world can't disguise the fact that a rack of ribs is basically a bundle of skinny bones. They were sitting there, all shiny on the plate, looking like a bigger version of a dead cat's ribcage, which took the appeal right away.

Here's another thing I learned. It's very hard to disguise that you're not actually eating a rack of ribs. It's obvious you're not lifting them to your mouth. I was pushing them around the plate, trying to tuck a couple of shreds of meat behind the small bowl of chips and he got a bit irritated and said, 'What's wrong with them, Fussy-chops?' I didn't answer; I just pretended to be chewing a lot, and pointed at my mouth as if it was rude to speak. My mum was sucking on her cocktail and looking at me a bit wide-eyed, although I wasn't sure if that was actually the weight of the mascara. Things got worse because my imagination was really running with it now. I'd started thinking about matted cat fur, which turned into a fur ball and before I knew it, it was making me clear my throat a lot. That's an annoying sound, even if you're not annoyed by a person already. I could see he was watching me pick the ribs up to my lips and then put them down, and my mum threw another look at me and ate a couple of my chips to be helpful, and about ten minutes of this passed and then he said, 'Well if you don't want them, waste not want not,' and lickety-split his big ol' fat fingers were scrabbling across my plate.

Mum looked at me with her disappointed face. 'It's not like you to be unappreciative,' she said, her head tipped to one side. I felt like saying that it was alright for her, what with a chilli beef burrito looking nothing like a dead cat's ribcage.

He zipped his teeth along the ribs and reduced them to a pile of bones in minutes. He swooshed his fingers in the little bowl of water, wiped his lips, sat back and said, 'Well that's me done for.' Just like the cat.

We drove home and nobody really spoke in the car. He turned on the radio and when they spoke to each other I couldn't hear them very well. Mum leaned over and whispered something to him so I guess I wasn't meant to hear it. He took his left hand off the gear stick and gave her thigh a pat.

When we came into the house she made a big deal of some yawning. 'I am always so sleepy,' she said, 'after going out for lunch.'

That's not really true. Often when we've been out for lunch on a Sunday she's keen for a box set or a walk in the woods. When we do that, we have the conversation about what dog we'd choose if we were ever to have one. If we see one we like the look of, we stop and ask the owner the name of the breed. I have a list in a notebook, with accurate descriptions, so that if we do ever get a dog we make what she says is *a fully informed choice.* Anyway, she did another yawn, and added in some extra tiredness by stretching her arms up tall. Her blouse came up and you could see the skin of her tummy. He stroked it with his thumb.

'Time for a siesta I think,' he said, and winked. They both went upstairs and I decided to go out for a bit.

I was actually pretty hungry, but I figured they'd hear me if I got busy in the kitchen. I plumped for going to the park to see if any of my school friends were there but they weren't. It was quiet as a graveyard so I thought I might as well actually go to the graveyard because it was as good a place as any to go on a Sunday afternoon.

I don't know anyone who's buried in our nearest one. My grandad wasn't buried, he was cremated. That way Grandma could take his ashes to Florida, although since she met her new 'companion', I think they're now kept in what she calls her closet rather than on the mantelpiece which was where they started out, next to a photograph of them together on Slapton Sands. I don't know what she's done with the photo. Maybe she's put it side by side with the new one of her and Marvin on Venice Beach. Anyway, when I go to the graveyard I like to think about Grandad even though he's not actually buried because it puts me in the right frame of mind for remembering. It's a bit like watching the service at the Cenotaph on Remembrance Sunday when all the old soldiers in their medals go marching by. I always find myself standing up for the 'National Anthem' and the 'Last Post' even though I am not a soldier, am wearing my trackies and am at home on the couch.

The graveyard was busier than the park. Sunday is obviously a good day for visiting the dead. I sat on a bench by a grave that had its very own rosebush with big open flowers, and I looked at the yew tree and the holly tree, and was thinking about how there are always lots of dark green trees in graveyards and that there must be some reason for that. Someone would know. I also couldn't help thinking some more about the cat story.

First of all I felt sad for the cat because that must have been a shocker, the bike whizzing out of nowhere. Then, the unfairness of being a little bit reversed over by a car when it was dead already. Dying once is bad enough without a repeat performance. Next, his parents must have felt really bad; I bet they lay in bed talking about it, asking *how could we not have seen it,* and *surely it would have made some sort of noise?* Maybe the mum cried with how terrible she felt. Then they had to tell the neighbour. Did they carry it next door, holding it out like a present? Maybe the mum tried to find a box, and then put it on an old towel to make it look at least a little bit comfortable.

Was it a funny story? My mum put her hand over her mouth when she laughed at it, which I heard once is a sign that you know something is not actually funny. Whether the story was funny or not, if the visit to Sticky Ribs was meant to be some kind of start-over it wasn't. If anything it meant he likes me even less. *Fussy-chops.*

I don't know how long I'd been sitting and thinking in the graveyard but when I looked up towards the church I saw Minnie and her sister by a headstone near the stained-glass window. I shouldn't have been surprised. Old people are more likely to know someone that's dead. Minnie was holding a small bunch of flowers in her hand. Clara was talking to her but she didn't look like she was particularly listening. She turned and saw me and I gave her a wave.

I walked up to her and she smiled and said, 'What a surprise seeing you here, Max,' and then, 'What have you been doing, isn't it a scorching afternoon?'

I told her I'd been out for lunch and that it had been a bit unusual. She frowned when I said that and asked if I'd like to come back to Rosemount for tea. Clara didn't look very pleased, but I said yes anyway.

In the kitchen Minnie cut me a slice of seed cake which made me think of Horace the budgie, and then Mrs Hughes' lips spraying the buttered brazils, and I wondered if everything about eating today was going to be complicated, which was a shame because I was actually starving by now. I needn't have worried because the cake was delicious. Minnie put it on china plates, and poured tea into the same cups as before. She asked me why lunch was unusual and I told her about the cat. Not just what he'd said, but the parts I'd thought about on the bench in the graveyard.

'Thing is,' I said, 'it was told as a joke but I ended up sitting there feeling sad and a bit sick.'

She nodded and said, 'I can see how that happened.' Then it went silent and I picked up my teacup and turned it around. It was a very a delicate pattern.

I said, 'This must have taken ages to paint.'

Minnie nodded again. 'I think so. China is full of endeavour.'

I liked that thought.'Will you tell me something interesting about china?'

She thought for a moment and then looked the tiniest bit mischievous. 'Would it be acceptable if it continued along the theme of bones, but without any distress, and no lies told?' I told her I thought that in the circumstances it would be exactly the best kind of china story.

So here's my second tale of the day. Minnie went into what is called the drawing room and took a cup shaped like a small trophy out from a sideboard. It was bright blue and decorated with butterflies and flowers and fruit. She gave it to me to hold and said, 'This is like a party memento – I bet you can't guess why?'

She was right. I'd never have got it. The cup was Copeland Spode bone china from 1833. THE BONE IN THE CHINA WAS MADE FROM THE GROUND-UP BONES OF AN OX EATEN DURING A FEAST. The ox that the guests had eaten became part of the china that commemorated the occasion.

I like the idea of that. There's a ton more dignity in an animal's remains being transformed into something turquoise and gold and decorated with butterflies. Far better than being sneakily put under a car.

So when she told me it completely stopped me thinking about the cat. I said Wow! and turned the cup around and around in my hands. I should tell her that she's very good at distracting. And, as a bonus, now I know the answer as to whether bone china ever actually contains bone.

22

Minnie

My body begins to change with a determination and an independence of purpose which perplexes me. I do not give permission for my breasts to bloom larger, for my nipples to darken, or for a line to begin to trace itself from the part of me that he hurt upwards towards my navel. I have not bled since the summer. I take sanitary pads from the pile in the bathroom and hide them at the back of my wardrobe so that my mother will not know. My hair grows thicker, glossier. I am constantly ravenous. I eat my own school lunch and clear the plates my friends pick at and discard. 'Goodness, Minnie,' Daisy Shepherd says, 'you will be the size of a house.' I am not. My limbs remain as they were. It is only my belly which seems to be stock-piling the food I consume, so that it becomes packed, dense, round. I can cradle my interlocked fingers beneath it. My school tunic has buttons at the side which can be let out. My school sweater is over-sized so my silhouette is disguised. My mother and Clara show no sign of noticing anything different. I feel my step change, my stride become more dominated by what feels like a smooth roll of my hips. I am walking home from school one day in November and I feel a frantic fluttering within me. I stop by a lamp post and feel sweat prickle in my scalp. I have tried not to know what it is but certainty is dawning upon me.

At home I begin to wear a sweater which had belonged to my father and which I find in the potting shed. Perhaps he gave it to Hooper;

I take it for myself. It smells of soil, of bonfire smoke, of grass. I press the cuff to my forehead, my hand balled up into a fist. My mother sees me wearing it while I am doing my homework. 'That is an affectation of grief,' she says, and I let her words land on me without rebuttal. There is no one to tell. No one with whom even to begin. I lie in bed and bundle my nightgown around me, and recall Mr Lucas's pristine white tennis pumps and bite my forearm until it bleeds.

At school we are preparing for our General Certificate. The English teacher, Miss Potts, takes me aside and tells me she has high hopes of me. She thinks I should read English Literature at University, and should return in the sixth form and join the Oxbridge preparatory class. She is studying my face carefully, hoping, I think, to see if my expression lights up with enthusiasm. Deep in my abdomen there is a soft, determined kick. The door that Miss Potts opens – I imagine myself on a bicycle cycling to a lecture, and sitting in a library scribbling notes frantically and dwarfed by a pile of books – swings shut. 'I am not sure if I will be staying on,' I tell her, and she says, 'Minnie, you are one of our brightest hopes; surely not?'

Later in another lesson, she is discussing Victorian novels and makes an offhand remark about yet another innocent young virgin undone by an unconscionable squire. 'Thankfully not a problem for you girls,' she says and smiles beneficently at us. Miss Potts wears cyclamen-pink lipstick and dogtooth-print narrow-legged trousers, smokes cigarettes and carries an emerald green leather handbag. I would like to raise my hand and tell her that squires might now come in the form of tennis coaches who smell of Old Spice. I catch her looking at me again as we file out of the classroom. I know I will disappoint her.

Mother, Clara and I no longer eat in the dining room in the evening. We sit at the kitchen table where the maid and Cook used to eat, and the copper pans on the overhead rack throw out gleaming shards of light, and my mother cuts carefully through the suet crust of a steak and kidney pudding. As the gravy spills out it is all I can do not to weep. Mother keeps one crystal glass by the draining board for the glass of wine which accompanies her supper. It winks conspiratorially at me.

In my mind what is within me is shaped like a sea horse. I sit in my father's study with an encyclopedia on my lap, and I look at the picture of an upright, bobbing sea horse and see it within me, alive on a tide of fluid which I imagine swilling within me as I walk. In the study I lay my hands on the objects which are solid and to be trusted. In the nursery I look up at the moon through the lemon-drop coloured curtains and feel a force, an abstract potency, which flies in the face of it all.

It is in a Biology lesson where I become more informed. I am sitting next to Teresa Cartwright whose father is a publican and who over-hears all manner of things from the snug beneath her bedroom. We are looking at a diagram of a cross section of a womb. In it, there is a foetus, tethered by an umbilical cord. It has the beginning of a skull, and a spine coiled like an ammonite.

'That's the time,' Teresa whispers confidently, 'when something can be done about it.' I look at her, wide-eyed, as she continues. 'There are women in backstreets who give you pills made of treacle and gin and herbs and goodness knows what and which cause the baby to slip. If that doesn't work they make you have a very hot bath and poke it all out with a specially boiled knitting needle.' I wince.

Mrs Shaw tells her to be quiet. I spend the rest of the lesson looking at the curious, stubby foetus spooned to the side of the womb, and feel certain that there are no women in the vicinity of Rosemount who might do what Teresa just told me about. After Biology there is Games, for which I am excused because I say I have my period. 'That's a pity,' Miss Lane, the PE mistress says. 'You're a good little centre forward, and you look as if you might benefit from some running about.' I can't tell if she means I look pale – Teresa's comments have done for me – or if she's noticed my straining tunic.

Once home, I go to a bathroom on the second floor and lock the door carefully behind me. I sit on the edge of the bath with my head in my hands. *I wonder if a hot bath could do the trick by itself. I cover my mouth at the thought of the rest of Teresa's description. I slowly take off my clothes and fold them carefully in a pile on the floor, then I turn on the hot tap and run the bath scalding. In truth, I don't imagine anything will happen. The water looks so innocuous, so clear. I stand sideways to the mirror and look at my outline. I watch as the steam from the bath swallows my shape, as it clouds around me and obscures me, dampening the length of my eyelashes. I would like it to make me evaporate, disappear. That would be a solution. I watch myself doubly lost as the mirror blooms with the steam.*

My mother – likely hearing the boiler fire up in the scullery – comes and raps on the door. 'What are you doing in there?' she asks. I tell her I am muddy from hockey and would like to be clean before starting my homework.

I wince as I ease myself into the water, and blow out of my mouth in soft, quick, huffs until I can lie down. I watch the temperature cause scarlet ripples on the expanse of my belly. The baby swoops and dives; I trace its trajectory. The most unsettling thing is our mutual knowledge; it knows, presumably, when I am still, when I am moving, when I am speaking, when I am silent. And I am mindful of when it sleeps, when it wakes, of the increasing strength of its movements, a fresh distinction between a foot and a fist. So we are tied together, this tumbling thing and I. The only thing which knows of and shares my predicament is the very thing I think needs to be gone.

The water cools around me and the skin on my fingers shrivels and softens. Nothing else happens. I hear the clock strike downstairs and I get out. I stand bare-footed on the white tiles. I wrap my body in a towel and dry myself fiercely until my skin smarts red. When I unlock the door, I see Clara slip away on the landing. I am still a mystery to her, standing there in billows of escaping steam, my hair damp-tendrilled to my face, my fists clenched at my sides.

At supper time, I sit and cut lamb from a chop. I am impossibly hungry; I ask for another potato. My mother looks at me askance and says, 'You might want to check your appetite, you don't want to be getting plumper.' It is the only comment she will make.

I would like to say to her that I have recently learned that what I want seems to have no import at all.

23

Max

She's gone to yoga. That's a new thing. There's a class at 8 o'clock at the leisure centre. You can use their mats, and then buy your own if you decide to keep going. She's already earmarked on the web the mat she intends to buy if she likes it. It has a swirl of butterflies on it which she thinks will put her in the right frame of mind. She ummed and ahhed over what to wear for it. She said it was important for yoga-wear to be slouchy and yet not revealing. In the end she plumped for the leggings she used to wear when she had a go at running, and one of my old grey t-shirts which she said is *just the look*. I asked if the point of yoga was that the look and style of things didn't matter, but she said not exactly. She said in a room full of women someone is always clocking what you're wearing and whether your bum looks big in it. She watched a video on YouTube on how to say *Namaste* properly and we practised a few times and she was chuffed because she says she won't look like the newbie if they start the class by saying it. On the leisure centre website, it says the class is all about *getting rid of stress and tension and breathing in a new state of calm*. I'm not sure that's the effect it's having on her so far. She had two green teas to try and balance out the Twix and espresso she'd had at 5.30, and then fretted that with all that liquid she'd be needing a wee.

Just as she was leaving, she turned to me quick as a flash like she'd just thought of it and told me that he would be popping round to keep me company while she was gone. 'It'll be nicer than you sitting here all on your ownio.'

I think perhaps what she didn't add is that it would also mean he would be here waiting for her when she got back. He rocked up ten minutes later. He had four cans of cold beer and a copy of *Anglers Weekly*. He looked all set to make himself very at home. He greeted me by saying, 'Wotcha Maxy boy,' to which I just nodded, because I'm not actually sure there's a good answer to that.

We both went into the sitting room. We walked in and sat down, and the only way I can describe all our movements after that was as if we were playing a chess game with parts of our bodies as the different pieces. I moved my arm; he moved his foot; he cleared his throat; I touched my stubbly hair. It was like everything happened in alternate moves, and the silence between us felt thick like rice pudding.

I decided to get out a jigsaw puzzle. Partly because he was reading – or I'd say more like looking at the pictures because he was just flipping the pages, although perhaps if you've seen one fish you've seen them all – and I thought it would be rude to turn on the television. There wasn't anything I really wanted to watch either. I don't understand why there are so many programmes about gardening on in the summertime. If you have a garden and like gardening, you are most likely outside digging on summer evenings. If you double don't, and you're inside watching television, you're probably not interested in how to grow sweet peas. And anyway, our garden is really small and mostly paved. A jigsaw was far more appealing.

Mum and I have always done jigsaws together. We even re-do ones we've done already. We just swap round who does which part: the sky, the trees, the foliage. We have a specific way of going about them. One of us does the edges, the other focuses on the brightest patch of colour. Then, we pick an object or a person or a particular face. Before you know it we're slapping down the pieces and filling in all the gaps. She's usually sitting there with a glass of wine in her hand and she whoops and says, 'We're getting our eye in – look at us go . . .' When it's finished, we leave it on the coffee table for a couple of days, and when we go past it, we pat it, or smooth our hand over it, and then give each other a perky double thumbs up.

As I crossed the room to get a puzzle (that was three steps across to the sideboard) he adjusted his position on the couch, then I bent down to open the door, and then he scrunched the beer can he'd just finished. I wondered whether to ask him if he wanted to join in. I thought it would be polite and also if Mum came in and we were doing a jigsaw puzzle together, she might feel like doing a double thumbs up instead of the disappointed face from Sticky Ribs. I chose the puzzle carefully. Some I did with Grandad when he was really poorly, which gave Grandma a chance to go into the Powder Room and have a manicure. ('Connecting oxygen tanks,' she'd say, 'is an absolute killer for chipping nail varnish.')

We've got loads of puzzles. We've had phases of ones with landscapes, and ones of fine art paintings. She likes those because when they're done, if they have what she calls *a quality finish*, she says they'll look good enough to hang on the wall. I felt a heartbeat ... ...ing her as I looked at all the neatly stacked boxes. I hoped she'd said *Namaste* properly, and wasn't dying for a wee, and that the clothes she'd chosen to wear had cracked the difficult dress code. Then, I chose 'Lady with an Ermine' which is one she particularly likes. It's a picture of a woman in a blue and red dress, holding a kind of white ferret. Her hair is tied back and the animal is just sitting right there in her hands.

I turned round with the box, and he looked up and over *Anglers Weekly*.

'I think I've seen everything now,' he said. 'You're kidding me, Maxy; truly . . . a jigsaw puzzle?'

I bit at my lip for a minute. *Would you like to give me a hand?* would probably fall flat now. He clearly didn't want to join in which was probably better. I was suddenly feeling a bit awkward anyway about having him sit close next to me on the couch. His fat meaty arms would probably block my view of most of the pieces. It would be like sitting next to a great big gorilla. I went back over to the coffee table and tipped open the box.

'What are you, almost twelve?' he said, scratching his head, 'and this is what you want to do?'

'Mum and I do them together. We like doing them. It's usually a team effort,' I said.

He sat back on the couch and looked at me. 'For real? Looks more like a plan to give you something to do.'

I didn't say anything back. I just stared at the Lady with an Ermine and chewed at the inside of my mouth. I could feel my cheeks getting hot. His words felt like they were burrowing right down to my ear drums.

I've been thinking about it and I'm sure – almost positive – that we don't do puzzles because she's just trying to think of something for me to do. She'd have to be a brilliant actress to fool me for that long. And here's the smart part: SHE'S NOT A BRILLIANT ACTRESS! I know that for a fact. She joined a local Amateur Dramatics society once because she'd always wanted to be in a musical. She wanted one of the main parts because she thought she could pull off the tap dancing, but she didn't get one of those, and then not even a place in the chorus. The only role she was given was handing out programmes, so she stopped going after that. I'd say that's actual proof that she couldn't have faked liking puzzles. But then I tried to remember whose suggestion it had been to start the last few ones we'd done. I racked my brains for a bit, and I didn't feel quite so good after that, because I mostly came up with the fact that it had been my idea. Then, when I thought about it some more, all the time looking at The Lady with an Ermine, I realised that most of the things we do are my idea: a walk to the park, a trip to the cinema. I'm usually the suggester. That's also because after work she says things like, 'I'm going to lie down on the couch now and DIE,' which she definitely isn't, but which was worrying for a while. She often perks up if I suggest doing something.

Anyway. I started the puzzle and focused on the edges. The problem is that almost all of one side of it is a very deep black. It's hard to crack unless you really have your eye in. Hard too, to pay attention to the shapes you are looking for when someone has planted the idea – for the very first time – that maybe your mum does a little bit of pretending. And here's what makes it worse: I've just remembered that sometimes she *does* tell lies. Only small ones, more like fibs, and mostly not to hurt people's feelings, but it is a fly in the ointment.

If someone comes to the Powder Room with the outfit that they are wearing to their daughter's wedding, and they want *Special Day* make-up to match, she does it all beautifully and tells them they look fabulous. But sometimes, when they've gone, she closes the door, leans her back against it, rolls her eyes and and says, 'Oh my God who told them that suits them?'

Sometimes I want to say 'Well, actually you just did', but I know that isn't the answer she's looking for so I just stay quiet.

Also, there's extra evidence which I've learned from other things. Grandma seemed to love Grandad a lot, and to like living here, but then when he died she upped and offed super-quick. You'd think she might want to keep living in their house so she could imagine him still there with her. Grandad had never even *been* to Florida. He was *a Devon sort of guy* although that obviously didn't tempt her to move to the south-west.

While I was thinking all of that, he'd turned on the TV and

was watching that police car-chase programme. If I squinted sideways I could see his whole face. His mouth was a little bit open so that his bottom lip hung down, and he kept shouting things like, 'Put your foot down and catch the thieving bastards.'

I got hardly any of the puzzle done at all; just a few edge pieces and some of the lady's hair. I'd done the ermine last time, so it would have been against the rules if I'd started with that.

When I heard her key in the door, I thought I might quickly put it all away. We weren't doing it together so that wouldn't be a bang for her. Then I thought it would be interesting to see if she shimmied up to the coffee table and popped a piece straight in. If she did that, it would prove she *did* like puzzles. So, I sat back from the table, my arms folded, and waited for her to come into the room.

I don't think she even clocked it. She came in with her arms twisted around each other and said, 'Look at me, I am a Thai Goddess.' She bowed to us both and then said, 'Whaddyaknow, look what I can do!' and sat down on the floor like a rag doll, her legs straight out in front of her, and bent her body right over so that her face was pressed on her knees. 'I'm *made* to do yoga, the instructor said,' she added, but that part was a bit muffled because her mouth was squished against her thighs.

I'm guessing that means the mat with the butterflies will be delivered shortly. He laughed, and reached over and gave her foot a squeeze. 'So you're quite the slinky. I like the thought of that,' he said. She laughed as well, and gave him one of her big, bright smiles, and I felt there wasn't anything I could add that wouldn't sound a little bit lame. I just sat with my hands in my lap and felt a bit useless.

Then she got up from the carpet. 'I'm starving,' she said, 'I'm going to have a few noodles in a mug with some stock, chilli, ginger and garlic because my body is a temple! Would anybody else like some?'

Neither of us did. He followed her into the kitchen, and as he went past the coffee table he looked down at the puzzle and he raised his eyebrows as if to say *I told you so*.

So now I'm sitting here in my bedroom reporting it all, and it's funny because it isn't very much but it feels like a lot. Here's the thing. With Zorba, I don't know who he is, I've never met him, and he probably doesn't even know I exist. I don't double-think what he says because I've never talked to him. With my mum it's different. It's always been me and her, just getting on with our life, which is everything I can remember from when I was very small. And the thing is I've never even wondered if what she says to me is what she actually feels or thinks, or if she might be pretending. I've always thought everything was truthful between us, mostly because surely there was no need for anything to be hidden?

Until tonight, I never thought that our life together wasn't enough for Mum. And now that's what's popped into my head – that I might have been mistaken or just kidding myself. I thought she was happy. I thought we did happy things together. I thought everything we did – the Tesco order, the puzzles, going to the shops to spot the new season's colours – was exactly as she wanted it to be. And now, I'm thinking that I might be a little bit like a client who's wearing a dreadful outfit for a wedding and she says the opposite of what she actually thinks. The worst thing is, if I ask her about any of this, for example if she likes puzzles, now if she says yes I'll be thinking she might just be lying some more. It'd be a double-fib. I can't win on this one.

I've always thought the Lady with an Ermine had a mysterious face. Now I'm wondering if she looks sad. Or maybe that what's crossing her mind is that she doesn't actually know what to make of anything at all.

I've just looked out of the window and Minnie is sitting at hers. She looks down at the same piece of pavement at night and it looks as if she is both concentrating hard and yet also lost in whatever she is thinking. She doesn't notice me for a while, and when she does she just looks straight across at me and it doesn't feel right to wave.

When I was smaller, I thought that most of what was going on with people was shown on the outside. If they were running or laughing or eating, you could tell if they were happy. Now I see it's not that. I think most of the important stuff happens on the inside, and that faces, instead of being like a pane of glass which you can see right through to what's happening, are more like a door, shut tight, so that's it's perfectly possible not to have a clue.

I think Minnie has something inside of her that is sad. I don't think I'm a genius to be able to work that out.

24

Minnie

I go into a haberdashers and buy a pair of knitting needles even though I will only need one. It is two weeks since Theresa Cartwright has told me of such a thing, and I am spurred on by the fact that my school tunic will hardly fasten. I am not exactly sure what is inside me by now. I think that if I wait until April it will be a baby, but I gauge that on this cold, bleak, bare day in early February when the branches of the trees look like fingers beseeching the sullen sky, that what I have inside of me is something between the stumpy-headed foetus in the textbook and a baby. I know it swims in fluid, and I understand it as part fish, something that began its life by swimming right up into me. It exists as a roll and tap of sensations. I walk past a girl who can't be much older than me and she is wheeling a pram. An infant, puce-faced, is crying furiously within it. I crane my neck to look inside and the girl turns to face me. 'I get no bloody peace,' she says to me furiously, the wind whipping at her chapped cheeks. I nod and avert my eyes.

The needles are a size 7. I don't think it is significant but I register it anyway. They are pale blue, and grey tipped. The ticket on them carries the design for an ivory matinee jacket. My mother is out when I arrive home, and Clara too. She has begun working in a small prep school as the office administrator. I stand in the kitchen and boil the kettle until its whistle turns into a shriek. I fill a copper pan, and put it on the hob and watch the needles tumble and spin as the water boils and rolls around them. I think hygiene must be important and so I wait until the kitchen is billowing with steam. I watch droplets of it condense and run down the wall behind the range.

When I come into my bedroom I am still not entirely sure what it is that I am supposed to do. It is kicking softly, and seems to turn onto its side. I take a scarf from my dresser and tie it around my mouth. Whatever happens I plan to be quiet. There will be a symmetry with when he did this thing to me.

When I lie on my bed I am holding the needle like a pen. I would like it to have the power of a pen, to be able to rewrite what has happened, to create a different version of events so that it never happened at all; this time, my mother will listen to me when I say I do not like the tennis lessons. I will rewrite my story so that the summer ends with me essentially as I was when I began it. I will also rewrite my father alive.

In my mind his death has become increasingly bound up in my shame. It has occurred to me, with my patchy understanding of God, that even if He was not on the alert to save me, in allowing my father to die He perhaps chose to save him from the pain this knowledge would have caused him. I am not consoled by this. It occurs to me that this logic makes Father's death actually my fault. It gives me the courage to do what I do next.

I lie down on my bed, part my knees wide on the eiderdown, put the thin needle inside of me, and I wiggle it.

I think of the diagram in the textbook, and I push harder. I find nooks, crannies, curves. I bite through the scarf. The needle point is focused, meticulous, sharp.

There is suddenly a whoosh of fluid which is warm and silky against my thighs, and then a hot wave of pain storms after it, followed by cinches and cinches of tightening and crushing. I am overwhelmed with the fierce need to be standing on my feet. I get up and clutch the back of my dressing-table chair. My legs are planted wide, and between them there seem to be mostly roaring and billowing.

And quickly, more quickly than I'd ever thought possible (downstairs, the sound of my mother making supper, the slamming of a cupboard door, the clattering of a saucepan, the strike of the clock) comes an unbidden instinct to push, to expel, and after a time which cannot be calibrated in minutes and seconds but rather by heat, and pain, there is a crowning and a slithering, and then a waxy, white-blue mucousy mass on my carpet.

This is precisely when Clara walks in to tell me that supper is ready. She looks aghast, her mouth a round 'o' and then she screams, a thin, horrified scream, which brings Mother running, an empty copper saucepan still held in her hands.

She stands by the door and the sweep of her gaze takes in the enormity of what has happened. Her first instinct is anger, quick to ignite. 'You disgraceful, cheap slut. What shame you've brought on us.' She crosses the room to where I am crouched beside the infant.

He is tiny, like a doll, and perfectly formed, apart from a long thin graze along the length of his thigh which must be from the needle. I have hurt him. I lift his little chicken-wing of an arm, my fingers streaking with the white waxy smoothness which covers it, and I am unsure if his rib cage sucks in once, twice, in an attempt to draw breath. My mother reaches for a cord which I see still pulses between my legs. She pulls it sharply, as if she might be intending to ring a bell, a bell which will bring someone running, someone who knows what to do. There is a second slithering, this time without pain, a great plate of lividness blooming out onto the carpet. I crouch again, the infant motionless beside me. He has dark hair, very dark hair, slicked smooth over his forehead.

It is a baby. Not a sea horse, not a fish, not a stumpy foetus. Not something part-way between, but entirely a baby. Recognisably, perfectly, and beautifully whole.

Clara speaks. 'Shall I phone the doctor? Minnie needs a doctor; the baby . . .' her voice evaporates.

'You will do no such thing. Bring me a towel from the airing cupboard, not one of the best ones.'

'But, look at Minnie, look at . . .'

'I can see perfectly well. Clara, do as you are told.' Her voice brooks no disobedience.

The baby has fingernails like tiny pink sea shells. The length of his arm, from the elbow to finger-end, corresponds exactly to the length of my middle finger. He looks as if he is sleeping. He has a vivid ruby-red birthmark on his shoulder the size of a wild strawberry.

My mother steps around us both and turns to me with hot fierceness. 'I would have thought this was beyond even you. I am glad your father did not live to see this.'

Clara comes back into the bedroom holding a towel. My mother picks up the baby and wraps him in the towel as proficiently as she might a pound of sausages. She folds both ends of the towel in neatly, and the last I see of him is a tucked-away tiny foot.

I close my eyes. The image does not go away.

If you look for movement, you see movement; if the eye – inexplicably, unexpectedly, unbidden – wants to see the tiniest motion, it will. If the ear wants to hear the smallest cry, it will. A wriggle of a foot would confirm life and perhaps allow you to say Stop! Stop! whilst your mother wraps the towel tighter and tighter, until the bundle looks as if all it might hold is a bathing costume, wet from a swim.

I bite my lip.

Mother turns to Clara again and asks her to go to a cupboard in the housemaid's pantry. 'In the one to the right of the sink,' she says, 'there is a box, a green Clarks shoebox. The picture on it will correspond to my stout winter boots.' She is thinking clearly enough to choose the most apt word for her winter boots. They are indeed stout, the heel flat, the sole solid, the top trimmed with lambskin, and a wide bronze buckle.

Clara re-appears with the box, her lip trembling as she passes it over. Mother puts the towel in the box, and asks Clara to go again

*and fetch brown parcel tape from the drawer in the bureau. She wraps
the tape round and round until the lid is firmly secured, and then
tears it neatly with her teeth. She makes sure to fold over the torn
end of the tape so that it will be easily found next time it is required.
The side of the box has a black and white drawing of the boots and
the name of the design which is 'Rosemary'. He was conceived, with
violence, while I stared at bright white tennis shoes. He is being buried
in a shoe box. It seems cruelly apposite.*

*'You need to clean yourself up,' Mother says. 'Go and have a bath.
Clara, strip the sheets and the eiderdown from the bed and put them
in the laundry. I will go and get some newspaper for this.' She gestures
to the afterbirth, which is still in the middle of the carpet. 'It will need
salting to make sure there is no stain.' Her housekeeping proficiency
is calmly at her fingertips.*

*I am numb. I run the bath and stand beside it as it fills slowly. I
smell of iron, of earth, of rotting vegetation. I look down at my breasts
and see that they are softly leaking. When I sit in the bath it tinges
pink with my loss. Clara brings me a towel and hands it to me without
saying a word or meeting my eyes.*

*We have the ruined supper in silence. My mother eats with deter-
mined concentration, pressing over-cooked cauliflower deftly onto her
fork. Afterwards, she goes out to the potting shed and returns with a
spade and a torch. 'You stay inside,' she says crisply to me. 'Clara,
fetch the box from upstairs.'*

*Clara complies again, and comes down carrying it flat on her
outstretched forearms, her palms uppermost. Her evening has been a
succession of holdings and passings: towel, boot box, parcel tape, towel
again, and now the filled box. She follows Mother out of the door,
and I go to one of the front bedrooms and stand by the window. I
watch as our mother stands and casts her eye over the shrubbery. She
finally selects a large hydrangea bush, lies the torch on the ground so
that its beam shines silvery clear like a lighthouse, and begins to dig
briskly. Clara stands behind her, silently holding the box, her head*

bowed, looking as if she stands in obedient attendance beside an altar. Mother hefts out the soil and piles it at her side. She wipes her forehead with the back of her hand, and at one point steps back, appraises the size of the Clarks box and begins digging again. Neither of them say a word. Through the small open window, I hear the occasional clink of the spade against a stone, and Clara, once, clearing her throat as she shifts from one foot to another. When Mother judges the hole to be big enough she turns to Clara, takes the box from her and puts it in with the smooth, neat efficiency of a woman storing winter sweaters in a drawer at the end of the season. I may be mistaken, but I think that once it is in the ground she adjusts its position so that the box lies absolutely straight on the soil. She does not pause for a moment before beginning to shovel the earth back on top. She says something to Clara, clearly dismissing her, and my sister turns and comes back inside, walking like a stiff, stunned soldier.

Clara doesn't come to find me. Along the landing, I watch her go straight to her room and her light goes off almost immediately. After a while my mother appears at the top of the stairs. She has washed her hands, and is drying them with a towel, paying particular care to the skin between her fingers.

'I am tired. We will speak of this in the morning. You can either make up your bed with fresh sheets, or sleep in another room.'

She turns and walks away. I go to the linen press and take out some sheets. I walk to my father's study and press my forehead to the closed door. I am sorry, I whisper. My apology is not just to him. I remake the bed and try not to look at the damp mark on the carpet. I open the window and let the rush of night air chill me. Perhaps it will banish the smell – I am sure I am not imagining the smell – of innards, of birth, of bodily fluids. I press my fingertips to my nose, and try not to cry.

When I finally fall asleep, I dream of a baby falling, and of my hands outstretched, unable to catch it. I can see the darkness of its hair pressed to the softness of its scalp, and a blue vein pulsing, vivid, at its temple. I hold a tennis racquet in my hand and a curtain flaps forlornly in the breeze. My mouth tastes of orange barley water; ice cubes chink in a glass. I reach out and am given a mauve hydrangea bloom. I hold it in my cupped hands and it is the size of a skull. Clara is visible behind frosted glass; she seems to be receding, passively, until she vanishes entirely. My father appears, dressed as for work. He looks at me with his head tilted to one side, perplexed, and when I try to talk to him only billowing steam comes out of my mouth.

I wake early in the morning and stand at the window where I'd watched my mother digging. A blackbird teases out a worm from the freshly turned soil. The hydrangea is implacably, solidly there.

25

Max

Mr Helpful decided on a new project today. Cleaning windows. There used to be a window cleaner who came down the street but he charged £25 and Mum said he didn't even ask for hot water for his bucket, or change the water he'd actually got in it even if he'd already cleaned all four houses along from us. She said it was like paying to have your windows made dirtier.

She was delighted when he offered. He didn't have his ladder with him, so today would just be the downstairs windows, with upstairs following shortly. I bet his ladder technique won't match Grandad's.

He rustled up a bright red bucket from his van and a big yellow sponge, and he ran the tap water until it was boiling hot and used half a bottle of Fairy Liquid for the bubbles. He asked her for a clean rag for the polishing, and she came down from the airing cupboard with an old sheet and he ripped it in half with one big swish, his arms out wide.

I was sitting at the kitchen table eating a chocolate mousse. He looked at me and said, 'This isn't going to be a spectator sport, you can make yourself useful for once, holding some of the gear for me. Hup Two Three.'

He did a march like he was a Sergeant Major, and flipped the mousse carton across the kitchen into the bin. Lucky I was finished. Also I wasn't very happy about the *for once*. Who's he to say that when he's got no idea of what I actually do?

Mum said, 'This I have to see,' which surprised me because I'm not sure what's so amazing about cleaning windows. We went outside and she stayed in the front room giving us a thumbs up through the glass and he blew her a kiss and she put her lips right on the window pane and he put the tip of his index finger on the glass as if she was actually kissing that.

I stood there with the balled-up bits of sheet held out in front of me like a tray of drinks, and he put the bucket right by me and dipped in the sponge until it was properly drenched and then he started cleaning the window with great big rainbow swoops of his arm, his t-shirt tugging because of all his muscle action. I looked at Mum through the window and she was just watching and watching his arm like it was hypnotising her, and I remembered how I used to look at the windscreen wipers going in Grandad's car and it was the very same thing, except she bit her bottom lip and flashed her eyes like she was winking, and he laughed some more, his bigness just rumbling with it. Then he reached the end of one window pane and he flicked the sponge right at me so that a string of water flew from it and went right in my eye and he said, 'Stare stare like a bear,' so I looked down at my feet. Water with that much Fairy Liquid in stings quite a lot. I blinked and squinted and twitched a bit but kept on holding the sheets. He'd started singing 'Love me Tender', and seemed to be having a fine old time.

A couple of boys I know from school cycled past and I shrugged a bit and shuffled my feet to try and make it look as if I was standing there casually, rather than just waiting for the next instruction which actually I was. There was something about him which I think looked playful from her side of the glass but didn't feel like it on mine. He finished swooping across the last bit of the bay window and he said 'CLOTHS' really loudly and I reached over to pass them to him and he took them very quickly in one hand and then tossed the soaked sponge at me – fast like a rugby ball straight at my stomach. It was only a sponge so it didn't hurt but it wet my t-shirt so that I had a big damp patch and made me look like a dopey catcher which I'm not, given any kind of proper warning. I was glad Tom and Alfie had cycled out of sight.

He dried and polished the window double-handed in fast circles, and it was really shiny with the sun bouncing off it, and she couldn't have looked more delighted; she was clapping her hands and pretending that the light streaming into the front room was dazzling her.

He finished doing the smaller window and she opened it a little bit and said, 'That is the most champion window cleaning I have ever seen and deserves a special reward which will begin with a nice cup of tea.' He laughed and rapped on the pane with his finger knuckle, and she disappeared into the kitchen and I was still standing there, like a soldier, wondering if he was going to tell me I could stand down, or stop, or just go away. It felt as if there was a funny crackle in the air between us, and as if I needed to wait for his permission for whatever it was that would happen next. What did happen next was unexpected. He tipped the dirty water from the bucket into the drain and then, quick as a flash, put the empty bucket over my head. Lights out, the last drops of water dripping down my cheeks and my neck. Then he knocked on the side with his knuckles twice and said, 'Ding dong bell! Pussy's in the well,' and laughed fit to bust. He was still laughing when he went into the house.

I stood for a minute, the bucket swinging from side to side and then coming to a creaky halt, the wet sponge still in my hand and my t-shirt sticking to my stomach. I felt like one of those things at the fairground that you whack with a hammer, and the weight chases up to the top and makes a big bell ring. Tom and Alfie cycled past again; they must have been doing laps of the block. *'Great look!'* one of them shouted.

I listened for the sound of them going away – which was hard with a bucket on my head and what with my left ear with drips in, and then I listened some more to check that he hadn't come out of the house again. I knelt down and put the sponge carefully on the concrete because it occurred to me that if he was watching from the window, his cup of tea in one hand and the other one probably somewhere on my mum, he'd probably *take exception* to his yellow sponge being chucked on the ground. Then I took the bucket off and put it right-side up next to it. I rubbed the water off my face and took a big breath because I couldn't think what else to do.

After a bit I went and sat on the front wall, and thought about trying to catch Tom and Alfie up because maybe they'd be playing football in the park or something by now and I could just join in and not think about him and his big stupid bucket, but I didn't really feel like it. Instead, I looked up and there was Minnie at the window, looking right at me, and I guessed she'd seen all of it, and I just sort of nodded to her, and raised my eyebrows, and she beckoned to me and a moment later opened the big, wide Rosemount door.

'Not your best day,' she said when I went in, and she had a faded towel with a rose pattern on it in her hand. She passed it to me and I dried my head and rubbed at my t-shirt. 'Would you like a cup of tea?'

She has tongs to pick up sugar cubes. She says she and Clara don't use them all the time as they use loose sugar most days but while the kettle was whistling to a boil she took some cubes out of a silver tin and put them neatly on a little saucer, and passed me the silver tongs and said, 'Have it as sweet as you like.'

I started piling the cubes one on top of each other, and she smiled and said, 'Do you think you could build the Eiffel Tower?' I told her I didn't think so, but it was a nice thought and it was good to be sitting in the big, calm, white-tiled kitchen and not to be standing next to him and feeling his thoughts crackle like pylon wires across to me.

Clara came into the kitchen and said good afternoon. She didn't look exactly pleased to see me but she didn't look like she very much minded either. I made my tea as thick and sweet as treacle.

Afterwards, Minnie asked if there was anything I would like to do. I asked her if she would show me another antique. This time I got to go upstairs.

If I describe Rosemount it won't do it justice. It's amazing but also quite sad, and depending what you are looking at, one of those things is in your mind. So, as I walked up the staircase I could see properly the big stained-glass window. The stairs continue up a second flight and the light comes down like in a cathedral. Its colours look like jewels, and it feels like the space above the stairs is full of ruby fire-flies. Then, when you look at the walls, there are what Minnie told me are called cornices, and they are made with patterns of vines and flowers and fat, flying babies called cherubs, and some of them are a bit flaky, and some are covered in massive cobwebs which are too high to reach, but it's easy to imagine a time when it was all clean and perfect. On the landing there are carpets which were spun in Persia and the patterns are complicated and colourful and quite difficult to stare at. When you kneel down close, you can see parts of them are worn through from all the people walking on them for years and years, and when Minnie straightened one out, up puffed a small cloud of dust.

She took me into her father's study. It felt like no one had used the room for a very long time. There was a dark-red leather armchair and a big desk, and a very shiny pen stand. There were shelves of books, and another patterned rug, and very heavy curtains. There was a jar which used to contain humbugs. It still smelt a bit minty. She showed me two things. The first was a cabinet – *a Queen Anne walnut bureau*. The doors were mirrored and inside there were shelves and compartments and pigeon holes and all kinds of secret spaces.

'I don't think there is anything particularly secret in any of them,' she said.

She let me look anyway. There were tiny buttons which she said were studs for a dress shirt. There was a receipt for a hat bought from a shop in Cirencester and a business card for a man who worked for Lloyds of London.

'I wasn't much older than you when my father died,' she said, and then I told her about Zorba. We stood there with all the drawers of the walnut bureau wide open, and the receipt and the studs in my hand, and it felt like we were also holding our vanished fathers and then she showed me the second thing, which wasn't sad at all.

It was a group of eight china monkeys – *Meissen*, she said – dressed as a band. They had little striped jackets and different instruments. When you tapped the tiny drum it made an actual noise. One of them had a bell on its cap which jingled when you touched it. I wondered if her father had sat here, thinking about business stuff or where he might buy a new hat, and then sometimes, just for the hell of it, tapped the drum and quietly tinkled the bell.

'They must have taken hours to make and paint,' Minnie said. 'Isn't it curious that someone would decide to do these?'

We agreed that we were glad they had. Minnie said she thought of them as *a little troupe of porcelain merriment*, and for a bit I forgot about standing on the pavement with a plastic bucket rammed on my head.

When I crossed the road to come back home I had a spring in my step. He was watching the football and Mum was doing the ironing so I came straight up here to make this recording. If I keep remembering all the antiques information Minnie is teaching me, perhaps when I grow up I can be an auctioneer. I'll have my very own hammer like on the television and most likely get really good at noticing small, secret gestures.

26

Minnie

My mother calls me into the drawing room the next morning. She is sitting in the pale-blue silk chair by the fireplace. She beckons me to be seated, and then she begins to speak. Her voice is cold, precise, clear; each word is enunciated so carefully that I am to be in no doubt as to what I am being told.

She begins with what she calls my disgrace. She tells me that she has no interest in learning how I came to be in my condition; she is confident that it is entirely as a result of a combination of my wilfulness, my excessive appetite, and my curiosity, which, she reminds me are all the flaws in my character which she has repeatedly tried to address. She tells me that I am both licentious and duplicitous because I have given myself to someone and then tried to conceal the fact that I have done so.

She waits a moment for her words to settle upon me. I look directly back at her, and wonder what would happen if I were to tell her what Mr Lucas did, if I told her that I gave nothing, and that what was lost was horribly taken. But as I look at her I see in her eyes such complete certainty of knowledge, such absolute judgement, that I realise that even if I were to tell her, she would likely not believe me and it would only confirm the opinion she has of me. She is also partly correct. I have *been duplicitous. I have told no one. Mostly through ignorance, and fear, and shame, but my mother is not interested in whys and wherefores.*

She reaches to the bureau and picks up a copy of Readers' Digest. *'I am going to tell you about two women,' she says, 'in the hope that it might help you to understand your position better. Are you familiar with the term baby farmers?'*

I am not, and I console myself afterwards that it is not a correct description of me, because baby farmers are paid to take other people's children under the pretence of intending to raise them through infanthood, and then they drug, starve and murder them, and keep the money they have been given.

My mother is using the term as shorthand for someone who has killed an infant. This is, indisputably, what I have done. She settles herself more comfortably in her chair and reads aloud. She has a habit of tracing the line of words she is reading with her index finger. I have always felt previously that it conjures a look of someone not entirely familiar with the act of reading. Now I think it is to add particular emphasis.

These are the women she tells me of. Amelia Dyer strangled babies with dressmaker's edging tape. She put their bodies into carpet bags and dropped them in the River Thames. The police found six infants, each with the same white tape around their neck. She told the policemen: 'It was how you could tell it was one of mine.' Her last confession filled five exercise books. When she was about to be hanged her last words were 'I have nothing to say'. My mind snags on the fact that there must have been nothing left, what with the five exercise books presumably giving the line and length of it. The second woman is called Minnie Dean. When Mother reads out her name, she pauses and glances at me for emphasis, as if I might somehow miss the coincidence. Minnie Dean lived in New Zealand and was observed boarding a train carrying a baby and a hatbox. She left the train carrying only the hatbox. When she was tried, hatboxes containing tiny baby dolls were sold outside the courtroom. Mother holds up the Readers' Digest to show me a photograph of Minnie. She has carefully dressed hair, a shawl, and a neatly pinned brooch.

'The law caught up with these women,' my mother says, folding the magazine in half and putting it back on the bureau. 'They were guilty of a crime, the same crime you have committed, and . . .' she pauses, 'the crime in which you have embroiled Clara and myself. You have endangered us all with your wilful ways.'

I wonder what would happen if I say that if she had called a doctor as Clara suggested, then she and Clara would not be implicated, and I alone would be accountable for what has happened. I keep my lips pressed shut.

She stands up and moves towards the grate so that her back is turned to me and she is looking at the fireplace.

'The three of us, now,' she says, 'have a secret to keep. The secret is your fault. You have blighted Clara's future as well as your own and we will from now on live private lives so that this does not come out.'

In the distance, the church clock is beginning to strike eleven. She turns her head, and then her gaze falls upon me again.

'I am going to leave you to sit awhile here and consider what you have done. I can only hope that knowledge, and shame and guilt, will temper this . . . this running at life which has been your custom since you were small.'

She leaves me sitting on the chaise longue, and closes the drawing-room door behind her with a precise click. Although it is not locked, I am reminded of when I was a small girl and she would leave me in the nursery 'to think about what you have done and to come out a better child.' There is no chance of that now.

The sound of the final church bell thrums in my chest. God, a court judge, a policeman, my mother: no doubt they would all look upon me with the same austere face. I am doubly wicked, both for the child's life and the child's death.

I sit in the drawing room suffused with guilt, and I am snared, tugged back to the moment of the birth in my bedroom. What I am not sure of, and I wonder if Clara knows, is whether between my own unexpected cries which now strike me as sounding like an animal in *the field, and the terrible slithering noise, and the sound of the bedroom door opening, and Clara's own scream, there was actually another cry. Was there a brief, high wail, something akin to the mew of a kitten? Round and round in my head the thought goes, until I get up from the chaise longue and walk over to the lamp by the bureau and I take my thumb and press it firmly on the bulb where the filament shines bright. I look at the smooth red weal on my skin, and it is all that I know for certain.*

I go out into the hallway. The door to the music room is open and Clara is sitting at the piano, very still, very upright. I can tell she knows I am there but she does not turn to face me and she does not speak. Instead, she begins to search through her sheet music and I stand for a moment, willing her to turn to me, willing her to say something, but still she does not, and so I turn and begin to walk up the stairs, slowly, painfully slowly, my palm flat to the bannister. In my bedroom I fall to my knees upon the carpet which is damp and salty where my mother has cleaned away the stain and I cradle my head in my arms and my thighs press against the soft rippled slackness of my stomach, and as I kneel there Clara begins to play the piece she has chosen. The notes rise like balloons up the stairwell and she is playing Bach's Goldberg Variation 988 very slowly which I recognise because I have turned the pages for her when she has practised it. The plangent melody rises up and speaks to me of grief and guilt and a loss so deep that I know it will be with me for the rest of my life. I begin to weep a spill of silent, enormous tears because I feel so sad and so wretched, and because I have killed something that is small, and perfect, and innocent.

Clara continues to play and the music is both a requiem for the tiny boy and for my innocence, which I thought had been lost six months previously but I realise has been truly and wholly lost now.

I understand as Clara reprises the Bach that she is speaking to me in a way that her tongue, her words, would never allow, and I remain balled-up on the floor of my room, the music washing over and over me and I know she will never bring herself to speak of what has happened, and that I will not ask. I am correct in this; we will go on to live our adult lives like two spiders spinning side by side in a kind of horrified silence and she will never play the piece again in all the years that follow. I lie there until my limbs are locked in numbness and chill, and until the clouds thicken, and soft, dense snowflakes begin to fall from the gunmetal sky. I think of him in his shoebox being gradually blanketed by a coverlet of snow. I think of the ground freezing and hardening around him, and of his tiny hands, purpled, and of the startling redness of the wild-strawberry birthmark. I think of all the weather that will blow in over where he lies, and I know that I will never be able to stop looking at the spot where he is buried, the hydrangea placid, resilient, marking him with massive indigo blooms.

As Clara's notes continue to rise up through the blue, fading light of the stairwell I weep because what has happened is so very, very wrong and can never be made right, because I am as indelibly stained as he is pure, and because Clara's Bach is his song, and it is all I have given him.

27

Max

Minnie is crying. I'm standing at my bedroom window, and I'm looking down into the room they call the morning room. She's been writing in her diary again. Whatever she has written has upset her, because she has looked up and she is staring across to the street light, and she uses the back of her hand to wipe away the tears from her cheeks.

I don't give her a wave. Sometimes you know when someone wants to be alone. It happens more often than you might think. By the seaside once, I saw a woman standing by the sea wall, and she was making no sound at all, but tears were just pouring down her face, even though she was surrounded by chattering people eating ice cream and fudge and carrying buckets and spades. Nobody noticed her except me.

I haven't had a great day, although not on the crying scale. Mum's had a full book of appointments and he's come over to see her now. She's giving him a luxury foot massage on the couch. It's meant to be in the Powder Room but she says for him she'll make an exception. He's telling her she's awesomely talented, which is a nice compliment for her to have.

I was at a loose end earlier, just sitting with the TV not even on. I haven't got completely used to the fact that it's not my job to be on call for the Velux. It was quite a stuffy afternoon and I had to remind myself that she wouldn't need me scooting on in there. I decided instead to go and see my friend Eddie. He's my friend in a particular kind of way because friendship is more complicated for him. He was in my class for all of junior school but in September he's going to a school which is more suited to look after children like him, children who prefer things exactly just-so. Where I'm going wouldn't fit the bill. Eddie has quite a few rules. Once you know them, it's easy to step your way around them; it's the people who can't be bothered to learn them who make him scream and flap his hands like a bird trying to take off. Eddie's rules are actually quite simple. The first is that you don't touch him without telling him first; it's not your skin on his skin that he minds, just the surprise. The second thing is that you mustn't ever have the door to a room closed. He likes to see there's an obvious escape route. The last rule is about colours; there are some he will never, ever wear, and there are others – yellow, for example – which are his favourites. He likes to wear bright socks, and for you to notice the colour. The last part is particularly easy to deal with. I say things like 'Hello Captain Orange Socks' when I see him, or 'Hey there Redfoot', and there's that hurdle cleared. The last thing is that he likes to carry an oat bar in his pocket at all times in case he misses a meal. He checks on it all the time by tapping his thigh. He is never actually going to miss a meal. His mum is a really good cook and feeds him like it's her actual proper job. She also lines his socks up in rows so that he can pick the colour he wants each morning. She calls him a *funny old bird* which is as good a description as any especially when he is flapping his arms. When you know his four things, and they're really not the hardest, Eddie's as normal as anyone. When we were in Year Three, his mum told my mum she wasn't sure if Eddie would ever get the hang of friendship, but I knew he would as he doesn't just think about himself. We were making pumpkins for a Halloween display, and I cut mine out too much and it collapsed in a mush. He offered me his, which was brilliant and much better than anyone else's, and I knew he had the hang of friendship because he'd guessed exactly how I felt. I didn't take his pumpkin, but this is what I noticed later. On the display table, you had to put a card with a name in front of your pumpkin, and he'd put both our names on his, even though I hadn't helped at all.

So today we were sitting in the tree house in his garden. It's more like a platform, actually. It was built by his dad and he's given Eddie plenty of exits. There's no door; you can get out anywhere around the edges and find your way down through the branches. So we were sitting up there, Eddie whittling at a stick, and just talking quietly to himself. He wears big glasses like Joe 90, and the shavings from the stick kept flicking up at them. Every now and again he'd put the knife and the stick down and tap the oat bar in his pocket. He asked how my school holidays were going. I said how things were all a bit scratchy. Scratchy came to me as the right word, watching him whittling away. That's what I like about Eddie; he just took the word right on the chin. I told him what he'd said about Mum not actually liking puzzles, and also about putting the bucket on my head. 'He's kinda messing with me,' I said, which sounded a lot cooler than I feel about it.

Eddie stopped whittling the stick, put it down, and didn't tap the oat bar, but patted my hand instead. That was a first.

'Thing is, Max,' he said, after a short pause, 'just be glad you're not a chimpanzee.'

I blinked at him, and then he explained.

'Male chimpanzees sometimes kill the babies of their new mates. They do it to make sure all the female's energy is spent just looking after their future babies. It's called self-preservation. It's to make sure their genes survive.'

I sat back on my heels to digest that a little bit.

'It's not only chimpanzees,' Eddie said. 'Lions do it, and

dolphins. A female dolphin looks after her baby for four years. With that in the way, she won't want to mate with the new male for a very long time.'

You've got to admit there's a lot there to take on board. I told Eddie I was going to shake his hand to say thanks for the advice, and I did, and then we talked about cricket for a bit before leaving the tree house.

So here's the thing:

1. I'm lucky I'm not a baby chimp, lion or dolphin with a single mother. That doesn't sound like it would result in what Mrs Winters would call *a good outcome*.
2. A dolphin may look after her baby for four years but I'm almost twelve, which just shows human parenting is a much bigger deal. It also helps to understand why he might think I shouldn't be her number one priority. Maybe he reckons my time is up. Maybe it actually is.
3. It's made me think that Nature can be all-round brutal. Especially human nature, if you think of him and his brothers and the cat.

It's also reminded me of a wildlife programme Mum and I watched together. It was about a bird called a shoebill which hatches two chicks but only rears one of them. The mother decides which chick is stronger, and then she just stops feeding the weaker one until it withers and dies RIGHT UNDER HER FEET in the nest. SHE CAN'T EVEN PRETEND NOT TO SEE IT. *Cheep cheep;* it begs for food but the mum only stuffs it in the other one's bill. So, thinking about what Eddie told me today I am now glad about a whole number of things. I'm not a chimp, a lion or a dolphin, and I don't have a stronger sister or brother. That'd be a whole new complication. If Zorba were around maybe none of these things would be relevant, although that line of thinking isn't going to get me anywhere. It's probably better to think about Mum's friend a little differently; maybe it explains why he would dislike me from the off.

Mrs Winters once said that to understand someone better we needed to walk a mile in their moccasins. After what I've learned today, I can try and see it a little bit differently. If I imagine him as a chimp – and he is pr-et-ty hairy – it's more obvious why he might not like me. He probably doesn't even understand it himself. Perhaps I should think myself lucky that he only put a bucket on my head.

Minnie has come out of the house. I've just looked up from the Dictaphone and she's standing by the dangling gate. That's unusual for her, especially at this time of the evening. She's not crying anymore, but her face looks very still and sad. She's standing on the pavement between the third and fourth street light and she's just walked back and forth a couple of times. Her lips are moving a little bit, as if she might be counting. I think I'll go outside and see her. Maybe she needs a distraction.

I'm back. I went out to her on the street and touched her arm because she hadn't seen me come out. Before I touched her arm, I nearly warned her I was about to do it, which just shows how quickly you get used to behaving in a particular way.

'How's your day been?' she asked me, and I told her not the best. I said Mum was giving him a luxury foot massage, and that I was learning lessons from wildlife, which she said was an unusual combination. She asked if I'd like to come into Rosemount for a glass of elderflower cordial, and if perhaps I might be interested in seeing another antique. She didn't have to ask twice.

The first thing she showed me was basically dangerous if not used carefully. It was *a Hunting Horn table lighter made by Alfred Dunhill in 1930 from polished brass and silver plate.* It looks like a regular hunting horn, but when you tip it upside down a great WHOOSH of flame comes out. Apparently they caused lots of fires in country houses when they got left on the table after supper. They might have looked impressive, but if there was a draught they'd fall over, and before you knew it the tablecloth was on fire. I bet that caused a stir; housemaids running around carrying buckets of sand. It never happened at Rosemount, obviously. It was kept in a stand, completely the right way up. I put it to my lips and liked the thought that I might blow fire. Minnie said best not to try, what with my hair just starting to grow back.

The second thing was kept in a glass cupboard called a *vitrine* in the drawing room. It's the first time I've been in there and I think it's the biggest room in a house I've ever been in in my life. The fireplace is so big I think I could hide up the chimney, but when I said this Minnie reminded me it would have been built not so that a child of my size could hide in it but scoot up it and clean it. That put a different shine on it.

Minnie opened the vitrine and took out *a pair of famille verte models of Buddhistic lions*. Each lion had a huge grinning mouth, wide open with a red shiny tongue. They had bulging eyes, and curls in their manes made of actual snail shell. One lion had its paw resting on a playful little cub, and the other on a ball. They looked as if they were having a right old laugh, and the red of their tongues made me think of a circus clown's mouth. After we put them back we went past the parlour where Clara was doing some needlework. She said, 'Here again?' but her voice wasn't properly stern.

I'm back now and Mum is making a stir-fry in the kitchen. She's made some for me too, and I'm going to go down and make a special effort. I wonder if there's a way to show that I'm no threat to the survival of his genes? Self-preservation really isn't his problem, especially when he's got ol' Jasmine carrying them already. I know most likely he wouldn't think of it in that way, but thanks to Eddie, I certainly am.

28

Minnie

I return to school two days later. My mother has said I have a cold. She gives me a handkerchief to tuck ostentatiously into my sleeve. I hold it to my face in assembly and press at my temples. This is not an affectation; the heat of the hall, the number of people present, are making my heart race. I feel a soft sheen of sweat prickle on my upper lip. I touch the skin of my cheek and it feels cool as alabaster. My form mistress, when taking the register, says she hopes I am no longer infectious. I tell her that I am not. I walk along the corridors in a state of remove. The girls' gossip and laughter filters as if from very far away. I sit in lessons and the words in my textbooks turn into legions of soldier ants which march off the page leaving it white and bald. I do not hand in homework. I barely listen. I carry a sense of my own wickedness and guilt like ash in my mouth. I taste it each time I swallow.

One lunchtime, a group of girls are conjecturing about sex. Their expectations are as romantically heady as mine would have once been. I stand near them, and it is all I can do not to turn and say to them, 'It is not like that at all, it is more terrible than you could ever imagine,' but I don't want them to think that, to know that, to begin to clench their skirts when they pass a man in the street, to feel anxiety if he turns his gaze upon them. I start to go to the library at lunchtime, not to read or revise, but mostly to stare at the rows of books. It becomes a form of self-torment, a reminder of all that I have lost.

Miss Potts stops me in the corridor. 'Minnie, I am worried about you,' she says, 'you are not your usual self. Is there anything troubling you? Would you like to come and talk to me?'

I stand for a moment, my eyes fixed on a ring on her finger. The stone is amber with a tiny leaf fragment within. The leaf seems to spin in the warm glow of the stone. The possibility opens, for a moment, of telling her the truth – what Mr Lucas did, my pregnancy, what I did, and how I am drowning in my own guilt. And then I remember what my mother has said to me. I have made her and Clara my accomplices; I have made them culpable too. I think of Clara in her job at the prep school. She files school reports. She takes the headmaster tea at eleven. She answers the telephone when parents phone to say their child is unwell. She is respected and well thought of. I cannot jeopardise that.

I look Miss Potts straight in the eye. 'Everything's absolutely fine,' I say. 'I'm just not really interested in school anymore. My plans are changing and I am looking forward to leaving in July.'

She does not reply. She looks at me carefully, and then reaches forward and touches my shoulder lightly with her fingertips. 'As you were, then,' she says and continues along the corridor. I stand for a moment, not moving, biting my lip very hard, and then I go to the cellar cloakroom which is barely used. I stand with my forehead against the locked door of a toilet and I stay there until the bell rings for afternoon lessons.

In my general certificate exams I write very little, even though some of the answers are easy. My pen is heavy in my hand. When I sit the English paper it is all I can do not to weep. I read the questions on Othello, *on* Wuthering Heights, *on* John Donne. *Even with what little work I have done, I could still answer after a fashion. Instead, I write* I'm sorry I'm sorry I'm sorry *over and over in very tiny writing. Miss Potts is invigilating the exam and I see her notice me writing and she gives me the faintest of smiles. Perhaps she might look at it when she puts the scripts in the envelope.*

On the last day of school we line up in our uniform on opposite sides of the playground – one side for those who are leaving, one side for those who will be entered on the register to return in the sixth form. I stand with the leavers, who have begun to autograph each other's blouses as they will no longer be needing them. Miss Potts comes over to me. 'Minnie, surely not?' she says, and then, 'Perhaps I can speak with your mother?'

I shake my head and say, 'It's my decision and I am happy with it.'

After we are dismissed, I walk for one last time into the school hallway. I stand before the gold-lettered boards with the names of all the girls who have gone on to Oxbridge. I let go of that particular rosary. I walk away with the thought that I have managed to disappoint both my parents. I have not the accomplishments that my mother would wish for me. I have not achieved the academic success that my father had hoped for. I am also irremediably blemished and no longer a nice girl.

When I get home, my mother is out and Clara is at work. I linger by the umbrella stand in the hallway, my hands clasped in front of me. The tiles where I cartwheeled stretch out before me. A question comes to me, audible as if whispered directly into my ear: 'What do you want of the world?' and an answer comes back, 'Nothing, absolutely nothing.' And when I ask myself a second question: 'And what can you give to the world?' the answer is the same. 'Nothing, nothing at all.'

My friends call for me for a little while. One scorching day in June when they are going to the river to swim, they knock on the door, their bathing suits rolled inside towels under their arms. 'Come with us Minnie,' they say. 'Come, it will be heavenly,' and I shake my head. 'No, thank you,' I tell them. My voice is cold and polite. My mother watches approvingly from the door to the drawing room. I have become quieter and more obedient than she could ever have hoped. After a while they stop calling and I spend my time doing chores she sets for me, polishing candlesticks, scouring the white enamel of the baths, and hacking at the Japanese knotweed which has run amok since Hooper has gone. The grass on the tennis court has become rank with coarse-leaved dandelions. I try to pull one up, and it stains my hand yellow and rancid. I press my hands to my face and stand there, inhaling, lost, until my mother raps on the window and calls me in for tea.

In the dog days of the summer, the civil engineers, the architects, the estate planners begin to arrive. All around Rosemount there is striding, and counting, and measuring; men with pencils behind their ears, clipboards, and vast spooling tapes which they wind back in with a handle. They put red crosses on trees which are to be felled, and paint white lines to show where the new road will go. They drink tea in tin mugs from a stainless steel urn and make wide sweeping gestures with their free arm to illustrate where all the new houses will go. They have the air of magicians who will conjure up a whole new bold landscape.

The chief architect takes it upon himself to keep my mother informed. He removes the waterproof jacket he wears on site, and comes into the dining room with rolled plans under his arm. He unfolds them for her and outlines the progress they are making. I sense my mother enjoys these encounters. It is her last opportunity to play the lady of the manor. She rests her fingers on the papers and says 'I see, I see' gravely as he talks about their proposed schedule of work.

I watch the men from the morning-room window. I watch as they measure beyond the hydrangea, as they line orange traffic cones to show the curvature of the road. I watch as they drain the pond and then fill it with three lorry-loads of rubble. I listen all day when the tree surgeons come, and the aspens fall, one after another, to the scream of the chain saw. I open the window and the air smells of resin. I stand watching it all. The men do not acknowledge my gaze.

When the planning is done, and the ground is made ready for the building teams to arrive, the chief architect comes in one morning *and says he will have something impressive to show my mother later. It is a to-scale 3-D model, he tells her, which will show how the estate will look in two years when it is completed.*

Later in the morning, it is carried in like royalty in a sedan chair, two men either side of the plywood base it is built on. It is four feet by four feet and they have to manoeuvre themselves carefully through the front door. The double doors of the dining room both have to be opened to give them safe access. There is much fussing and consultation to ensure that it is not chipped or damaged. It is to be displayed later at the town hall; it is, the architect assures her, highly innovative and progressive. They place it on the dining-room table and the chief architect beams at my mother. She nods her head as if graciously accepting a gift, and I feel that the fact that the land has been sold has somehow slipped from the equation. My mother looks pleased with the model. 'Such neat, intricate work!' she says. I am reminded of Elizabeth the First being shown discoveries from faraway lands. My mother fits the bill.

I wait, quietly, next to the curtains, just beyond the eye line of them all. They eventually process out of the room, my mother having given the chief architect a theatrical round of applause. I close the doors behind them and study the model at my leisure.

Rosemount looks marooned. It looms up in the middle of the shoals of tiny houses like a maritime, vast-bellied creature that has swum into waters too shallow for it. I trace my finger along the line of the eaves, and the roof. It is made of tiny, red clay bricks and the windows are made of carefully cut rectangles of actual glass.

The new houses are made of balsa-wood and are positioned in neat, orderly rows. The front door of each one is painted in a bright, contrasting colour. Tiny, symmetrical, square lawns have been picked out in emerald green felt. The aerial view emphasises the order and uniformity of the crescents and cul-de-sacs. Each of the street lamps has a tiny orange wick inside of it to give the impression of light cast. I am reminded of a doll's house, except on a grander scale. The model maker has added figures of people to give reality and occupation to the estate. They are a little over-sized for the scale, but they bring it to life. There is a woman in a headscarf with a tiny navy pram; a man holding a bucket by a red car; someone with rolled-up sleeves pushing a tiny matchstick wheelbarrow in a garden. Clusters of people are chatting in doorways. There are two small boys, one holding a football, and a woman walking a little dog. A milk float is parked on one of the streets. The impression of crates of milk is given by tiny scrunches of foil glued onto a little tray. I brush my finger along a tiny slide in the play park. They are oddly comforting, these happy miniature people going about their busy, normal lives in their clean, uncluttered streets. The model maker has added a tabby cat, curled up on a doorstep, and also a girl, holding a yellow kite, in the playground.

It is only when I stoop to examine the detail of the kite that my eye is on the same level as the morning-room window of Rosemount. I catch a flash of colour, and look beyond the kite and into Rosemount itself. I notice he has given this window curtains; it is the only one which is dressed in this way, with a small pleat of velvet which echoes the smoke blue of the ones that are actually there. And I am there too. I see that instantly. When I crouch to look properly, there is a figure looking out from the window. She has painted hair which is plaited like mine, and he has coloured her with a rose pink sweater and a navy skirt, which I have worn while I have watched the men work. He has noticed me, and included me, as I watched Rosemount dismantled before my eyes.

The roof has a hinge. I carefully open it and put my hand down into the morning-room space. The figure is almost the width and the height of my smallest finger. It is the size of something which might go on top of a wedding cake. The other people have faces painted on them – mouths round 'o's, broad smiles, or lips straight with intent – but my face is unpainted. It is totally blank. I touch where he has painted the plait of my hair so carefully. Perhaps he ran out of time;

perhaps he thought no one would peer in and catch sight of me. I don't actually think this is the case. I wonder if his eye, which has registered everything so carefully, and which has created a vision of the estate as somewhere where happy, purposeful people live, has seen in my face an emptiness which the blankness of the figure's face flashes whitely right back at me.

I cradle the figure in my palm. I am protective of it, and wish to spare it anyone else's gaze. I fold the hinge of Rosemount's roof back down and leave the room quietly. My mother is having a sherry with the chief architect and does not notice me climbing the stairs. I wrap the tiny figure in a soft paisley handkerchief so that her blind eyes are concealed, and then I place her carefully in the drawer of my nightstand. I remember the tiny dolls sold in hatboxes outside the courtroom at Minnie Dean's trial. I go and stand by the bedroom window and watch as another earthmover rolls up. I prepare myself for the ground being broken up around me.

29

Max

Well that didn't go so well; the first part at least. While I was in my room recording, he'd taken out a bottle of tequila from his rucksack and they were drinking it from little glasses, banging them on the kitchen counter. I think I'm right that tequila is a Mexican drink, so I'm not sure how that fits as a starter for a stir-fry, but they seemed to think it was OK. When I went down into the kitchen there was a saucer of cut-up lime and another one of salt which had spilt everywhere, and Mum's eyes were looking very bright and shiny. They were both laughing and she kept folding herself over the kitchen table and saying 'Ohh my Gaaad', which isn't one of her usual phrases.

She wasn't paying much attention to the stir-fry. Those packets of Rainbow Cut vegetable strips only take about two minutes to cook, also the noodles, and she was busy having some more tequila while they started to stick to the bottom of the pan. I quickly cut the sachet of sweet-chilli sauce open – not that she noticed as they were dancing down the hallway – and stirred it all together before putting the food out on the plates.

It was hard to join in. One, I hadn't had any tequila, and two, not much of what they said needed me to answer. Showing him I wasn't a threat to his gene pool wasn't really working out. And then, to make matters worse, he looked at me and said, 'More tea, Vicar?' and burst out laughing. She giggled a bit, and he mimed raising a tea cup to his lips. 'I could see you,' he continued, looking straight at me, 'as a man of the cloth. A little bit prim.' He folded his hands neatly in his lap.

'You'd make a lovely vicar, if that's what you wanted to be,' Mum hiccupped. She'd rubbed at one of her eyes now, and her eyeshadow had gone onto her cheek. I could tell she wasn't used to drinking tequila. Rosé wine never messes with her face like that.

He was rummaging in his bag, laughing his head off. 'It's in here somewhere,' he said. He pulled out a dog collar and lead. Apparently, he had a Staffie until three months ago and he can't bring himself to throw it away. Mindful of the cat, I can't bring myself to think what might have happened to the dog. He unbuckled the collar, leaned over with his lips all wet and shiny, and put it round my neck. 'A dog collar for you, Reverend,' he said, and guffawed away some more. He was killing himself with how funny his joke was.

I just sat there, very still. Here's the thing. When I was smaller, Mum used to ride a bike with me strapped on a little extra seat at the back. I had a helmet to wear with frogs all over it. When she buckled it on me, it was always a nervous moment. Someone might catch her eye – coming out of the shop we were leaving – and say Hi, or she'd drop something and need to pick it up, and then she'd do up the buckle with only half an eye on the job. Unless you've had someone put a cycling helmet on you, you won't know that there's a very soft piece of skin where your throat meets your neck, and if they're not watching what they're doing, it gets caught in the clip. And then, once they've realised that, they have to pinch at the clip to open it again which gives it a second bite at your skin. The bruise was always as red as a grape. Mostly, when she started to put on the helmet, I'd shut my eyes and just hope for the best. So, when his big meaty fingers were practically round my neck, my instinct, again, was to sit very still. No kidding; your body remembers this kind of thing. I reckon sitting still made it look like I was joining in, as game for a laugh as he was. He paused for a minute, just looking at me all moony-eyed and then clipped the dog lead onto the collar, gave it a tug and said 'Walkies, walkies' in a high voice like he was an old lady dog-trainer. A tug with arms his size was enough to get me to my feet. He jiggled the lead a bit, and then he sat down, laughed some more and put his big ol' head on his arms.

'You're daft,' she said to him, 'and you'd make a rubbish Barbara Woodhouse.'

'Take no notice of him,' she said to me, although that wouldn't actually have been possible in the circumstances. She seemed to think the whole thing was as funny as he did. Perhaps I did look funny with a lead on. Mrs Winters says there's laughing at and laughing with, and I guess you can't always be in the 'with' camp. They'd started arm wrestling now, with him using just one finger and Mum her whole clenched fist. I sat down again, with the lead trailing in my lap. It's harder than you'd think to take off a dog collar when you can't see the buckle. Also, when the collar is a bit thick and twisty from being around a dog's neck for years. It was quite difficult to undo. I thought about lifting my chin and asking her to give me a hand, but I thought we'd be back where we were with bicycle helmets, and back then she hadn't even been drinking alcohol. It would probably not have ended well. When I finally got it off, they didn't pay any attention. My fingers smelt of dog, so I got up to wash them. That probably counts as *prim*, but it would have put me off my stir-fry. When I went up to bed, they were in a heap on the couch.

I don't know how to report this to Eddie. There's probably something to be made of it.

She's not looking so bright this morning. She's texted to cancel her first two appointments which is unheard of. She told them she had food poisoning. I hope she didn't say I cooked the stir-fry. He left early for work – I heard him thump down the stairs – and I've just gone into her bedroom. She's lying propped up on the pillow with a Refreshing Cucumber Mask stuck across her eyes. It'll take more than that to fix them. One of them actually looks bloodshot. She kept saying 'ohhh godd', but this time in a very, very small whisper.

I got into bed with her. I always used to do that, before him, on a weekend morning. She'd read a magazine and I'd have a comic, and sometimes we'd have pancakes with maple syrup and eat them off a big tray. She'd whack a dent in the pillow next to her and say 'Hop in!' as if I was a little bunny. She didn't look like she was up for that this morning. I just quietly lifted the corner of the duvet and crept in beside her.

The bed smelt different. It was a combination of the aftershave he wears, the tiniest bit of sweatiness, and something else. On the pillow was one of his dark hairs. I picked it off and dropped it on the carpet. There was no danger of her seeing me do it – the eye mask was still plastered to her face.

I offered to go down and get her some breakfast. I said maybe some food would help and she just nodded, her hands pressed to the side of her head. In the kitchen, the empty bottle was still on the side. I threw it away because I guessed she wouldn't want to see that again. I made her a boiled egg, and I cut white toast into neat, thin soldiers. I thought dainty food might help. That's what she makes for me whenever I'm sick in bed. I carried it upstairs on a tray and put it gently on her lap. She took off the eye mask and said, her voice a bit croaky, 'You're an angel child.'

I got back into bed with her and watched as she started dipping the soldiers in the yolk.

She looked across at me and said, 'What have you done to your neck?' See, it always happens, a bruise the size of a biro lid.

I told her it was when he put the dog collar on me. 'Remember,'

I said, 'more tea, Vicar.' I mimed the tea cup motion. She furrowed her brow. She looked at a bit of a loss.

'It's all a bit misty I'm afraid,' she said, 'after the fourth or fifth one. I can't even remember eating supper. The last thing I can remember is opening the bag of noodles. I don't know what came over me. I'll never drink tequila again.' She finished her egg and put the tray down on the carpet. 'Oh my God,' she said, 'I feel like death.' She squinted across at my neck. 'Does that hurt?'

'Only a little bit.'

'I'm sorry about that. Sounds like too much high jinks, as well as too much tequila.'

I nodded, and looked down at the tray. It came to me it was now or never. She wasn't going to leap out of bed anytime soon, so I might as well go for it.

'Thing is,' I said, 'Even though I'm no threat to his gene pool, Eddie says that's probably what's happening. It's like we're chimpanzees.'

She put the pillow over her face and groaned. 'I so do not know where this is going. I thought I was beginning to rally after the egg.'

I stuck at it. 'It boils down to the fact that my dad is someone else. I'm another man's child. A different blood line. It's all down to biology.'

She looked mystified. 'I have the worst hangover of my entire life and you're talking biology and blood lines. Excuse me?'

My main point was still up my sleeve. 'The thing is, it's all about knowing who's the daddy. I've been thinking if I knew who mine was, and if he did, things might be a bit more straightforward.'

'Who's the daddy?' she said weakly.

'Yes, my dad. I was thinking about it last night in bed, and maybe now, what with me being punished for it, because me and Eddie think that's what's happening, it might be nice to know.'

She sat up, turned sideways, and put her feet on the carpet. She knocked the egg cup over, and she put her hand to her forehead and leaned over sideways, slowly, to pick it up.

She turned and looked at me. 'I don't know how we've got to this point. Punished? I'm failing to make the connection between dog collars and biology and you asking me about your dad. This conversation isn't the easiest to follow. I haven't really got past the bruise on your neck. Are you really asking me about your dad? Now? Today? First time ever? Straight off the bat?'

I nodded.

She got back into the bed and sat right next to me. She put her hand on my leg and was rubbing it as she talked, but she kept her eyes straight forward.

'Thing is, I'd love to tell you lots about him. I'd love to tell you the story of a lovely romance and beautiful memories, and I'd like to sprinkle it with loads of details so that you got a really good picture.' She tugged at the side of her fingernail and then said, 'But I can't.'

I didn't say anything. She took a deep breath and carried on. 'I can't because I don't have facts or details. None. Nada. Where it happened is pretty much all I've got for you.'

I thought for a moment. 'So where did it happen?'

'In a nightclub. A nightclub with a swimming pool in it, and loads of drunk people thinking they were having the holiday of their lives.'

'Do you know his name?'

She shook her head.

'Where he comes from?'

She shook it again.

'Not much to go on then.' I was trying not to sound sad but I don't think I did a very good job.

She nodded and bit her lip. She took hold of my hand. 'I could try and convince you that name and nationality tells you nothing at all, but I won't. Try not to be angry with me, although I'd understand if you were. I was twenty-two, which is no excuse at all, but when you're twenty-two you might have more understanding.'

She suddenly looked very, very tired, as well as hung over, and with last night's make-up still on and all smeary, which she never ever does.

She kissed me, got up off the bed, and stood by the door to the bathroom. 'I should say sorry. That's all I can actually do. I'm sorry.' She left the door open, sat down on the loo and started to wee. She had her head in her hands.

She doesn't even know his name. Turns out Grandad was riding to the rescue by calling him Zorba. She has no idea if he was Greek or English. That's probably the highest degree of not knowing; the most not knowing that's possible. I'm guessing it must have been very quick. He won't have a clue I exist or that I've extended his gene pool. If we were a pride of lions, he wouldn't be batting for me anyway.

I've just been to see Minnie. I told her all of it. We sat in the parlour, which is the smallest, cosiest room in the house, and she made me tea in my favourite cup. When I got there, we'd kicked off with *a collection of early twentieth-century sporting items,* which turned out to mean three pairs of wooden skis, a pair of ice skates, some hockey sticks and a pair of brown leather field boots. She says they belonged to an uncle who spent most of his time in the French mountains. We moved onto a Victorian easy armchair in the parlour itself, *upholstered in gros point needlework, on turned walnut front legs and with polished brass castors.* She was quick to see I was a bit dejected. I wasn't asking as many questions as usual, and I was mostly tracing round the chair's needlework flowers with my thumb.

She looked at me the way she does, her head tipped a bit to one side and her green eyes looking right at me as if I am the only thing in the world worth looking at, and she said 'What's troubling you?' Her words felt like an Elastoplast, both on the actual mark on my neck and on the fact that my mum only knew my dad for a few minutes in a swimming pool in a nightclub when she was twenty-two.

That's when I told her. I told her about the dog collar and lead, and then about the conversation with my mum, and she sat there and she thought for a while and then she told me two things. Firstly, that with too much alcohol things seldom end well, which could be applied to both occasions now I've had time to think about it, and then she said, 'But don't think badly of your mother. She chose to have you and to bring you up and that's a much more loving, brave decision than a lot of girls would have done in her position. She would have had a choice, and she chose you.' She went quiet after she said that and looked as if she was thinking about something else.

What she said has made me think about it differently. It had never occurred to me that I might not actually have got born. I came home and when I came into the kitchen, Mum was sitting at the table with her eyes shut and her head resting on the back of her hands. A client had just left. I came up behind her and gave her a kiss on the cheek.

She looked up and said, 'Not cross with me?'

I shook my head and said, 'Not cross at all. I'm your gene pool. It's like we are dolphins.'

She stood up, looking puzzled. 'Sometimes, I really don't know where you're coming from.'

I don't think that matters. She gave me a big hug, and it felt safe and cosy like before the boiler was serviced.

30

Minnie

The workmen arrive in hordes on a morning in March. It is just over a year since my disgrace. I move more slowly now. My mother looks at me with a degree of approval. Whatever was within me before has been first stilled, and then extinguished. In the summer, the hydrangea bloomed blue for a boy and I stood beside it and wept. Now, as the workmen arrive on site, it has just started to leaf again with vivid curls of green which are smooth to the touch.

I watch from the window as the ground breakers arrive. The York stone of the terrace is dismantled square by square. The glasshouse shatters with a squeal with one swing of a wrecking ball. The gravel driveway disappears in the scoops of the digger's mouth.

The workmen have a series of caravans where they take tea breaks and lunch. Outside them are two rusty braziers which they fill each morning with coal. They stand warming their hands as the coal spits and glows, and talk in low voices. They hold rolled cigarettes pinched in their lips while they speak. When it rains they sit in the caravan and play cards. I do not know if they notice me. I watch them as they thread string where each of the houses will go, and as they line-mark with paint the shape of the road that will run right in front of the morning-room window.

On the side of my waist is a small silvery stretch mark. It is shaped like a fish and is smooth and thick to my touch. When they stand by the hydrangea, finessing the curve of the road, I tuck my thumb into the waistband of my skirt and allow it to rest upon it. It is the only physical sign that he ever existed.

On this morning, the men are disquieted. Something is not correct. They fetch a large plan from the caravan and unfold it next to the gate. The foreman taps it, traces something with his finger, scratches his head, consults with one of the surveyors, and then knocks on the door and asks my mother if he can use the telephone. The chief architect arrives. Another drawing is laid beside the first. One of the younger lads paces first the length of the road with a trundle wheel and then the width across to Rosemount from where the first houses are marked out. He stops at the morning-room windowsill. He looks up at the last moment and I startle him, standing there. He says 'Ghost Girl' to me through the glass and mimes a shudder. Is this what they call me?

The chief architect knocks on the door. My mother takes him into the dining room and he unfurls the drawings on the table. I stand by the curtain and listen to what he says. There has been a miscalculation, a mistake in transcribing. The land purchased actually comes four feet closer to the house. If the road is laid as shown by the existing painted line, there will not be room for the essential services. There are gas pipes, water mains, electricity, sewers all to be considered.

'What does this mean?' my mother asks. He tells her that he could delay a day or so and go and source the original contract signed by my father, which will detail the precise measurement of the land sold in relation to Rosemount's foundations, or, he says, she can take him on trust, and then they will just need to measure four feet closer to the house. My mother asks him to show her.

I fly back to the morning room and watch as she steps out amidst the workmen. She has put on her coat, and a headscarf, and the men step aside as she approaches with the architect. He gestures to the apprentice who has called me ghost girl, and the boy runs to one of the caravans and comes back with the trundle wheel, two wooden pegs and a large ball of string. The architect looks at the diagram again, assesses what lies in front of him, takes hold of the wheel and begins to walk purposefully from the windowsill to the paint-line marker of the road.

It happens in slow motion, and feels inevitable. A blackbird is singing in the forsythia. One of the workmen is tipping coal into the brazier. There is a small shower of sparks which catch and cascade in the riff of the breeze. Another of the workmen has finished a cigarette and is grinding the stub beneath the sole of his boot. The orange and white tape which delineates the foundations of the house opposite flutters and twists, and part of it unfurls from where it is tied to a metal stake. There is a dog crouched by a pile of damp sand. A cement mixer is churning. And while my eye, my ear, register all this, the architect steps forward with the new pegs and string and crouches down to press them into the ground and now the line falls between the hydrangea and Rosemount, whereas before the hydrangea remained within our house's footprint.

He secures the pegs and turns to face my mother. She is knotting her headscarf more firmly. I cannot see her face. She is nodding, and then she turns briskly and comes back into the house. The architect tells the workmen where to put the remaining pegs.

I go to her in the hallway where she is taking off her coat. She is folding her headscarf very precisely and placing it in her pocket.

'They can't,' I say to her, my voice shaking, and she says, crisply, 'They can do as they please, it is their land.'

'But—' I say, and when she reaches over to me and takes hold of my wrists, I realise I have raised my hands, imploring her. She puts my arms back down at my sides and says, 'But nothing.'

She sweeps past me down towards the scullery, and then turns and adds, almost as an afterthought, 'If there is anything I will tell them that it is a pet, a much loved family dog. Rover, Fido, Rusty. I will think of something appropriate.'

It occurs to me that these imaginary pets have a name, and he does not have even this small dignity.

I go back to the window and the orange and white tape now flutters between me and the hydrangea. I place my thumb back on the silvery stretch of skin and watch as one of the workmen casually steps on its lower branches.

In the nights that follow I am heady with dreams. I dream of diggers, crashing relentlessly forward, scooping wide-mouthed into clay soil and emerging holding intact a green Clarks shoebox. The box falls away in soft papery tatters, and from within it comes a shower of pale, tiny bones. In another, the foreman stands on the step of Rosemount, holding the box flat to his forearms as Clara has done on the night it was buried. 'Is this yours, Miss, is this something to do with you?' he says sternly, and then 'we'll have to let the authorities know.' And sometimes it is a policeman standing there, pointing to the hydrangea and shrilly blowing a whistle as it rocks open at its tangled roots, the Clarks box spilling up, completely intact, the brown parcel tape still tight. Miss Potts unrolls the towel, her fingernails polished scarlet, and when it is unfurled, she holds in her hand a green and white tennis shoe. And then, finally, it is the model maker, his overall daubed brightly with paint, his back inexplicably hunched, his eyes watchful, reserved, standing on the doorstep and shyly proffering on his palm the tiny figure of a baby. The infant has a scratch on his thigh and a wild-strawberry birthmark on his shoulder.

When the day of the ground breaking arrives, the digger is so close to the morning-room window that I could reach out and touch the man who is driving it. His cheeks are ruddy, and he is wearing thick mustard suede gloves. He has a scarf at his neck, and a rolled-up newspaper in his jacket pocket. He manoeuvres the digger into position.

My heart beats so slowly I think it may stop.

The leaves on the hydrangea convulse as the digger makes purchase with the ground. I think of the towel, wrapped neatly, tightly. Secrets come out; Mother said this on that morning in the drawing room. They work their way to the surface like worms. The digger scoop comes up, heavy with a knot of roots and red soil. Does it contain a tiny scapula or a forearm the length of my middle finger? If the driver were to see that, would he believe my mother?

The digger scoop falls and rises, falls and rises. I strain my eyes, looking for scraps of cloth, of cardboard, but there is nothing. Nothing but damp clay soil, the twisted roots of the hydrangea and the occasional vivid flash of its bright furled-up leaves. The driver stops for a cigarette, steps down from the cabin and stands beside the machine, the sole of his foot resting up against the wheel arch. He nods to me and begins to smoke his cigarette, the end of it glowing brightly with the pull-in of his breath. 'Is it time for a brew yet?' he calls to one of the apprentices. He walks off to the caravan.

I step outside and pick my way over the mound of soil. I look down into the hole and see nothing, nothing at all.

'Can I help you Miss? There won't be much to be seen down there.' The driver's voice startles me. He has extended his hand to me, as if he is unsure of my physical strength. I am evidently considered an invalid. I take his hand because it seems impolite not to, and I step away from the trench until I am standing beside the digger again.

'Makes quick work of it,' he says, gesturing to the pile of soil and I nod. I step away from him, and come back into the house. When I raise my hand to my face, it smells of tobacco, of soil, of diesel.

Later, when Clara comes home from work, I see her veer quickly over there too. She peers into the hole, a fist pressed to her chest. She looks at the mound of earth, picks a handful between her fingers, rubs it, and lets it fall to the ground. When she turns to the window and sees I am standing there, she makes haste for the door and goes upstairs without seeking me out.

She has said nothing to me; she has never commented on my decision to leave school or on my new solitary life. I have heard Mother telling her, the drawing-room door ajar, 'Minnie must always be watched, must be contained; she has a volatility which it will always be your responsibility to keep in check.' Clara looks at me side-on *after that, or at a distance from a doorway, as if I am something unpredictable which might suddenly run amok.*

The earth that is taken from the strip of land is later compacted and included in the hard core for the pavement. I watch intently as a row of kerbing is laid where the hydrangea has been, a smooth slick of hot tarmac poured and spread like icing to make the surface of road; I watch as the foundations of the houses opposite are filled with cement, raked smooth, and as the brickwork sprouts upwards, the spaces for windows like missing teeth. When the street lamps are finally put in, it is hard to accurately know where everything has once been. Was the hydrangea closest to the third or fourth one? I would like to know for sure. It is a comfort of sorts, the notion that if a loop of soft dark hair remains, the street lamp stands over it, marking its presence with light.

I decide to move my clothes from my girlhood bedroom to the front one. From its window, both street lights are clearly visible. My mother watches from the landing, her mouth pursed, silent, her arms folded tightly as I carry my clothes in bundles. Before I draw my curtains, I stand at my new window and watch the sodium light pool on the pavement and the pristine kerb.

In June, when the focus of the building activity has shifted to the parkland, I am in the drawing room, flipping through my mother's Reader's Digests. It is a warm afternoon but I do not venture outside. An article catches my eye. It is about the Foundling Hospital, which is more properly known as The Hospital for the Education and Maintenance of Exposed and Deserted Young Children. *In 1741 it opened its doors, with the hope of safeguarding abandoned babies, and of providing a means of reuniting if the mother's circumstances change. I am absorbed. The hospital required that each child should have something left with it, as an identifier, so that the child could be subsequently traced or claimed. The objects became known as 'tokens'. I look at the photographs and the descriptions of them. This is what the women have left: coins, carefully severed, or with tiny chinks carved* out of them; the sleeve of a tiny garment, the other kept to match; playing cards torn in half; a small bone fish; a brass cross; a thimble; an entry ticket to Vauxhall gardens; a medal commemorating a naval victory in 1739; an Irish halfpenny with eight notches carved into the edges; a scrap of sprigged linen; a hairpin; a spyglass; a piece of red linsey-woolsey embroidered with purple worsted thread; a padlock and cuff; a tiny ring with a red, heart-shaped stone; a coral necklace; a shirt buckle; a heart cut from parchment and decorated with ribbon; a smooth silver heart engraved with the initials E L; a brass button which says St Ethelburga and St Swithin; a label from a decanter which says, simply, ALE; a scrap of peach fabric, embroidered with the initials M D.

The tiny items express so much powerlessness and poverty, and so much desire to do right by one's child. I read the descriptions and feel my own failings freshly cut.

And then what undoes me are two of the last tokens shown. Most plain, and most simple, a hazelnut and a stone. I weep for the women who have made their way to the Foundling Hospital to give up their babies, and all that they can give is whatever they can find on the ground on their way. I imagine the coolness, the smoothness, of a hazelnut and a stone in my hand. They become, at that moment, my own rosary of loss.

I tear out the pages of the magazine and take them to my room. I put them in the drawer of my nightstand and I will look at them until I know them all by heart.

I take out the paisley handkerchief, and unwrap the tiny figure from within it. I lie it flat in my palm. Its colours are still minted fresh – the rose-coloured sweater and the navy skirt, the plait neatly secured with a painted blue ribbon. I stand the figure on its feet and lift it to my eye line. I see it anew, this time as my token for him.

31

Max

So Jasmine popped back up again. Turns out he has one contact weekend a month – *most of them they screw up*, she tells me. She keeps popping a great big bubble of pink gum. I'm not sure if this means she wants to see him or she doesn't, or just that both her parents are rubbish at making arrangements. Either way she was seeing him now because we were in the back of his car going for a weekend at Center Parcs.

I think we went as a kind of saying sorry. Not sorry from Jasmine, obviously. I think sorry would probably be the word least likely to fall out of her mouth to anyone. She'd probably rather lose a front tooth. I think there's a reason for this. I think it's because if you think the world owes you one huge apology, you're not likely to spit one out ever.

On the scale of things I don't think she's that hard done by. I'm not sure how she'd react if she was being bombed in Syria, or kidnapped in Nigeria. She probably wouldn't welcome me pointing that out to her. *There's always someone worse off than you* is the kind of thing you'd expect a teacher to tell you, or someone very old.

Anyway, when Jasmine clapped eyes on me again she didn't feel bounced into a late apology for what she did to my hair. She just gave a big ol' guffaw and said *Hey Sprouty* and stuck to calling me it all weekend. So I think the saying sorry – if I'm right about it being why we were going to Center Parcs – was mostly from my mum. I'm not sure if it was a sorry about my dad. It might be that it was a sorry for the way I found out. Jasmine might want to consider she's perhaps not the only one who's a little bit hard done by.

Whatever the reason we were going, Mum actually didn't need to apologise more anyway. She'd said sorry in the kitchen and that was just between me and her whereas in the car to Center Parcs whatever's going on is not private at all.

He whistles when he drives on the motorway. It's weird. It's not a loud, full-on kind of whistling, more under his breath as if he's waiting for something to happen. Maybe that's in relation to Jasmine; I can understand where he's coming from on that. If I spent much more time with her, I think I'd be looking at her sideways too, keeping her in my vision, just in case she bounced something unexpected on me. 'Look at us, little blender-family step-sibs for the weekend,' she said. It wasn't a good thought.

In the car, Mum read out loud from the brochure all the things you can do. *Go-karting Max! Zip wires!* There wasn't an activity I could name that wasn't listed there. He just kept on whistling, and occasionally looked across at her and winked. Once when he did it, Jasmine said, 'Get a room why dontcha,' and he gave my mum a quick little double slap on her thigh, as if that thought was a good one.

Here's the thing. When you're having what Jasmine called a little blender-family weekend, there's a lot of trying that goes on all round. Everybody gives themselves face ache from smiling. There's also a lot of attention paid to the other person's child, or you might as well have gone away with just your own son or daughter.

Mum really threw herself into the activities with Jasmine. She put her hair in a French plait when we'd checked into our cabin, and re-did her eye shadow in a pretty good copy of Taylor Swift's because Jasmine had decided she wanted to look like her for the day. They went to the spa and had a pedicure – Mum says it's nice when you spend your time doing it for other people to have someone do it for you – and then they had a cappuccino in a café. Jasmine bought a bikini in the shop and a small magnetic diamond ear stud for her ear.

Here's what he and I did:

1. Falconry. *Experience the wonder of a hunting bird landing on your own hand*, it said. Thing is, it can be quite a surprise when you're not expecting it. You can be wearing the big glove and watching some other random bird, like maybe a fat crow, up in the sky, listening to the trainer making a squealy noise to call it back, and you're watching and watching until your eyes go fizzy with the effort and suddenly *whump!* the actual bird lands from behind you on your hand and you jump a mile. It obviously looks funnier than it actually feels. He certainly found it funny. He was practically choking with how funny it was, and everyone joined in, and the bird looked at me sideways, and the trainer gave me an award for the *Most Surprised Young Falconer* of the day. He, meanwhile, has mastered an impression of what I looked like when it landed; he did it twice for Jasmine over dinner, and also to three people in the queue on the way out.

2. Aqua-jetting on a Sea-Doo. *Swim like a sea creature beneath the waves*. There's probably an equation in Physics you could sum this up with. If you are heavy, and sit on the Sea-Doo as if it were a big egg you'd just laid, no doubt you will be like an actual sea lion swooping beneath the waves. If you are quite skinny, and not the greatest at taking in a deep breath and holding onto it, you might find yourself mostly bobbing around on the

surface like a cork, which allows you to be ambushed from beneath – a bit like when killer whales grab seals off small bits of an iceberg on TV – and before you know it, you and the Sea-Doo are metres apart, and you've swallowed half of the not-very-clean-looking lake. Again, that's another opportunity for someone to laugh their face off at you, and to use their Sea-Doo like a raft, their arms folded across it, treading water, so that they can get a good old proper look at you floundering around out of your depth and then describe that later in detail as well.

3. Field and target archery. *Discover your inner Robin Hood.* I didn't. Mrs Winters once asked whether I might need an eye test. I told Mum she'd suggested it, but she was trimming her cuticles at the time which takes concentration so I'm not sure she was properly listening. She didn't arrange one anyway. Maybe Mrs Winters was right. The distance to the targets is adjusted by your age. If you end up firing at the target that is intended for six-year-olds and you still only just clip the edge of it, it could be to do with your eyesight, not your skill. If you, on the other hand, manage to achieve a double bullseye and Shot Of The Day, it would be better to be modest about it, not take three selfies and whoop-whoop all the way out of the park.

4. Canoe capers. *Capers.* I think they use that word to capture all the fun of pelting across a lake like a tribe of Native American Indians. Some people interpret it a little differently. If the first time you are finally stable – having already rolled under the canoe twice and got soaked – someone starts using their paddle to flat-splash a skim of water in your face, it's not the funniest. Especially when you've had a right old *caper* trying to

get upright, and especially when swimming, it turns out,
isn't your strong suit when applied to getting out of a
canoe.

5. Traverse wall.
6. Quad bikes.
7. Cable ski.
8. Tenpin bowling.

I could describe each one but they are all pretty much the same.
When we finished, and were due to go and meet Mum and
Jasmine, he lifted one hand up as if to high five me and then he
said, his voice suddenly a little bit hard, 'I won, Maxy, hands
down.' The first thing I thought was that he actually was proud
of beating a nearly-twelve-year-old at a bunch of Center Parcs
activities. The second was that it wasn't about hands down at all.
What I think he would have liked me to do – walking away from
the Falconry centre, the canoe capers, the tenpin bowling alley
– was to have said *hands up,* and stuck both of them right up in
the air, like in a Western when someone surrenders to the sheriff.
If I'd done that as we walked towards Mum and Jasmine – who
were eating tubs of frozen yogurt with different toppings and
giving each other spoonfuls to taste and saying *yum* and *ooh!* – it
would have been very clear there was an actual winner. Him.

We're back home now. I'm doing this in my bedroom. He's
taken Jasmine to the train station and this is what I think I know.
If he *is* always the winner, maybe he will be happy. Maybe because
he can't actually kill me like the male dolphin does, whupping
me at everything at Center Parcs is enough. Thing is it's not
much fun, at least not from my side. My face aches a bit from
pretending to smile, mostly because I could see my mum really
wanted me to be smiling and laughing and having a hoot just
like they were. Center Parcs is expensive and I know that she'd
have had to think carefully before splashing out on it. She said

to me once, 'If you earn your money doing manicures and facials and waxing, every penny you spend you calculate in terms of how many of them you have to do.' I think that was probably a ton of manicures and facials and waxings just to have a big bird land on my arm.

I can hear him coming back through the door from the train station. Perhaps I should go downstairs and pass him a note which says in capital letters CONGRATULATIONS YOU ARE THE WINNER. Maybe that would make everything alright. Just being myself obviously doesn't.

32

Minnie

One night in early January it comes to me what I want to do. I am standing by my bedroom window and the moon is pale and full in the sky. There are the beginnings of a frost; the kerbstones glitter, and the street lamps throw long, lean shadows. There is now glass in the windows of the new houses, and it shines blackly at me. I am holding the tiny figure in my hand.

I turn, suddenly with conviction, and walk quietly along the landing. I pause by my mother's bedroom; I hear her cough and turn over in bed. I stand by Clara's door and check there is no rim of light beneath it. Often she reads, and I am aware of her awake, vigilant. Her room is silent. I walk down the stairs in the velvet darkness, feeling the edge of each step with my toes. There is one slice of silver moonlight shining down through the rose window. As I step through its beam of light, it illuminates my skin. 'Ghost girl' they called me, and I feel it now. I tiptoe to the scullery, and quietly, so quietly, in case it scrawps or sticks, I open the drawer which I know contains a small trowel. I go back along the hallway, put on my coat over my nightgown and button it to my throat. I pull on my galoshes and stand before the front door. All the bolts are drawn, and the chain pulled across. I lift my hands to the first bolt, and see that my fingers are trembling. An owl hoots outside, and causes me to jump. A dog barks in the empty new streets and I wait, pressed close to the door, for any sound upstairs. Clara's door creaks and opens. I draw myself into the shadows and hear her walk to the bathroom. I hear the tap running, a glass filling with water. She walks back to her room. From where I am standing I can see just the trim of her nightgown as she crosses by the balustrade at the top of the stairs. I think I can hear it swish, but my ears are straining so hard I may imagine this detail. I wait for the sound of her door closing, and for her to settle back into bed.

I wonder if I should fetch a candle. A candle smoothed along the runs of the bolts will make them quieter to open, but perhaps it will leave curls of wax which will be visible to my mother, eagle-eyed, in the morning. The owl hoots again. I wonder what he can be searching for, wheeling over the bare, smooth pavement and the freshly line-painted road. Whatever used to scurry in Rosemount's parkland at night is long gone. I think of the aspen trees, of the shiver of their leaves in the wind, and I slide the first bolt back, my fingers pinching it tightly.

There are four bolts. I draw each one back, holding my breath as I do so. I press the sleeve of my coat against the links of the chain so that if it rattles or clinks the sound will be muffled. And then there is the key. It is the length of my hand. I fold both my palms around it and turn it, slowly, carefully. The clock in the dining room strikes two, and I hear my mother cough again. I wait for a moment, and check that the lock is fully turned. Glancing once behind me to make sure I am undiscovered, I put the door on the latch, ease it open and step out into the street.

It is so very cold. Through my galoshes, I feel the iciness of the stone step on the soles of my feet. The air slaps at my face, and my breath responds with a scribble of vapour. I wrap my fingers around the figure in my coat pocket. The steel edge of the trowel presses against my leg. I step out down the path, and slip through the iron gate.

I walk carefully to the third lamp post, and count the steps between it and the fourth one. I do it three, four times, each time turning to look up at the front bedroom window where I stood watching Mother and Clara. I check with the morning-room window for additional bearing. I eventually come to a halt somewhere between the two street lights. I turn and look back at Rosemount. It looms up like a galleon at sea, the moon high above it. I take the trowel from my pocket and fall to my knees.

The ground is freezing on my shins. I dab small crystals of frost from the soil with my fingertips and touch my lower lip to mark it with the cold. Digging is easier than I anticipated. The soil is friable because it has been freshly laid by the workmen in a runnel between the kerbstone and the pavement. They have raked it ready to be seeded with grass in the early spring. I dig a small hole. When I am satisfied it is deep enough, I take the figure from my pocket. I lie it flat on my palm and stroke the length of it with my fingertip. I kiss it – I am not sure why – and lay it in the earth. I scoop the soil back over it, and press the surface back into place. When I put the trowel on the pavement beside me, the ting it makes sounds to me as loud as a peal of cathedral bells. I still it with my hand. Then, I sit, my head bowed. I blow between my clasped fingers, and tremble as the cold bites at my bones. In my peripheral vision something moves fleetingly and I look up to my bedroom window. There is no one there. High overhead, the owl hoots again. Something else cries out. A cat? A vixen? I look around me warily. The street is totally still and empty. The frost is lacing its way along the orange and white tape. It feels as if I am the only person outside in the world, there, on my frozen knees in the shiny new street.

When I can bear the cold no longer, I stand up and brush the soil from my coat. On the night he was buried, I do not think my mother thought to give him any kind of prayer. I do not feel clean enough, worthy enough, to offer him one either. Instead, I say, 'I'm so sorry, little one,' and stand there, my head bowed, still, my hands clasped before me.

I push the front door ajar and tiptoe inside. I sit on the bottom stair and pull off my galoshes. My feet are like ice. I creep down the hallway and replace the trowel in the scullery. I climb the stairs again, and make it safely to my room.

I lie in bed, my knees flexed, rubbing the soles of my feet against my flannelette sheet. I continue to blow on my hands which are blue with the cold. It feels as if I will never warm through. I curl in a ball, my arms folded around my knees, the eiderdown pulled over my head, my breath warming the cocoon I have made for myself. I hear the dining-room clock strike three.

In the morning, when I wake, my bedroom has a steel-blue light. I pull back the covers, go to the window and draw back the curtains. The street is covered in snow. It lies thickly over all the contours of the kerbs, the walls, the gates, the eaves. It spangles dispassionately at me.

January 1963 is the coldest month of the twentieth century, and the coldest since January 1814. The builders shut up shop, and all construction on the new estate stops. Most of England and Wales is snow-covered throughout the month, and the ground starts to freeze solid, with temperatures almost as low as minus twenty. The sea freezes for a mile out to shore at Herne Bay and for four miles at Dunkirk. The Thames also freezes, and a car is driven across it at Oxford. Icicles are over three feet long. In February, more snow comes, and the drifts reach twenty feet deep.

Through all of this white, cold, smothering, the figure lies in the soil, keeping vigil. It is my token to him, and I watch the blanket of snow, and feel that he is no longer unmarked.

The 6th of March is the first day of the year without frost anywhere in Britain. The thaw sweeps in, and the workmen come back, stamping their boots, lighting the braziers, shaking snow off the mound of shovels. The temperature climbs quickly and the snow snakes away in rivers of melt water. The workmen sow the verge with seed and it sprouts tender green grass with the first soft, fresh rains of April.

Clara knocks and disturbs me with the pretence of bringing me afternoon tea. I can tell she has something to ask me. She stands hesitantly by the night stand and holds the edge of her cardigan in her fingertips. She looks at me warily.

'I want to ask you about Max. Why do you continue to invite him here? What is there to be gained?'

I look up at her carefully. I am surprised that she has cut to the heart of the matter. She shifts in the shadow of the door.

'Perhaps you mean what harm might it cause? Is that what you fear?'

'We do not have visitors, Minnie, we have not had visitors for years. We have been as we have been. Is that not enough for you?'

'I do not know what is enough for me,' I say to her wearily. 'How could I? I have tried to be content with very little. Very little in comparison to what I hoped for when I was Max's age.'

'Why would you . . .' She falters. 'Why would you start to talk about old wounds, things that happened so long ago? Is that what you are doing, writing in that book at all hours of the day? Every time I find you, you are writing furiously.'

'I want to think about those times, those things,' I say gently. 'I think the truth of it should have a place amongst the rest of our daily words about candlesticks and vegetables and needle-point. Don't you?'

'I don't want you to talk like this. No good will come of it.'

'I won't if it upsets you, but you started the conversation. You asked me about Max, so let's just talk about him. It is not about me. I invite him in because he is unhappy. It is clear to me that he is unhappy. I cannot hope to make him happy, or to change what makes him unhappy, but I can be kind to him. Is that so unforgivable?'

Clara turns her face from me and places her hand on the door jamb. 'Always, Minnie . . .' she says, and then she stops and bites her lip. 'Your tea is getting cold,' she says, and leaves the room.

I am left here wondering what she was going to say to me. It would be reckless to follow her, to say to her *finish what it was that you were about to say*. I hear her go down the stairs, and close my diary.

I have damaged Clara. I see this in moments of clarity. My burden is her burden. My wickedness contaminates her. My mother appointed her my keeper. If it were not for me, perhaps she would have received callers, sat on a bench in a park somewhere and received the attentions of a respectful young man with a slim volume of verse. An older man more likely; perhaps the shy Latin teacher from her prep school who telephoned once and whom she told me to tell that she did not want to receive his calls. He stammered, and apologised, and did not call again. 'We will live together, always,' she told me one day with conviction, as if we might still be in the den we made in the bean canes next to the fig tree. Hooper would pick figs and pretend not to see us. I am sorry that Clara did not want to receive the calls of the Latin teacher. I am sorry that my mother's words scorched her as forcibly as they did me. I am sorry that she leaves my bedroom with the weight of me heavy in her heart.

I continue to sit in the room and watch out of my window. Max is sitting in his room. He waves to me, and continues to talk into his Dictaphone. His mother is out on the step, talking to a neighbour. She shows her something on her phone, and laughs, running her fingers through her hair.

I realise she was not much beyond a girl when she gave birth to Max. Somehow she has managed to preserve some of that part of herself; it is visible to see as she laughs on the step.

It makes me wonder what it must be like to live in a world where this is not a disgrace, where one's actions are unaccountable, utterly free. Shame has lost its heft. This is what has happened. This was inconceivable to me in 1963.

33

Max

Tonight I sat in the kitchen while my mum cooked supper. Before these summer holidays, I could have sat there even with my eyes shut and mufflers over my ears and known how it would be. But I can't now. It's not that everything is super-different, it just feels like something flat has tipped a little, so that everything slides along a bit and is in the wrong place.

This is what usually happens in the kitchen if she is not working and she is cooking supper: Sometimes, she has a playlist from her iPod playing, and she dances while she is cooking, particularly if she has to sieve anything, and then she taps the side of the sieve as if it is a tambourine. Her favourite song is 'The Girl From Ipanema', and when that's playing she swishes and wiggles from the kitchen to the hallway. Sometimes I follow her, doing it too. If she has made a casserole, which is more of a wintertime thing, she puts up the ironing board and irons a few clothes while it is cooking. She pours herself a small glass of Bailey's and she takes a sip after she's finished ironing each thing. She hates matching socks, so she waits until she has a big pile, and then she tips them on the kitchen table and we sit either side of it and turn it into a game to see who can win the most pairs. These are the sort of things that happen when we are in the kitchen in the evening.

Tonight she had different music playing. He's given her a CD which she's added as a new playlist. There was no dancing or swishing. The songs are mostly love songs. I was talking to her and she wasn't really listening. She kept taking her phone from her jeans pocket, and texting, texting, texting. She took about seven selfies and Snapchatted them to him. For one of them she stood close by the fridge and I think she put the phone down the top of her shirt. I'm not sure why she'd do that as I'm guessing it isn't anything he hasn't seen already. They spend hours in her bedroom and I doubt she's wearing all her clothes.

When she'd finished browning the chicken pieces and put them in the oven, she turned around, took off her apron and said, 'I've got a surprise for you!' She handed me a box, and inside it was a phone. 'I've set it all up for you,' she said. 'It's ready to use.'

So here's the thing. I was supposed to be getting a phone ready to start secondary school. I've wanted a phone for a long time, and she said I could only have one then. We'd agreed we'd go to the phone shop the same time as we bought my uniform and my shoes and my rucksack. There's still three weeks of the summer holidays to go. We haven't even discussed when we are going to buy my uniform, and now the phone's all done and dusted without me having even the smallest bit of choosing.

'Look, see!' she said, in her most enthusiastic voice, 'I've sent you your first text.' And that's what nearly made me cry, even though the look I was going for was that I was pleased to have my own phone.

This is what it said: *Greetings from the mother ship.* And she'd added an emoji of a flying saucer.

I need to explain why this made me sad. In Year Five I did a topic on the Apollo trips in space. In it, I learned that when Neil Armstrong took his first steps on the moon, Michael Collins circled around it in orbit, invisible on the dark side. Buzz Aldrin was in the lunar module, sitting right there on the surface. The whole world was listening to what Neil Armstrong said, and watching him make the first steps on the moon, but when I read about it, all I could think of was Michael Collins in the mother ship, spinning away in the darkness, totally invisible and completely on his own. And sometimes, when I feel sad or lonely, that's what I think about, a spaceship moving away by itself into the vast black sky. And that's what the text made me feel, as if the mother ship was moving steadily away.

Because *greetings from the mother ship* are the exact opposite of sitting next to someone sorting socks. They're like little pips of sound, bouncing through space from a long, long way away. The phone suddenly didn't feel like the promise of new things for big school, but instead something which would allow Mum to step right away.

The next thing she said showed I was on the money. I was busy scrolling down the numbers she'd put in – our landline, her mobile, his mobile (like I'd ever phone that), school, Mrs Philips for emergencies – and she said, suddenly, putting her arms above her head like a dancer, 'Guess what, we're starting tango lessons next week. You can be home alone and if anything bothers you, you can send me a quick text.'

'Cool,' I said, and gave her a thumbs up.

When I was small, I used to sit on her lap, with my thumb in my mouth and my other hand stroking a length of her hair and I used to tell her that I would live with her always. She'd say 'That will be lovely' or 'Of course you will my baby', which made me feel cosy and safe. And suddenly the phone, all shiny in its box, and with cellophane still on the screen so it gets no smudgy fingermarks, seemed to be saying the opposite. *Greetings from the mother ship* confirms I won't live with her forever, and that it's not me who is up and off, because almost twelve isn't when that usually happens. Instead, it looks like the girl from Ipanema doesn't just go walking, she walks away, walks right off, with a quick first stop to learn the tango.

She ruffled my hair quickly before she took the chicken out

of the oven. I realised she hadn't looked at my face once in the whole conversation which is probably a good thing because I was mostly trying not to cry.

'And you won't be able to guess another happy thing,' she said, 'I've had a great idea which involves all three of us.'

I didn't see this one coming. Not a clue. I was stuck on wondering when we became *all three of us*.

'Dads and lads soccer. A one-off tournament in the park on Sunday. I'll be clapping my hands off for both of you,' she said.

He's not my dad. I'm no way his lad. I pointed that out to her; not in a sulky way, but focusing on whether it would be allowed.

'Not a problem,' she said, 'I've already double-checked. Sophie French is playing with her dad and she's not even a lad. The Frenches have three girls, so what's Dave French meant to do?'

Play with Sophie obviously, but if Mum knew how Sophie tackles, she'd understand Mr French had everything to play for.

She hummed washing up. That's a new thing. I'd say she was dancing in her head even when she's standing still.

After supper I phoned Eddie. I had his number written down in my notebook, all set for when I finally got a phone. He was obviously surprised to hear from me. He knew I was getting a phone, but quickly twigged it was three weeks early. I was worried he might not be okay with that kind of surprise. Turned out I learned a new rule. He likes you to start the conversation by giving your full name and where you are calling from; that way, even though you are mobile, and could be talking to him from anywhere, he can place you exactly. I can see his logic. I told him I was at home and then we were good to go. I added my compass direction, which the phone flashed up at me, and that gave him a real bang. It might become a new rule.

Eddie digested what I told him and then pointed out the upside. He said he might not be my dad, but at least now I can play in the tournament. Eddie said from what he knew of my mum, she wasn't going to be putting on football boots any time soon.

'You'll be on the same side too,' Eddie said. 'That's a step forward.'

He's got a point. He reminded me it's always better to try and look for the positives. I've never played in a football tournament before. I decided to stop thinking about the mother ship flying away, and I went to see Minnie because that would cheer me up.

She was sitting in the parlour. I think she had been writing in her book because she had that expression on her face which looks as if her thoughts are very far away. I told her I had something new to show her and I took out my phone. I showed her all the things it could tell me, and then gave her a quick run through emojis. I showed her texting, Whatsapp, Twitter and Instagram too. She sat back in her chair, clapped her hands and said, 'Who'd have thought it?' She looked properly amazed.

I pointed out that half of the antiques in Rosemount wouldn't have been made if craftsmen were busy tweeting instead of working carefully away at wood or porcelain.

That made it time to look at some. We went into the pantry first and looked at a Copeland-cow creamer. A creamer is a jug in the shape of a cow's body, and the lid you open to fill it is in the middle of the black and white cow's back. 'It's from 1870,' Minnie said. The milk is poured out of its mouth, which we agreed looked a bit like the cow was actually being sick.

On the wall down to the scullery there was a painting of a dead rabbit and two dead birds. She showed me where it was signed by William Henry Hunt, and dated 1825. On the rabbit's back legs Minnie pointed to where you could see the marks of the snare, which is a kind of trap made of wire. The rabbit looked completely dead; that's the only way I can describe it. Really *real* but completely without any life at all.

In the drawing room, we looked at a china figure from 1765.

It was of a map seller, holding a map in his right hand, carrying others in a sack strapped to his back, standing on a base that was turquoise and gold and *applied with slight bocage*. *Bocage* means making leaves, flowers and plants in clay. I taught Minnie words like Whatsapp and emoji, and she taught me bocage. We both think it's a fair swap. As we were putting the figurine back in the vitrine I spotted that it had the workman's mark – D for Derby – on the base in red. Minnie said it was probably the closest thing then to a selfie. I laughed because she had turned the new word so quickly back on me.

In her father's study she showed me a Persian *Jambiya*, which is a kind of dagger. It had a double-edged blade, so I had to be careful touching it, and the handle was all silver and carved with birds and a tiger.

Minnie said we could finish up in India, and so we went to the library and looked at a book called *The Adventures of Pandinoodle and His Man Jungo*. She thinks it came from her mother's nursery in India when she was a little girl. It tells the story of a hunting trip, in which Pandinoodle and Jungo fight lots of horrible monsters. At the end of the book, when they've beaten them all, they go back to their rooms and retire for a nightcap and a smoke.

When I came home just now, he was here and they were downstairs on the couch. I didn't know this from seeing them but from the sound of their voices. My mum called out 'Hiya' as I came into the hallway, but not in a 'why don't you come in and sit down and join us?' kind of way. It's funny how one word can make that very clear.

I came straight upstairs to bed. I pretended I was Pandinoodle and I marched up and down a little bit on the landing. I saluted Jungo goodnight and pretended to brandish the Jamiya. If it had been old times, I'd have called down to Mum and told her I was retiring for a nightcap and a smoke.

34

Minnie

I am a past master at closing a life down. Having closed his down – completely, before it even began – it seemed only fair that I should correspondingly do so with my own. In the aftermath of my disgrace, I learn to walk along the edges of the hallway, to press my body into pools of shadow, to stand in the corners of rooms adjacent to the folds of curtains, to move so quietly that I cause my mother and Clara to jump when I speak behind them. The colours of my clothes are muted – grey, smoke, dun. My movements are measured, careful, precise. My fingers never break or chip any china I hold. Each thing is grasped as if I am responsible for preserving it.

If I could make myself disappear I would; I would breathe myself out in tiny exhalations until I become invisible to anyone's eye. I leave Rosemount rarely; my skin becomes alabaster white; a vein at my temple emerald and distinct. I clean the house as my mother has instructed me. I think it is penance of a kind. I wash and scrub and polish in the hope that I might feel cleaner. I do not. I feel myself to be as stained as if my limbs were inked blue. Sometimes, I go into my girlhood bedroom and stand by the mark on the carpet. In truth I am not sure if there is a stain anymore. I think an outline may persist, the faintest of traces, and that my eye compounds it until it is as it was that night. Sometimes I fall to my knees and press my palm to it and I say, 'I'm sorry, I'm sorry,' my body curled into a ball.

Guilt seeps into bones, into cells, into pores; it smokes through veins and arteries, curls itself like a cat in the chambers of the heart. I look at myself in the mirror, aged nineteen, and see only what I have done. My face is obscured by what I was capable of.

It dawns on me that I am also something of a hypocrite. I bring as much focus, as much intensity, to not living, to whiting myself out, as I did to the intention and hope of living with vivacity. I find I cannot completely extinguish my imagination. Despite my attempt to be as plain and as unobtrusive as a mouse, my mind still conjures up images which give my daily life colour. One day, on my knees in the hallway, I am reminded of a devotional painting, heavily daubed in ochres and reds, and I see myself as a novitiate in an Italian convent. I am tempted to stretch out, prostrate, across the hall floor. It is only the thought of my mother coming upon me which stops me. I stand up briskly and put the polish away, and will not allow myself the indulgence of the thought of my forehead pressed cool to the tiles. The image of a supplicant young woman, however, takes hold. I see myself as performing some kind of expiation, and this informs every-thing I do. I take comfort that even though I have not faced the censure of a judge, a policeman, a newspaper, a neighbour, I can punish myself; sentence myself to a life that is as far removed as possible from the one I hoped for. I do so with precision and care. In the summer, when my mother buys white-skinned peaches and I find myself anticipating the pleasure of biting into the warm, fragrant fruit, instead I eat an apple with my lunch – a Golden Delicious which I do not care for and which is not pleasing to my eye. If the apple skin catches in my teeth, I work at it with my tongue until my gums bleed. If I am hungry, I remain so until I am a little light headed, until my fingertips tremble when I extend my hand. I read about women in workhouses who were sentenced to unpicking tarry old rope. I like to imagine the feel of it shredding my skin.

I walk to my father's grave each Sunday with my mother and Clara, and I stand by his headstone and take solace in the fact that

*he would find me unrecognisable. I am as changed as he no doubt is,
as stripped to the bone. Sometimes I wonder what Miss Potts would
think of me now. Perhaps she would not recognise me. I think it is
likely that I look older than her. I seem to be catching my mother up,
in posture, in stance, which is unexpected.*

*And then, suddenly, when I am almost twenty it becomes necessary
that I also work. Clara's salary is no longer enough. The stock portfolio
– written out in blue-inked figures in the feint-lined margined paper
and checked by my mother, reading the columns of the* Financial
Times *with her tea each morning – has not performed as hoped. 'You
must find work,' she says to me one day, and adds, 'preferably somewhere quiet, where you can be discreet.'*

*I wonder if she thinks that evidence of my crime shines from my
skin, or carries its own fragrance, or is written in tiny indigo letters
across the palest skin of my brow.*

*I choose to work with death. Actually not death, but in the time
which precedes it; the hours that lead up to its crunching
advancement.*

*I see my choice as apt. I was no comfort to him, so I will spend
my working life being of comfort to others. I will make the moment
of others dying as comfortable as possible. There is a circularity to
this which I like. I train as a nursing companion in palliative care.
I am taught to administer pain relief, and to provide basic care.
'You're very young to be in this line,' a patient's relative says to me,
and I am, but it suits me perfectly.*

*My hands are kind and gentle and careful. I lift beakers to lips,
apply salve, place a cool cloth on a brow, or an extra blanket over
limbs that will not hold heat. I spoon soup gently into mouths, make
clean what is soiled, bring a small posy of flowers for the bedside,
balance on a chair to open a window to let in the smallest breath of
fresh air. I stay awake through the cold stillness of the night, a shawl
around my shoulders, my ear alert. If whomever I am sitting with
stirs, or murmurs, I am ready to ask them what it is that they need,*

or what it is that they are dreaming of, and ready, if they would like it, to read aloud. I read novels, poetry, women's magazines, and for one man, an entire volume of Wisden.

I become attuned to the world beyond each sickroom, to the time, to the seasons, to the wider world which rolls and spins beyond me, through the night. I can place, instantly, the cold, dense, dark weft of a February midnight, and the soft, dusky weave of the same time in June. I carve for myself a routine which is meticulous, arriving at sickrooms at 7pm each evening, and leaving at 7am, often as the newspaper is delivered or the milk bottles jangle onto the step. There is always something welcoming about the familiar sounds of the morning as they begin to jostle their way into the day. The milkmen and the paper boys treat me with an awkward shyness; mostly they know why I am there. They step aside to let me pass, my small bag in my hand, my face pale from being so little outdoors, and, I am sure, with a trace of antiseptic, or of sickness, or of old age, clinging to me. My hair I wear in a severe bun in the nape of my neck. It is finally tamed. One morning I walk out of a terraced house, after a night in which a man has cried out in anguish, and I stand on the step and allow myself a deep breath, and do not notice the woman next door who is smoking a cigarette and drinking a mug of tea. She reaches across, takes a tendril of my hair which has obviously worked free and tucks it behind my ear. 'You look bushed,' she says kindly. 'You're only a scrap of a thing.' My skin burns where she has touched.

I arrive back at Rosemount each day as Clara leaves for school. I eat a boiled egg, and a pear, and am particular about only eating from white china. It satisfies my craving for plainness. I sleep until mid-afternoon, and wake to the sound of the schoolchildren threading their way home. I watch by the window until it is time for me to leave again. I do not drive, and so a taxi collects me and takes me to wherever I am working. It is usually the same address for two, three weeks, and then change. The taxi drivers do not speak to me. Only once, a Mexican driver, appraising me carefully as I gather my coat *around me, says, 'Death angel,' without any anxiety, as if such a thing is to be expected and part of the community. In his taxi, a model of the Virgin Mary swings from the rear-view mirror. Her arms are outstretched, and as he turns the steering wheel, she appears to be beseeching whomever we drive past. Each time we stop at a traffic light, he kisses his fingertips and then touches her gently; the cab is infused with his certainty.*

I spend my working life mostly listening. I do not flatter myself that the sick talk particularly to me, or seek to share confidences particularly with me. I think the fact that I am listening means that what they say, what they tell, is heard, and in that way becomes more authentic than something that is only privately thought.

People cherish their words, their stories. They spend them like precious coins when pain tightens and whitens their lips. They also take refuge in their senses, and take comfort in what is familiar to them: the soft, worn edge of a paisley counterpane, the ticking of a familiar clock, the strike of a church bell, the mouth-feel of a particular glass, the sight of a pair of much-worn, sturdy walking boots kept by the bedroom door.

These are things I know, and yet I am also repeatedly taken by surprise, finding poetry where least I expect it. The taciturn banker, who has said nothing but that which directly relates to his care – more water, a tissue, a little lip salve, please – who then, the clock in the hallway striking two on the morning he is to die, speaks like a poet, his voice melodic, about a man he'd loved at twenty. He uses a Gaelic term and translates it for me to 'man of my belonging'. He tells me of a beach in Galway, and a terrified embrace. He weeps. A woman, in her appearance wholesome and plain as a plant pot and without any trace of personal vanity, who, in her last words – daybreak a few heartbeats away – recalls a pompadour taffeta dress she wore to a ball, and how exquisitely beautiful she felt. She tells of standing in a college quad under a firework-filled sky and kissing her own arm. And another who tells me that she lay each night in her marital bed and thought her heart would crack like an egg with loneliness and despair, and with the yearning to hold the hand of someone she loved. 'I would have given everything,' she said, 'for kindness, simply that.'

I, who have never even been kissed, collect their stories like buttons. Even though I cannot say I have ever loved or been loved, I think that at the end of my life I will be able to say, 'Yes. Love, I can say what that is.'

I see it refracted in the love of the friends and relatives of the people I care for. I begin to understand that romantic love takes up an unfair share of our collective attention. I watch friends come and sit by bedsides and laugh themselves to tears. I watch a teenager sit by her grandfather and carefully file his nails. I watch as the identities of the people I sit with slowly crumble away as they loosen their hold on life, yet watch that same identity burn bright as a gas flame in the eyes of those who love them. They hold it, pieced together, when it is all that remains.

For some people, there is no great truth, no startling revelation to impart – mostly, an observation of something they wished they'd done more of. Listening to birdsong features large. It means I pay attention to the robin in the forsythia by the scullery window, and a blackbird one morning in June, its song strung out like washing on a line.

The years slip by like the loops of wool from Clara's knitting needles, with the same steady rhythm, the same repeated shape. I sit with the dying until I am sixty-five. A woman, her eyes panicked, asks me to hold her hand. 'You're like a midwife, but all wrong,' she says. She has a point.

I find, somewhat to my surprise, that I am catching them up; my hand once smooth upon theirs, now snaked green with my veins. 'How spritely you are' the relatives say to me now, or, 'what enviable posture' as I sit by the bedside. 'Would you like a nice cup of tea?' they ask me in the morning, looking sometimes a little sheepish because I have kept vigil, not them. When I reach to open a window they offer to do it for me.

The last shift that I work, I bring a small posy of Michaelmas daisies and white sweet peas to leave beside the man's bedside. I walk out into the morning, and empty my small Gladstone bag into a dustbin. I come home and eat my boiled egg and my pear, and go and stand in the shower, and run the water scalding to my skin until it blooms red. I have sat by the dying for forty-five years and I am hopeful that this goes someway to penance and forgiveness. I have been quiet and discreet. My mother cannot fault me on that.

35

Max

She packed a picnic. She made a Spanish omelette, which she's calling *tortilla* now after she read it in one of her magazines. *The perfect summer food.* She bought some ginger and lime fizz, and a punnet of strawberries, and she made some chocolate brownies and cut them all neatly and put them in a Tupperware tub. She even bought paper napkins which I think were meant for a football birthday party, but which were printed with goalposts and whistles and balls. She packed it all into a coolbox, and then she told us to wait ten minutes while she nipped into the Powder Room. We stood there, looking at each other. He was wearing a Man City strip which was a bit tight across his stomach. I thought about the vine tattoo, struggling to spring free. I was wearing a Liverpool top which Grandad bought me when I was nine and which is now also a bit small. We certainly wouldn't have won any medals for being the best-dressed non-dads-and-lads.

When she came out of the Powder Room, she was doing jazz hands and saying *Whooo!* It took me a moment to clock what she'd done, because the first thing I noticed was that she'd lipsticked her mouth bright red even though it's not late Autumn. No grey polo neck in sight. I realised that what I was meant to be noticing was what she'd written in henna on her hands. His name, and mine, and in capital letters across her palms. She did some more jazz hands. 'Go you two,' she said. 'Look, every time

I lift my hand it's a living banner.' He laughed, and told her she was crackers. She said she was going to raise them every time we scored a goal. I felt a little bit uncomfortable at her saying that; she's never actually watched me play football. If she had, she'd have known her hands weren't likely to be that busy. She might even be able to keep her arms folded right through the game.

She passed him the coolbox to carry, even though it wasn't that heavy and I could easily have managed it, and she said, 'Isn't this great; we don't even have to get into the car because we can walk to the park,' and she laced up her wedges and balanced her sunglasses on her head. We went out onto the street, and she took his hand, and also mine, so that she was right in the middle of us, although she was holding my hand quite carefully – and his too, I guess – perhaps because the henna was likely still a bit damp. I think her goal-cheering hand-banner wave would have been less of a hit if she'd opened her fingers wide and there was just a messy smudge.

We walked off down the street in a row – she was positively cock-a-hoop. As we went round the corner all set to go into the park, I looked at her and she was beaming, just all round absolutely smiling her face off, and it suddenly came to me, what with how I used to wonder about Zorba and how it would be to have a dad, that maybe this was what she had been wanting for years, to walk into the park holding hands with a man and a child, and be able to stand on the sidelines and cheer in a competition for dads and lads. She'd never given the smallest clue.

She unfolded a blanket and sat right next to the half-way line. She offered Sophie French's mum a bottle of ginger and lime fizz, and then she started putting sun cream on her arms and her legs, but just with her fingertips to keep the writing safe. He and I were just standing, a bit beyond her, on the pitch, and I noticed we both kept looking in her direction. When we caught each other doing it, we both looked at our boots.

Turns out he knew one of the dads from a job on a new-build house. A man called Mike came up and shook his hand and slapped him on the back.

'The things you've gotta do . . .' he said to Mike with a bit of a roll of his eyes, and looked sheepish and patted his stomach. 'It's been a while since I've played a blinder up the wing.'

Mike laughed and said, 'The things we do for love, mate.' Then Mike said, 'Which one is her lad?' and he tipped his head towards me to where I was standing on one leg like a flamingo and stretching my hamstring. Mike just nodded.

Mum had turned the other women on the side into cheerleaders. As the referee started the warm-up, she got them all doing a little dance with their hands.

'Looks like your mum's having fun,' said Sophie French as we bent down to double-check our laces. She was right. Mum looked like she was enjoying having all the people around her, all joining in like a supporters' club. She was tying the hair of two little sisters into very high bunches with ribbon so that when they did the cheerleading dance, their hair swung to and fro. *Super-cute*, she was saying and clapping her hands.

The referee was explaining the rules to us. 'Keep it clean, no rough tackles on the little ones, good sportsmanship at all times. We're all here to enjoy ourselves.' The dads gave him a big clap.

We had to play four fifteen-minute games to get through to the quarter finals. If I was a reporter, writing how our team did, this is what I would say:

Game 1: if there are only two of you on your team, you can't win if you don't pass. You can't dribble the length of the pitch if running is not your thing (him) or if dribbling is not your thing (me). When people on the sidelines shout things *(Pass! Pass!)* it's not useful to pretend you can't hear them (both of us).

Game 2: if there are only two of you, and one of you falls over, not because their boot lace is untied because they have checked that carefully before each match begins, but because there is an uneven part of the pitch with a dip and then a big lumpy bit of grass, it is probably good sportsmanship when you walk by them to stretch out your hand and help them up, like some of the proper dads did when their real lads fell over. You shouldn't walk past, and almost step on their hand with your football boots, and then lean over and cough and spit because you are so red in the face from running. When you are the one lying level with the grass, a bit of phlegm wobbling on the end of a blade of grass can make you feel a bit sick, especially if you are feeling a little bit sick already from winding yourself when you first fell over.

Game 3: same old same old. The referee said no rough tackles on the little ones. He didn't say what the deal was on girls. Sophie French is better than me anyway. If I am marking her, and she is playing attack, it is not a surprise that she scored seven goals. I could have been a bit more aggressive, but tackling and barging a girl is always tricky. Also, what doesn't help is when she has gone round you in a circle for about the seventeenth time, and your teammate says – loud enough for other people to hear so that they join in for a good old laugh – *Jesus, I'd have been better off with Jasmine,* which was probably true. I don't think she'd have any difficulty barging anyone. Sophie French might have been poleaxed.

Game 4: which you need to win by one goal in order to qualify for the quarter finals and where the score is one goal each with three minutes to go. I don't know why they call it an open goal. Firstly, it suggests that the ball will be drawn towards it as if by a magnet or something and the goal will be scored without any effort at all. Secondly, if the dad who is meant to be marking the goal has tripped, it's a little bit awkward to just run right by him and boot the ball in while he's lying there holding onto his hamstring and yelling. It's very easy – when your mum is jumping up and down on the sideline screaming '*GO MAX! GO MAX! SCORE THE WINNER!*' and doing jazz hands so fast it looks like they will spin off her wrists – to take your eye off the ball (literally), whilst looking at the dad on the floor and hoping he's alright, and also being a bit surprised that your mum can actually jump that high, and before you know it you kick the ball a little bit on the top of it, a little bit to the left of it rather than properly, and so it just rolls to the left of the goal and lies in the long grass. When this happens, and when your opponent has a higher total goal score from the previous games, it's game over. Completely. No quarter final. Eliminated.

Then three things happened. First, the whistle blew, and she came over to him where he was standing with his hands on his knees practically being sick from running around so much, and he said, 'I'm sorry babes, I hate to be a loser. I'd have loved to win the whole damn thing for you. Losing sucks.' That's not good sportsmanship, which was what the referee asked for. The second thing was the way she answered. She knelt down and gave him a big kiss on his red, sweaty, dripping cheek and said, 'You're my winner, you're my hero,' and gave him a special clap with her hennaed hands so that they looked like a pair of fluttering bird's wings cooling off his face.

Then, when we were standing on the sidelines taking off our boots, and he was tipping a bottle of water over his bare chest and it was dripping down him so it looked like raindrops falling on the vine tattoo, Mike came past and said, 'Bad luck, not much you could do,' and when he replied he sort of nodded in my direction even though I don't think he thought I could see. 'Two left feet doesn't even begin to cover it,' he said, which I think meant me. I'm sure it meant me.

So here's what I thought, when we were sitting on the rug eating the tortilla and the brownies. If you've never done anything to do with dads and lads until you are aged nearly-twelve maybe you are not going to be as good as someone who has practised with a dad since they were about five, like Sophie French, who comes to the park with her dad all the time. And then maybe, even if you *had* practised every Saturday morning, maybe football is not your thing. Liking something is not the same as being good at it. Minnie says 'It takes all sorts'. This means I might not be the best at football, even though my mum is evidently the best at cheering it, but it means I can do other things.

Listen to these words: *tazza, paterae, brocade, gros point, bocage.* The antique words stick in my mind like they're super-glued. Minnie says them once, and they zoom like homing pigeons and roost right in my head.

That's something to hold onto; especially when, not on purpose but accidentally which is still upsetting, during the picnic your mum has opened the screw cap of the ginger and lime fizz with her right hand which means your name is completely wiped off. Whereas her left hand, with his name on, is completely fine, so when she waves with both hands at someone walking past, and she does this a lot, it's actually like she's only really supporting one person.

36

Minnie

What I tell Max, I know because of Great Uncle Leonard. In my
father's office there are leather volumes, catalogues of all that Rosemount
contains, written in Leonard's china-blue cursive, page after page.
There are descriptions of each item and its approximate value. If he
is unsure of anything he adds a small pencilled question mark in the
margin. For some of the spellings of the Chinese items, he offers two
or three alternatives. Occasionally he adds a phonetic clue, as if
anticipating difficulties in reading it out loud. He completed the cata-
logues in 1920. He returned from the Great War two years previously
and apparently said to my great grandfather, standing on the doorstep,
his kit bag over his shoulder and his cap in his hand, that in the
future he intended to focus on lists; lists cataloguing objects of beauty;
factual, accurate, and without human emotion. In the trenches under
bombardment, he had closed his eyes to the flares, and shut his ears
to the wail of the guns, and in part of his mind he walked daily
through each room of Rosemount, holding pieces of porcelain and
silver in his hand. Still standing on the step – the maids clustered in
the hallway, their aprons pressed to their mouths – he concluded by
saying that he knew nothing, absolutely nothing anymore about what
it was to be human, but that he would know exactly what Rosemount
contained. His work is meticulous. He sorted through all the accounts
books which were kept in what was then my great grandfather's study.
At the back of each volume, there is an appendix of receipts, cross-

referenced to where the item features earlier. '*A pair of Chinese famille rose figures of cockerels, purchased in April 1912 for £325 from W. Dickenson and Son, Wigmore St, London.*'

I am grateful that he catalogued all these things, that from the chaos and terribleness of all he must have seen in France he came home and sat quietly, and ordered what was around him into coherence. I imagine the maids cleaning the grate in the study while he sits hunched at the desk, skirting around him and avoiding meeting his eye. I like it that now I can tell Max details of the antiques with accuracy. Down through the decades, I have played a kind of elaborate, protracted hide-and-seek with Leonard; bringing a plate or cup to the catalogue and seeing if it matches his description. I have allowed myself this.

I trace my fingers over Leonard's initially fragile writing. His grip on the pen becomes firmer as the cataloguing progresses. In the first volume, which begins in January 1919, it's clear that the hand holding the pen shakes; there are blots when the cartridge must have just been re-filled. Writing 'George III silver set of four dessert stands, of circular pierced form with applied floral garlands and bead border' becomes a raft which carries him back to the possibility of a life.

The day he finishes the catalogue, he gets up from his desk and walks twice around the parkland, and then tells his mother he is planning on catching the next boat to America. He leaves in 1921 and meets and marries a young woman called Kitty in Boston. He makes a fortune selling refrigerators, and starts a restaurant selling cocktails and clam chowder. On his deathbed, years later, he says, '*It was the cataloguing that saved me,*' which makes no sense to Kitty who does not know what they are. It is only when she writes to my grandfather that what he has said makes sense.

Writing saved Leonard. Is it what I expect, writing this diary now? That somehow, just as Leonard achieved some kind of *redemption, so in writing what happened to me I will somehow finally save myself?*

I have brought the diary from the study into my mother's bedroom. Everything, it appears, will always spool back to her. She has been dead for several years, and yet this room remains as if she occupies it still. I enter, my fingertips sensitive to the memory of a tray held carefully in my hands, and expect to see her sitting upright in bed, a shawl around her shoulders, her voice imperious, 'Minnie, have you brought my lunch?'

Living alongside her, Clara and I galloped towards old age. We caught her up, a blurring between our generations happening quietly, unobtrusively; our knuckles united in a twinge of arthritis, our skin bruising more easily, blooming dark as a grape. Rather than an elderly woman living with her daughters, I think to our neighbours we became three old women who lived in the vast house. And yet, when she was dying the gap widened again.

Her possessions are still in the room. Perhaps we should have emptied it, but there seems little point. Her good winter coat hangs in the wardrobe. I can see her buttoning it firmly to the neck, preparing to walk to church. For years, I accompanied her to my father's grave every second Sunday, to the service for Matins one week and Evensong the next. I knelt beside her, mutely, for Compline prayers. She would not mouth the words, and neither would I. 'Lord, now lettest thou thy servant depart in peace according to thy word.' That would be a fine thing.

I went to the library with her each Tuesday afternoon before work. When her eyes began to fail in the yellowy light, I read from the book jackets to help her choose. I stood beside her when she worked the small herbaceous border that remains at the rear of Rosemount, passing her hyacinth bulbs from a hemp sack under an October sky and watching her dig with a precision that always had the power to pain me. In old age, her austerity became more pronounced. Looking out of the window, she had the mien of a hawk.

There is still a strong sense of her presence in this room. Her Mason Pearson hairbrush is on the dressing table. When I look at it carefully I see it contains two strands of her fine white hair. In the drawer is a lipstick, the shape worn blunt. I wonder, if I press it to my mouth, would it be redolent of a ghostly maternal kiss? I touch the pot of Ponds, which each night she rubbed into her face in a circular motion. If I open the lid and inhale, her cheek is before me again, tilted to be kissed goodnight, my lips then tacky with the surfeit of cream.

In her dressing room there are things she hasn't worn for years. A wide-brimmed hat, worn to go to the rowing at Henley, decorated with a midnight blue feather which trembles at my touch. Cream silk opera gloves, mother-of-pearl buttons to the elbow. A corset, tiny, made with whale-bone stays. A thick rope of pearls with a pavé diamond clasp. A woollen twinset the colour of windswept heather, with the elbow darned.

My mother has not gone. It is not just her possessions which remain; her rules and routine still hold sway. Clara and I continue to behave as she wishes. We move around the house in familiar, customary patterns, like a tiny dance of bees, meticulously over and over the same ordained shape.

And here is the thing: I have learned not to blame her. It is not her fault that my life seeped out of the soles of my feet into the floor of Rosemount. I realise, especially as I pass the age she was at my disgrace – her early forties, which now seems to me to be impossibly young – that what she did was right by what she knew. In functional terms, a battening down of the hatches, a desire to protect me from further disgrace. The fact that she did not consider that I might be innocent shows a naivety which matched my own. Perhaps she also could not conceive that men might do such things unbidden, her own experience limited to a childhood in India, debutante balls, to my father's shy courtship, to dance cards on wrists, to the jocund flattery of a red-faced Major at a Hunt ball.

I am glad I understood this before she began to ail, so that I sat beside her with compassion as I had done for so many others. I came to see that it was not only love and years of shared domestic routine which bound us but also that night which held us together in a complex connection. We moved through Rosemount in the years that followed like a soft swirl of dust.

I think I also learned to accept that it was not her intention to find me so provocative. In the years preceding the birth, my disposition simply baffled her. And so I forgave her for being incensed that as a child I ate honey directly from the jar with a spoon, that I climbed the apple tree in my best tartan skirt, that I pleaded incessantly for a pair of golden shoes in the hope that if I wore them and danced, it would be as if my feet sparked fire. I recognised that there was a restlessness about me, a beating and a tapping, which for her would not do.

And so through the years I managed to become her daughter. In the face of what I had lost, this is what I achieved. In the years in which I managed to white myself out, I became the daughter she wished for, a pigeon pair with Clara.

Rosemount dilapidated around us, and suddenly she was eighty, and we were sitting in the parlour for tea, Clara slicing an almond tart. We were playing a round of whist, and beyond us the house was cavernous and respectable and silent, the rooms laden with furniture and items which were never used. And it was hard not to turn to her and say, 'Is this what you wanted?' but I feared the answer would be yes and I could not bring myself to hear it. So I ate the almond tart neatly, and I held my hand of cards like a fan before me, and my mother shuffled and dealt, and the shadows fell long until the corners of the room were steeped in twilight and Clara turned on the lamp so that we could see in the darkness.

So now, as I sit on the edge of her empty bed and write in my diary, she is momentarily lying there again; I see and feel her so clearly. The charcoal light of a November afternoon is traced on the wall and I have bolstered her pillows and lifted her into a sitting position. I am spooning food into her mouth, careful that none spills on her nightgown. I take her hands in mine and rub in lavender hand cream, taking care to massage each of her cuticles. I use her hairbrush to brush her hair in soft sweeps to the nape of her neck and dip a flannel in rosewater and hold it to her temples. I fill a hot-water bottle and place it carefully beneath her feet. And she is mostly silent, although I can tell she watches me intently, her eyes retaining their force. We exchange simple pleasantries; we talk of the cardigan that Clara is knitting, of the sharp frost, of the need to wash the eiderdown and dry it on the line in the spring. The skin of her eyelids, as she lies dozing, is almost translucent. Her breathing becomes shallower, more hesitant; I recognise the sound of lungs giving up their pull on the breath. Clara sits with us each afternoon. The sound of her knitting needles punctuates the silence of the room. In the stillest hours of the night, when I hear the clock in the dining room strike one, then two, then three, I begin to wonder if my whole life has been leading up to this moment; if my mother and I have been midwives to each other's protracted forms of dying.

The winter progressed and the nights became cold. Often, I would get into bed beside her and lie with her as she lightly slept. One night in February, she suddenly woke, more alert than she had been for weeks, and asked me to open the curtains. There was a cold hard frost on the pavement outside, and the car windscreens were glinting in the pale white of the moon. A cat yowled by the lamp post, and a man, staggering a little from drink, his voice persistent and mournful, sang 'Come Home to Me Kathleen'. She pushed back the bedcovers and walked slowly over to where I stood by the window, and we looked, the pair of us, at the stretch of pavement between the third and fourth lamp post. I thought she was going to say something but she was just watching intently. She bit at her lip and the silence looped between us. I could bear it no longer.

'Are you remembering the aspens, the lake, the driveway? Remember how the trees used to whisper?'

She did not meet my eye.

'No, not that,' she said, and turned to shuffle back to bed. We did not mention it again. She asked me to re-draw the curtains and she turned her face from me.

In the last days of her life, her left side was numbed by a stroke. Clara and I lifted and turned her, and washed her to keep her skin comfortable. The side of her mouth was drooping and her left hand lay limp on the covers. I was holding a glass with a straw to her lips and encouraging her to drink. I smoothed the hair away from her forehead, and she suddenly placed her right hand on mine. I could see her struggling for mastery of her mouth.

'You are a good girl, Hermione,' she said.

As I write this, I realise, for the very first time, that it is something I had to wait almost a lifetime to hear.

37

Max

After I told Minnie about the football, she showed me how she knows so much about all the antiques. We went through the catalogues her great uncle wrote. Page after page of writing, with each thing described. Then she said I could choose some descriptions and we could go and find where they were in the house. It felt like a treasure hunt, up and down through Rosemount, looking and looking until we spotted what I'd chosen. Minnie knows where everything is; I think Clara does too. She was in the kitchen making tea and she looked up, almost smiling, and said, 'Maybe try for that one by the sewing room on the upper landing.'

In the scullery cupboard we found the silver two-handled tray by William Hutton and Sons Sheffield, 1911, *with a bead and scroll border*, and along the corridor to the attic rooms, just where Clara said, the mahogany chest *in the George II style on moulded bracket feet*. We finally found in a drawer in Minnie's mother's bedroom the *English porcelain navette-shaped perfume bottle from 1815*, which has landscapes painted on the sides. I opened the top and it smelt of old roses. Minnie sniffed it, paused and said, yes, that was how her mother smelt.

In her father's study, we found a *nine carat stock pin*, and a *George II mahogany concertina action card table*. Minnie opened it and inside was a yellowy pack of cards. She asked me if I knew gin rummy.

I do now. Here's the detail:

It's a card game invented in 1909 in America. There are just the two of you, and you're meant to reach one hundred points before the other person does. You have ten cards each, and have to form these things called melds, and *eliminate dead wood*. There are two types of meld; sets and runs. If you want to really throw down some sparks, you say you are going gin.

Here's the surprise. Minnie can shuffle the cards really fast and cleanly. Literally like someone on a TV programme about Las Vegas. I asked her where she learned to do that. 'Practising right at this table, about your age,' she said. 'I think at that time I'd decided I was going to grow up and work in a casino in Monte Carlo, and wear a costume made of scarlet sequins and a long white feather in my hair. Also, I think,' and she touched her ear with her finger, 'if I remember rightly, eardrops made of emeralds and diamonds as big as acorns.' She smiled at the thought. I told her she would have looked very sparkling. We played gin rummy with the cards face up, and when I'd got the hang of it, we played it for real. Turns out we mostly alternated in turns to win, and she told me some more things from when she was a child. She wanted to have a pet monkey on a turquoise collar and lead, and she wanted to run away to the circus and live in a caravan with its very own stove and chimney. She laughed when she told me, and I think the sound of herself laughing maybe surprised her, because she put her hand on her throat and her eyes widened as if she'd shocked herself. Clara came to the doorway with her tapestry frame in her hand, as if she thought the sound of Minnie laughing might make the roof fall in.

And then, when we'd finished playing gin rummy, we were back in the morning room and over the road I could see my mum and him. I think they were practising their tango because they were dancing towards the window, and then he twirled her around and she bent back over his arm, and then she was laughing and laughing and he scooped her up so that her feet must have been off the floor. A big tear rolled down my cheek, which was actually unexpected, and plopped right down onto the wooden arm of the chair. Minnie reached across and put her hand over mine, and I said, even though she hadn't asked, 'I'm happy that she's happy, it's just that he's not kind to me. And before him, when I thought she was also happy, maybe, it turns out now, she actually never was.'

Minnie said nothing for a little while, until my tears had stopped plopping on the chair arm, and then she said, 'There are all kinds of ways to be happy, and as many ways to be sad, and sometimes you have to think very carefully to understand why you feel as you do.'

I asked her if that was what her diary was about, and whether she was working out why she felt as she did.

She didn't speak for even longer, and she turned her face away from me, and I wasn't sure if maybe she was joining in with my crying and finally she said, 'I think so. I think I am writing about something that happened in order to understand it more clearly. I am not sure I am telling it to myself to be anywhere different or better, I think perhaps just to have said it all, finally, once and for all. Is it the same for your Dictaphone?'

I told her that it started just as a fun thing to do; to be a reporter or a secret agent, to collect everything I noticed. But now, when I play it back to myself in bed at night, I realise it's the story of this summer holiday, and of how everything changed when he came to service the boiler. Fun doesn't really describe it.

'Maybe you should play it to your mum,' she said. 'Maybe her head's been so full of the things that she has been feeling and thinking that she hasn't had time to think how it all might be for you. It's an easy thing to happen.'

I shook my head.

She asked me what I'd do when I got to the end of the tape and I told her I'd probably go right over and start again at the beginning, so that there would be layers and layers of things laid down on it that happened in my house; my mum saying *emery boards, shellac remover,* and then me talking about Jasmine cutting off my hair, and then whatever will happen next, which I'm beginning to think might involve him moving in, and which would mean everything the way it was before being completely gone for good.

Minnie said that maybe I should keep the tape as it is and not talk over it, so that when I am older I can listen to it again and perhaps understand it all differently. 'There's always the possibility of a different point of view, a different way of seeing, even though that may seem impossible to you now. There might be a way of seeing what he does, how he is, differently.'

Her voice was very soft and gentle, and I could hear Clara moving around in the kitchen, and suddenly everything felt very quiet and serious, and it was like Grandad said, as if our ages had leapfrogged and met in the middle. I thought again about her diary, because even though I've no idea what she writes in it, I'm sure we've been doing the very same thing.

'Is that how it is for you?' I asked. 'If you are writing about what happened long ago do you see it differently now that you are old?'

She paused for a moment, then she stood up and smoothed down her skirt and said that parts of it, yes, she understood a little better. But other parts no, she said, they remained the same as they were on the day they happened, and then she walked to the window and looked out over the pavement.

'Will you ever let anyone read it?' I asked her, and she shook her head and said no, and her face looked very sad and it was hard to believe that earlier Clara had come to the door because she was laughing so hard.

'Maybe I'll burn it,' she said, 'when I get to the end. That would appeal to my childhood sense of the dramatic.'

'You could burn it,' I said, 'and imagine yourself wearing your costume of scarlet sequins with the white feather in your hair.'

She smiled, but her face was what I think is called wistful. I've just Googled what that means and it was definitely wistful. Her face had so much regret in it, it looked as if it was crayoned onto her bones.

'This won't do,' she said, giving herself a little shake and moving away from the window. Beyond her, Mum and him were kissing goodbye out on the front step. Someone was walking down from the park carrying a football. It suddenly felt like it had been a very long day.

And now, just as I was about to stop recording, my mum came into my bedroom. She sat on the edge of my bed and she smoothed my hair.

'Did you enjoy today?' she asked, and I nodded because that seemed like the best bedtime version of a thumbs up. 'I was very proud of you,' she said, 'I could see you were trying fit to bust,' and I thought she'd chosen her words very carefully because she didn't admit I was rubbish.

'Wasn't it fun? It's great to spend time all together isn't it?' Her eyes went a bit wider as she said this, which I think is perhaps what happens when you know what is coming out of your mouth is mostly not true. I waited for a moment longer, and I could feel my heart beat getting thumpier. I thought, now's when she tells me that he's going to move in. But she paused for a moment, and then she got up and twitched the curtain a little to make sure it was properly shut, because it was almost ten o'clock, the room was filled with the nearly darkness, and she came back over to me and sat back down on the bed and she kissed my forehead and hugged me for a very long time like she used to when I was little, and I could smell her perfume and her face powder, and I thought of Minnie holding the porcelain bottle to her nose and the smell of her mother being there, even though she has been dead a long time.

And I just said, 'It's complicated isn't it?', because it felt like the most truthful thing to say, and also because lying there, it suddenly seemed like things didn't get any simpler even when you lived to be old like Minnie. She nodded, and tucked my quilt around me and went quietly out of my room.

38

Minnie

Clara is sewing as I write. We are sitting in the drawing room as we often do on warm August nights and we have the French windows open onto what was once the terrace but is now a short stubby piece of ground. Beyond the fence are the sounds of other people's busier, messier lives. Someone is barbecuing, and someone is mowing a lawn, and two voices are quarrelling, and a child is crying, and Clara and I sit, quietly, as we have for years and years.

Clara looks across at what I am doing, and she knows better now than to ask. Her face is pained and increasingly resonant with my mother's austere beauty and the only sound from within the room is the scratching of my pen upon the paper. Around us, all the artefacts Max finds so captivating slip into the shadows of the twilight, leaving two elderly women sitting in a vast house that is full of ghosts and faded grandeur and unspoken sorrows. Clara's hands continue to sew steadily and carefully and I think we are like a pale, sparse wishbone, fused in our endeavour and routine and unable to escape what was dealt to us by a man who behaved with impunity and whose wickedness was then compounded by my own.

As the moon rises and hangs low in the sky, there is something I want to do, something which suddenly, irrationally, comes to me as the one thing which will bring what I am writing to a close, so that just as Max with his Dictaphone will begin to erase his own words, I can stop writing, the purpose of it complete. I will have told how it was, for me, brought things full circle and that will be enough.

Clara puts down her sewing because the light has become too dim. I can feel her eyes upon me and I wonder what it was that I did to deserve her loyalty because now I understand that that is what she has given me, constant through the years. She gets up from her chair, closes the French windows and draws the bolts, and then goes to make our bedtime tea, and as she walks by me I think of reaching out and touching her as she passes. I do not. Instead, I look at the pale-lemon watersilk chair where she always sits; the fabric bears the imprint of her body and the chair tells as much of a story of her as I can.

I hear the kettle begin to whistle on the range, and I know she will reappear with the tea cups on a small, oval, silver tray, and we will drink our tea together and another day will circle to a close.

In the morning I will ask Max to help me with what I want to do.

39

Max

Today has been a very strange day, maybe the strangest ever.

I don't think I understand properly what I saw today. All I know is that it was something important.

On the surface what happened was not spectacular, but I think I can best think about it like something I learned in Geography, which is that under the earth's crust are tectonic plates, and sometimes, as the earth turns in space, the plates move about, and although nothing changes on the surface, beneath it everything is held together differently.

This morning I was eating my toast in front of the television. Mum and him were still upstairs, but because her bedroom is above the kitchen I could hear them talking and laughing and even though I wasn't eavesdropping it felt like I was, so I came into the sitting room and turned on the Test cricket. And I was eating my toast and wondering how the day would turn out because the weather forecast had said it would be sunny but there was drizzle falling and it already felt like back-to-school weather and I still have ten days more holiday.

I looked out of the window to see if the sky was cloudy, and I saw Minnie, out in the street, standing on the pavement between the third and fourth lamp post. I think she may have been standing there quite some time. She was only wearing a cardigan even though it was raining and perhaps she should have been wearing a raincoat because her cardigan was already quite wet. I would not expect Minnie to be someone who'd go out in the rain without a mac. Also she was holding a trowel in her hand, which was weird.

I went over to see her, just dressed in my t-shirt and shorts because they had said it was going to be warm, and I thought they would dry soon enough – faster than Minnie's cardigan anyway. As soon as she saw me she asked me if I would help her with something she needed to do. I could see Clara at the morning room window, and she was standing with her hands pressed to her mouth as if she was upset, but Minnie did not turn to face her, instead she kept looking at me and although her face was all white, and she was biting her lip, she looked very determined.

She gave me the trowel and it was like something Mr McGregor might have had in *Peter Rabbit*. I think the handle was once painted pale blue, but it was worn from years of holding and only the very end still had a scrap of paint. 'This was Hooper's,' Minnie said, 'he looked after the garden when it was at its most beautiful. The handle has been worn smooth by his hands.'

She looked away from me, to the lamp posts and she walked up and back, up and back between them. In the window Clara looked as if she might start to cry, but Minnie just looked as if she were thinking about something really hard. She said nothing for a while, and I just stood there holding the trowel. My first thought was that Hooper must have had very big hands because the place where his thumb must have gone was darker and spaced wide apart, and that made him real to me, his hands as clear as if I could measure them, even though he must have been dead for a very long time. And I was just holding the trowel, standing there, and thinking that was why I liked the antiques because they made people's lives exist again after they were dead, and I waited for Minnie to speak and then she knelt down and smoothed what is left of the browned scuffed grass on the verge, and she said, 'Max, please will you dig here, just here, not deep, just a few inches.'

I didn't answer because I didn't know what the right thing to say would be. I knelt down beside her, and when my body was next to hers it felt like perhaps we were in a church saying our prayers together except without those tapestry cushions which make it softer for your knees, and without me knowing what I was supposed to be praying for. She patted my leg and I gave her the smallest of smiles because I wanted her to know that I was happy to be digging for her, whatever the reason and whatever it was that she was hoping to find. She said, 'You're a good boy, Max, a precious and good boy,' and I remembered when I first saw her and she looked like a religious painting, standing in the red light from the circular window, and I had the same feeling again, as if her words were a blessing. It was like when we go to Church for the school carol service and the Vicar puts his hand on your head at the communion rail and says, 'May God preserve you and keep you,' and you think *That would be nice, I hope so too,* because it makes you feel safe and as if someone is looking out for you which is not always the case.

Someone cycled past us, and a milk float trundled by, and in my house opposite I think my mum and him were still likely upstairs and the Test match would be playing to an empty room and all of it seemed a long way away and misty, whilst the verge and the trowel and Minnie looked extra-real and magnified.

I started to dig and Minnie stayed close by my side and when I looked up I could see Clara was closer to the window, her palm flat to it, and she was watching everything we were doing and I found I was digging and completely holding my breath.

The edge of the trowel made chips into the soil which, even though the drizzle had begun to dampen the top of it, was hard and dusty from all the weeks of fine weather. I dug up a lolly stick, and two pebbles, and I tried to push the soil apart with my other hand but it was pressed down hard from all the years of people walking on it and pushing pushchairs over it, and the drivers – like him – who park their car with two wheels up on the verge so that it doesn't stick so far out into the road.

Minnie picked up the pebbles and the lolly stick, laid them on her palm and turned them over carefully with her fingertip, and she scooped a little more soil away with her hand, and she said, 'No, no, maybe a little more in this direction.'

I started to dig again, and this time the soil was a bit easier to dig in and quite quickly I had a hole that was the size of my fist, and Minnie felt around it, and patted at the edges as if she was making a sandcastle and she shook her head again and pointed to another place a little further along.

This time, there was an old root; it must have been from a long ago plant or bush, and it was twisty and tough, and it still had very small hairs on it which must have once sucked up water, and Minnie tugged it until it came out of the ground all shrivelled and brown, and even though it looked to me like we had found nothing at all, she seemed to be pleased with it, like it was a clue. She tilted her head to one side and looked at the three holes I had dug, and also at the lamp posts, and she turned and looked up at her bedroom window, and then she pointed to another bit of ground and said more firmly than before, 'Here, yes here. I think dig here.'

The rain was starting to fall a little heavier as I began, and my t-shirt was beginning to stick to my back. Minnie's cardigan must have been properly soaked through and I think it is not good for old people to get cold and wet, but she didn't seem to notice. Her hair was damp on her forehead but she was just looking and looking at where I was about to dig and so I began again, and the trowel hit a stone and then another, and I scooped away some earth that was a bit looser and then there it was, the thing she was looking for. I knew this immediately, because she quickly took it from me. She lifted it up, blew the dirt off it and held it out on her hand.

I didn't get it. It was just a tiny doll, like the ones you get on a wedding cake, but simpler than that, like a little peg doll someone very clever at models might make.

It looked like a girl. She was wearing a skirt and a pullover that I think were once painted. Like the handle of the trowel, they had little spots of paint; blue on the skirt and pink on the sweater. The face was blank but there was some brown painted-on hair which looked like it was in a plait. Minnie was turning it over in her hand, as if I'd found something miraculous and finally returned it to her.

She smoothed the soil back into the hole so you almost couldn't tell what we'd done, and then she stood up and asked me to come into Rosemount.

When we went into the hall, Clara was standing there. It felt as if everything around us had turned to glass and that if someone spoke it would all smash into a million pieces, so I just stood beside Minnie, the stillest and the quietest that I have ever been.

Clara and Minnie looked at each other and didn't say anything, and then Clara turned and walked to the music room, and Minnie and I followed her, and she lifted the lid of the piano stool and started looking through the music. Right at the bottom she found a yellowy folded piece of paper, and I could see that it said Bach at the top, and really slowly she put the lid back down on the stool, and sat down and played. The music was beautiful. It was so sad, and it made my heart turn over as the notes climbed and climbed, and Clara played it very slowly, maybe I think because her hands are old and quite stiff, but maybe also because I do not think that she had played this for a very long time. I looked at her and at Minnie's face and I was certain it was music they both already knew.

Minnie was holding the little figure wrapped tight in her hand, and I think Mrs Winters would probably have said that it is a symbol of something, but I didn't want to ask because she was holding it like it was the most precious thing ever. I wondered how many years it had been there for, and when Minnie put it there because I am certain that she did. Clara played the music over and over, and Minnie was crying so I held her hand tight, and I thought again about what my grandad said about old and young people, and I kept on holding it and she held mine right back.

Clara finished playing and stood up and said to Minnie, 'I saw you bury it, out on the street that night. I watched from your window, just as you watched me, and I could not help you, could not make it right.' She came over and kissed her cheek. 'I think you were never to blame; I was just never brave enough to say it and I hope you can forgive me for that. You were a child too.' And then Minnie said: 'There is nothing to forgive.'

She was crying more then and Clara put her hand on my shoulder and I didn't really understand what was happening, but we stood there for ages, completely quiet, the three of us – four of us if you count the tiny figure in Minnie's hand.

40

Minnie

Max has just gone home.

After we walked out of the music room, I went and changed out of my damp clothes and I found an old dress-shirt of my father's for him because his t-shirt was wet. I gave him a pair of cufflinks to match, and Clara said how fine he looked, and that perhaps we ought to eat breakfast in the dining room. I poured milk for him from a silver jug into a crystal glass, and served him bacon and eggs from a William IV silver presentation salver. Clara sat with us and it was the closest to merry I think we have ever been.

I have put the figure – my token – on the mantelpiece in my bedroom. I think I can look at it, now, as my past. Mine and Clara's past, from which we can move forward together and which I have reclaimed on my own terms.

After breakfast, Max sat in the morning room with me and I saw him glance across at his own home. He told me that sometimes now he feels more welcome here than there. I told him that there were many things I wish I had known when I was not much older than him but that most of all I should have spoken out and said what I felt. Miss Potts gave me that opportunity and I did not take it, and so I told Max that he should speak his truth boldly.

41

Max

When I got home, they were sitting in the kitchen and Mum was wearing a fluffy white bathrobe which I think he must have given her as a present, and she had made a big stack of pancakes.

Her first question (and she was standing with her back to me) was whether I'd like some pancakes and I said I'd already had breakfast, and then she turned and looked at me properly and asked, 'Where did you get that shirt from?', quickly followed by, 'What have you been doing? Where have you been?' The answer to the second part of that would have been complicated because I don't exactly know what I'd been doing and it was difficult to find a place to begin so I told her that Minnie had lent it to me because mine was wet, and that we'd been looking at Rosemount antiques like we usually did. The first part was true and the last part was sort of true because the tiny figure looked old. It felt like a decent answer.

He chipped in with, 'It's a bit weird isn't it, hanging out with some old lady looking at antiques,' and what he said didn't make me angry, it made me calm, which was a bit unexpected, although the whole day had been unexpected so far. I pulled myself up as tall as I could, which felt taller because of the shirt, mainly because the collar made me hold my neck very straight which says a lot about old-fashioned clothes, and I said to him, 'It's not weird at all, I'm learning a lot, and Minnie's really interesting,' and he rolled his eyes and said, 'But not anything that's actually likely to be useful in your real life.' And I remembered what Minnie said about the fact that you should speak up for yourself even if you're a child and I thought about how she'd spent her whole life in what looked like one big regret for not saying something or not telling, and it suddenly seemed a really sad waste of all that time and all the things she might have done instead, the card-dealing, the circus, the scarlet-sequinned dress, and I looked at him and decided right there in the kitchen that I wouldn't let him mess with me and how I felt about myself, or about home, and my mum, and everything we did together up to when he first came to service the boiler. I stopped looking at his silly tattoo and instead I looked him right in the eyes and all the time I was speaking I was also thinking of Minnie who had led a life that was much quieter, and mostly spent at Rosemount, which seemed a waste, especially when she could deal cards super-fast like that.

So this is what I said. His mouth was wide open from beginning to end.

1. You don't know what's going to be useful in my life. You work with boilers and all the words that belong to being a boiler engineer, and I know what I'm going to be interested in – antiques – and you may not think it's interesting but I do and you have no right to try and make what I like sound silly.

2. You might love my mum, and from what it looks like to me, you make her happy. I'm glad you make her happy. I think she likes doing lots of things with you but you shouldn't rubbish me, because she was happy before you too, just a different kind of happy and you should be kind about it.

3. I live here too, and this is my home as well, and as you can't just kill me like a lion cub or a dolphin or a

chimpanzee, you have to find a way to be nice to me and to do things with me without having to always prove that you're better or bigger or stronger because you obviously are but you won't always be and if you stay with my mum for a long time I will be all of those things one day more than you, so it would be better if you would be kind from the start and I will be too. Fair's fair.

The kitchen was completely silent for a minute and then I saw my mum was crying which made me feel bad, but then she got up and kissed me and said, 'I'm sorry, truly sorry. I've been thoughtless and only thinking about me and I understand now how it all looked to you, and I can't believe you just said all that so clearly and fairly, and it feels like you've been the most grown up of the three of us.'

He stood up from his chair and it was hard to tell from his face what he was going to do. He blinked a bit, and rubbed at his chin and I thought for a minute he might walk off out of the door which would have been the wrong kind of choosing, but instead he took a step forward and he put his hand out to me, and I put mine out (third time in my life) and he shook it, slowly and for a long time, with his other hand also completely containing mine and he said, 'Max mate, I'm sorry, I've been an idiot, I'm not sure what I was trying to be, but I can see now how it looked. Let's start over, I'll make a better job of it; you and your mum are worth it.'

My mum cried some more, and then she said she'd make some tea, and he said maybe we could all watch the cricket for a bit, which we did, and it was better because he actually knows something about cricket and he explained some of the fielding positions to me, and Mum sat in her new white dressing gown with her mug of tea. When the players went off the field because rain stopped play, she turned and said to me, 'I get all of it, everything you said and felt, but the lion and the chimp and the dolphin . . . what's that about?' and we laughed, the three of us, and it felt cosy, for the first time, with the rain falling softly outside. I looked across the road and the morning room was empty and I hoped Minnie and Clara were snug in the parlour, with the little figure, like a good-luck charm, making everything come right.

42

Minnie

This morning, in bright sunshine, I have woken and walked the length and breadth of Rosemount. I began on the upper landing, in each of the attic rooms. I opened a drawer and out flew a flutter of moths from someone's sweater. My grandfather's? Leonard's? Beneath one of the beds I found an empty pigskin trunk, and a canvas suitcase painted with my mother's name. I found an enamel chamber pot, and a small, red felt sewing kit in a drawer, and in a wardrobe, tucked at the back, an embroidered panel of a saint, standing on a serpent with Jesus in heaven above him. It is worked in silk and gold thread and edged with seed pearls. I do not think Leonard knew of this – maybe it is not ours. I remember an Irish maid from when I was very small, who showed me her rosary and taught me Hail Mary. Perhaps this was her room. I went into my mother's sewing room, where her old black Singer sewing machine stands watch at the table. I turned the handle and watched the needle dip and rise. In a drawer I found, wrapped in tissue and brown paper, the christening gown both Clara and I wore. The silk rustled at my touch. I found a tin of buttons, thick leather ones which I think must have been from my father's cardigans and waistcoats. I went into the nursery where Clara's doll's house is still beneath the window. I lifted the brass latch to open it, and it was as I remembered: the fender in front of the fire, the miniature mirror on the wardrobe door, a coverlet for the bed made from raspberry damask. On the table, a tiny tea set, the cups the size of peppercorns. I closed it carefully and went to stand by the lemon-drop curtains. The rocking horse eyed me warily, its dappled grey coat faded to a series of smudges. In the pantry I looked at silver sugar bowls, sets of tea spoons, a silver-gilt pair of grape scissors. I stopped and looked at each of the paintings on the walls, pausing before one of cattle watering in a river, of which I have always been fond. I went to the satinwood linen press and looked at the piles of folded sheets. It is years since many of them have been anywhere near a bed. In the corner hangs a faded lavender sachet. The lavender would be from the garden; I think that Hooper would have cut and dried it. I went into bedrooms and opened mahogany and ebonised wardrobes, and rosewood banded ones, and satinbirch chests. I found a collection of Malacca canes with white metal tops. In the dining room I opened the lowest drawer of the walnut and elm commode, and I found, tucked at the back, a receipt from Harrods for £325 dated January 1914. I stood in the drawing room, finally, and looked at the George II mahogany china display cabinet, and a Chinese blue and white baluster vase, and the mahogany wheel barometer and a Copeland stick stand, and all of it weighed so very heavily in my hands and my heart, and I went to find Clara who was sitting in the kitchen, having tea.

'You have been busy,' she said, 'I have heard you all about the house. What are you doing?'

'Just looking; just looking at the weight and substance of it all.'

And then I sat beside her and took her hand in mine, and I said, 'What if, Clara, what if we decided to sell everything, to have an auction of the contents of the house, and then to sell Rosemount itself? After all these years of living here within its walls, maybe we can use the money to buy somewhere small and manageable which isn't crumbling down around us and which doesn't need endless dusting and cleaning and polishing and then we can finally live a different sort of life.'

Clara looked at me as if I had suggested we might fly to the moon. It has evidently never occurred to her.

She smiled slowly. 'I might have guessed that your boldness would come back. But isn't it too late? Not for you to feel different but for us to walk away from all this? I thought we would die here, in whatever order it happened.'

I told her that was a horrible thought. She looked at the expanse of the kitchen around us, her gaze taking in the row of copper pans that hang above us, and I told her it isn't too late, it isn't too late at all, because I was suddenly certain that it was the right thing to do.

There is one Yellow Pages remaining which we did not burn on the fire last winter. We searched through it until we found what we were looking for. I phoned an auctioneers, who arranged to send someone to see us, and then an estate agents, who said yes, yes, they knew the house and would very much like to come and value it. Clara looked at me wide-eyed as I made the arrangements.

When I put the phone down, we sat and gazed at each other across the table, as if we could not believe I had the temerity to do what I had just done.

I went to my bedroom, and sat on the edge of the bed. I closed my eyes for a moment and had a clear memory of swimming in the lake as a child; of diving to its depths and then turning up towards the surface. I remembered the feeling of my body pointed towards the light, and of the surface of the water breaking clean across my skin, so that my hair was pressed smooth and sleek to my scalp, and I remembered feeling so stream-lined, so light, like an arrow ascending, and I felt like it again, as I stood to go downstairs, as if I will fly free of everything that is Rosemount and my past.

When Max came over for tea, I told him of our plan. I told him he can help arrange the whole auction with me. He was brim-full of his own news; he has stood up for himself. I hugged him. I think he is also the catalyst for my own redemption.

43

Max

If you've spent the summer holidays realising you want to be an auctioneer when you grow up, it's absolutely the best thing ever if your friend decides to auction the entire contents of her house, and you get to watch the whole thing happening.

First the valuers arrive. They go in every cupboard, every wardrobe, every drawer. They take pictures on their iPhones and send them back to the office to confirm a date or a price. They hold things out and say 'Wow, look at this,' or 'I haven't seen one of these for years,' or 'Look at the mint condition of this.' They use Leonard's catalogues and match everything the same way Minnie and I did on our treasure hunt. Turns out he saved them a lot of time. I would like him to have known this; that would have given him a kick. I looked at the woman who was matching the receipts to the items and scanning them on her iPad, and I thought that Leonard could not ever have imagined this. But the thing I like best is that for all the in-between time, the antiques are the same and still beautiful and still useful for what they were made for, and I told Minnie this and she told the auctioneer and he said he'd better watch out for his job because I will be after it shortly.

Up in the attic they found lots of clothes in old canvas trunks. There were shooting clothes which belonged to Minnie's grandfather, tweed jackets and 'breeks', which means trousers, and one jacket with a silk lining that is still really bright blue like the sky. There was a dress that was her grandmother's, all stitched with seed pearls, and another one that they said was from the 1920s which was all heavy around the hem because it was weighted to make it better for dancing. Minnie and Clara decided that it must have belonged to their mother, and Minnie held it up by the tiny thin straps and told me she could hardly imagine her mother dancing, but that she liked the thought of it. I told her mine seems to be dancing most of the time.

The valuers looked at items with magnifying glasses and put them all in pairs and sets and gave them lot numbers. All the china got washed in the copper sink in the scullery. They told me sinks for washing china were made of copper because it is softer and so there was less chance of porcelain getting chipped.

Now I spend every day at Rosemount watching them value it all. It's like all the doors and windows are wide open and there's a fresh breeze blowing through. The people arrive in the morning and they carry paper coffee cups, and thermos flasks, and lunch from Pret or Itsu, or sandwiches in brown bags and Tupperwares. Minnie and Clara let them put it all in the big fridge in the pantry, and at lunchtime they sit on the small patch of grass outside the drawing room, and usually Minnie and Clara have their lunch in the parlour and watch them through the window. They look a bit shy as if they can't believe it is all happening around them.

Photographers came and put lights in the dining room and covered the table with a cloth and started taking pictures, and someone stood there with a polishing cloth making sure all the items looked their best.

They've printed a catalogue and it's called *The Contents of Rosemount House: Pictures, Ceramics, Silver, Clothing, Works of Art and Furniture. September 30th, 2014.* It's like what Leonard wrote, but with even more detail. I'm now going to read out a bit of it, so that what I'm saying is an accurate record:

> *James Stuart Park (British 1862-1933) roses, oil on canvas; Manner of Melchior d'Hondecoeter* – I'm not sure I've said that right – *circa 1800, a cockerel with two pigeons in an open landscape, oil on canvas; A late nineteenth-century, Worcester part dessert service, painted with botanical specimens on a pale celadon ground, comprising four various comports and sixteen plates; A late nineteenth-century porcelain vase, of lidded baluster form, encrusted with flowers; Five Victorian cranberry glasses with clear wrythen glass handles; Victorian silver rose bowl, Sheffield 1890, with swag decoration and gadrooned base.*

How cool is all that. I love all the words and one day I'm going to know them properly myself.

On the morning of the auction my mum came over early with me to Rosemount, and she did Minnie's and Clara's hair so they'd look their best when all the buyers arrived. She put foundation on them, which was a first for them both, and then a bit of blusher. Minnie sat there, her eyes all bright, while my mum made her look lovely, and I could see how she would have looked when she was young and wanted to run away with the circus.

Mum and Tony looked at everything arranged for the viewing, and Tony said, 'Very impressive,' and patted me on the shoulder, and then he said, 'I can see this is quite a line of business,' and I smiled because I can see that he is trying, and he's called a truce on all the other stuff, and we're learning to live in a triangle shape that includes me too.

So this is the last thing I'm taping. After this, I'm putting the

Dictaphone in the drawer. One day maybe I'll listen back to it, and remember the summer of 2014 and how it was for me.

Here's the best bit to finish with:

1. The auctioneer let me bang his hammer after some of the lots.
2. Minnie let me choose three things to keep and I'm looking at them right now: the Meissen monkeys, the hunting horn and the pineapple stands which were the first things she ever showed me.
3. Grandad was right. Inside every old person, there's their young self right there.

So that's me, all set for big school. Over and out.

44

Minnie

This will be my last entry.

The auction was a huge success and Rosemount is sold. It is to be a healthcare centre for the community. It will be busy anew, which is a happy thought.

Clara and I have bought a house on the old village green, across from the pear tree and the farmhouse I knew as a child.

We are adjusting to our new life. It turns out there are actually walking boots which dry almost as soon as they are wet, and I have bought some, and joined the Ramblers, which Clara jokes is a step in the right direction.

Max calls in on his way home from his new school and we play gin rummy or talk. His mother is marrying Tony, and Max says he is ready for them to be properly dads and lads.

And here is what I have learned, in this summer in which every-thing has changed. In my book from the library this week, George Eliot says 'it is never too late to become what you might have been'.

As I sit at my window, gazing out at the clear light of a beautiful September, I have decided she is right, and that my time is now.

Acknowledgements

Thanks to:

Charlie Thomas, Director of the House Sale and Private Collections Department at Bonhams, London for helping me with antiques with back stories. Some of the contents of Rosemount also have a cheeky debt to the contents of Trelissick House, Cornwall. All errors, inaccuracies, and embellishments are obviously my own.

Coram, and The Foundling Hospital. The tokens Minnie learns about are part of their collection, and testament to their dedicated, centuries-long work on behalf of mothers, children and social justice.

The team at Hodder and Stoughton. Suzie Dooré is brilliant at the precise, intuitive, alchemy of editing. Sara Kinsella's fresh eyes and dynamism have contributed greatly to its final form. I am indebted to them both. Auriol Bishop gifted me the title, for which many thanks. Francine Toon and Sharan Matharu shepherded it through from manuscript to publication with efficiency and grace.

My agents Helenka Fuglewicz and Ros Edwards – long standing allies.

The Way Back to Us

Kay Langdale

Coming August 2017

Since their youngest son, Teddy, was diagnosed with a life-defining illness, Anna has been fighting: against the friends who don't know how to help; against the team assigned to Teddy's care who constantly watch over Anna's parenting; against the school who refuse to let Teddy start until special mobility specifications have been met; and against the impulse to put Teddy above all else – including his older brother, the watchful, sensitive Isaac.

And now Anna can't seem to stop fighting against her husband, the one person who should be able to understand, but who somehow manages to carry on when Anna feels like she is suffocating under the weight of all the things that Teddy will never be able to do.

As Anna helplessly pushes Tom away, he can't help but feel the absence of the simple familiarity that should come so easily, and must face the question: is it worse to stay in an unhappy marriage, or leave?

Read on for an extract . . .

Anna

I wake abruptly with a terrible start, because it feels like I'm holding something very, very precious, and I've dropped it. When I snap my eyes open, heart thumping, it's always just fallen from my arms. It's Teddy I'm dropping, even though I never actually have. In my half-waking, half-sleeping state I see it happen, as if I am both in and out of my thrumming body.

Teddy's still a baby in the dream, and he's wearing a striped red-and-white romper. My right hand is cradling his head, and my left hand is curled up and over his knees. Looking at us – and I can see that my crossed elbows are an additional hammock beneath him – dropping him couldn't feasibly happen, but it's always the sensation I have, my mouth parched, my arms flailing.

The babygro – the red-and-white-striped one – is an accurate memory. I'm confident of that. I must still have it, neatly folded in a cupboard somewhere. We're not by ourselves in the dream. The health visitor who was assigned to Teddy is there too, a woman who yawned constantly, her hand barely covering her mouth, her broad face placid and bovine. Perhaps she was bored, or tired, or maybe in need of more oxygen than the series of rooms provided.

The sequence begins as I put him in the scale pan, and he lies there, soft as butter, wearing a cotton-knit hat shaped like a strawberry. The hat accentuates the colour of his lips, and his tiny Cupid's bow, and I resist stretching across to kiss him because I know it would get in the way of the weighing, the measuring, the calibrating, and the jotting in the red book with her cheap biro that smudges. And so, while the health visitor writes, I am self-contained, sitting with my hands in my lap, my back straight, surreptitiously checking my watch, and with just the beginnings of a sprightly fretfulness that Isaac will shortly finish school and I will not be at the playground gate.

The health visitor looks at her notes and her tick-box charts, and gestures to indicate that I can pick Teddy up again, and as I lean to gather him to me, that's where the accurate recall stops. Instead, there's the chest-punching horror that I've dropped him, my arms flung inexplicably wide, my palms facing ceilingward. When I look down to where he should surely be falling towards my feet, I can't see him there either. There is nothing other than a dizzying blackness that tilts and shifts around me, as if we are in fact both tumbling in free fall, our arms and legs spread wide like stars, with Teddy invisible beyond my reach, cartwheeling down through space.

If I look over my shoulder – and the room is shrinking behind me and is suddenly bleached of all colour – the health visitor is still sitting plumply by her scale pan, her pen poised in mid-air. Her expression doesn't change, however many times I dream it. She is not startled, or concerned. She doesn't even drop her pen. What her face mostly shows is disappointment. She is clearly disappointed in my failure to scoop up Teddy properly.

Tom

Is it Eliza? It takes a moment, looking through the smoked grey glass of the hotel in Geneva, to confirm that it is. Her swimming costume is red; a red so bright she is as vivid as a scarlet poppy when she walks out from the changing room. The colour is unexpected, almost startling. Her work clothes are usually muted – neutrals and greys, and sometimes a blue that is almost black. Occasionally her lips are red; the only clue that would suggest her choice of swimming costume. When they are, I find it hard to look directly at her as she speaks, instead focusing on her temple, or her hairline, or the space beyond her. She wears blouses that are cleverly tailored and which have neat little tucks and seams and move entirely with her. A seamstress would understand the mechanics of that. I do not, but recognise that they are pieces she must have chosen with care and insight.

Eliza walks to the poolside shower, tilts back her head, and momentarily lets the water drench her. She shivers as it touches her skin. The act of observing her, even though in a public place, seems an intrusion. She pauses momentarily by the deep end of the pool and leans to look out of the window at the street below. The snow, which began thawing earlier, has continued to do so, and the pavement is slushy with gritty melt. It is much warmer than yesterday; unseasonably so. She won't need to wear the coat with the high lambskin collar that she wore on the way from the airport.

From her cupped palm Eliza produces goggles, which she

snaps on with a surprisingly practised hand, licking her fingertip and quickly tracing the lens. She blows out through her lips, rises to her tiptoes, lifts her arms above her head and stretches.

Anna and the boys look up at me from my iPhone screen saver. Isaac is standing next to Anna in the garden, his hands held behind him like a soldier standing to attention. I look at the photo fixedly to navigate myself back to them. Anna is smiling, but – seeing her freshly in the clean Swiss light of this calm and neat breakfast room – it occurs to me that it is a grim, stoical smile, which ends at the corners of her lips and is firmly staunched by the clamped press of her jaw. Teddy is on her lap, his head spooled back on her collarbone.

Time for a quick chat?

Her response is instant.

What do you think?

Perhaps I should send an emoji with a downturned mouth and a question mark beside it. Perhaps then she would respond. Likely it is just one of those mornings and she is best left alone. She has said, many times, 'Just let me get on.'

My gaze is drawn again to Eliza, who dips her chin to her chest and dives in. Without pause, she begins to swim an efficient crawl, her hands meeting momentarily at the front of her reach so that she seems to spear effortlessly between strokes. Her body skates through the water.

I should text my assistant and confirm the time of today's flight back from Geneva. The 10 a.m. meeting should not overrun; most of what was required was successfully completed yesterday. Eliza, at the boardroom table, going through the PowerPoint presentation, her grey eyes fixed purposefully on the client. I make the image of her dissolve, as if it is occluded by blotches of snow.

The waitress appears with the breakfast menu which is loaded with waffles, pancakes, Viennoiserie.

'Just an Americano, please.'

Am I only a heartbeat away from sitting here old and unfit, instead of forty-two and in reasonable shape? The other guests at the hotel are mostly the former. Perhaps the pool was built next to the breakfast room as a kind of subliminal taunt.

Eliza is still swimming, completing each length with a neat turn, her hand outstretched to touch the pool wall.

I'm reading a newspaper when she arrives beside me, dressed in a skirt that is possibly blue, possibly grey; it is hard to call it. She has on a jacket cut exactly to the curve of her body, which is somehow clearer to me now that I have seen her in her swimsuit. The waitress appears again.

'A flat white and some bircher muesli, please.'

Eliza's hair looks perfectly dry and is secured into some kind of chignon with a curved pin that has a small flurry of seed pearls at its tip. It's only when she reaches forward to return the menu to the waitress that it becomes visible: one small, damp curl stuck to the palest skin at the side of her neck, just behind and below her ear. I turn away, guilty with the noticing.

Anna

I've lost count of the times I've said, 'Don't text first thing.' It's not that I don't understand the inclination; can't remember perfectly, in fact, the impulse to do so: arriving early for a meeting, grabbing a coffee in a café, or sitting in a bland hotel lobby waiting for a taxi; the reflex to touch base, to check in, to report back.

Not now, though. The possibility of silence, first thing, is something to be safeguarded, like a small rectangle of lustrous matt whiteness snipped from a paint chart and held carefully in my palm. A window of opportunity, even though my use of it is increasingly questionable. Cleaning. Sanitising. Scrubbing at nooks and crannies in the kitchen with my lips pursed before the day has even begun. Who would have guessed that my grip on a mop could be so accustomed, so adroit? I think habits can be tracked back to their source, like long twisty rivers, or birds that have made complex migratory flights. All of this – all of what I begin each weekday with – flows back to a junior doctor, her hair held high in a swinging ponytail, who examined Teddy when he was in hospital for a chest infection last winter. She washed her hands at length, meticulously soaping between her fingers, the mechanised procedure still freshly learned. 'It's amazing quite how much infection can be prevented if people wash their hands regularly and thoroughly. Cleanliness makes a real difference to children like Teddy and their level of exposure to risk.'

Bullseye. Thoughts gain traction and heft, and now I sanitise all the kitchen surfaces, even though I can't rationally say what contamination I think happens during the night. Flies do not drop from the ceiling; cats do not pad in through the letter box; germs surely don't sally forth from the sink.

I repeatedly scrub my hands like the doctor did, so much so that the skin between my fingers is cracked and sore. If I stretch my hands wide it flashes at me like small, cross-hatched ensigns. At the table with Tom I keep my fingers pressed together, as if they are contained in invisible mesh mittens. On my phone I have googled the definition of 'open-handed'; it means *giving freely*, or *generous*. Perhaps now I don't qualify as either of these; instead I am a woman with a masterful grasp of a mop, who wrings it out into a second bucket so that the original water is not sullied with dirt.

Isaac will appear in a moment. For a child of almost ten, he is unusually obedient to his alarm. ('Snooze button? Lose button,' he said once. 'Why would anyone want one of those?') He will tiptoe into the kitchen, trying his best to avoid the patches that are not yet completely dry, and pick up the bowl of cereal I have put out for him on the counter. He will sit on the stool and hold his legs bent at ninety degrees so that I can swoosh past him more easily. He pours the milk carefully and makes sure not to spill it on the clean surface. I should tell him that I am grateful for this; for this gesture of allegiance, of tacit support. *I get it*, his body language seems to say, his elbow suspended at a right angle above the worktop.

Most mornings there is just the sound of him eating his cereal, and the clink of his mug of milk as he puts it down. I worry that his almost-silence is because I give the impression of listening for something else, a sound that will come from just beyond us and which I might miss if I don't give it my full attention. Only yesterday, I shushed him mid-sentence and then waited in the hiatus for the sound of Teddy stirring, while Isaac held the cereal spoon midway to his mouth like someone caught in the shutter of a camera frame. Perhaps this is why we start each weekday in the kitchen in what I'd prefer to think of as companionable silence – my elder son eating, me mopping and wiping, the street lights blinking off outside as the daylight increases.

Even now, as I empty the bucket into the sink, my head is cocked like a gun primed to smoke blue. I knead the side of my neck with my fingertips, aware of a tightness that tracks to my left ear. It is constantly tilted upwards, as if a particular sound will be poured into it abruptly, like water from a jug. Teddy frequently wakes with a coughing fit and can be promptly sick. On these days it is not just the bottom sheet but all the bed linen that needs changing.

Weekends are not like this. The cleaning and sanitising does not happen when Tom is sitting here, reading the papers, a coffee in his hand, filling the kitchen with his solid certainty; the length of his femur, his hand span, making me feel that germs are surely vanquished. If he saw me doing this, he would look at me, baffled. When I used to have a cleaner, I saw her wiping the side with the same cloth she'd just used for the floor. I told her – white-lipped – that from now on I didn't want her to touch the kitchen. She looked at me sideways with a flintiness in her expression that suggested detached, dispassionate evaluation. *See how you'd deal with it*, I wanted to say to her. I fired her shortly afterwards, relieved to be free of another set of eyes scrutinising me, and at the same time wondering how I became a person who might audibly crackle with internally generated bolts of lightning.

I take down Isaac's jacket from the peg in the hallway and put it next to his school bag. At least it isn't raining. The guilt is worse on wet mornings, when he goes off by himself, his feet nimbly hopscotching the puddles. He has walked to school alone for almost a year. I comfort myself with the fact that it's only a short distance and there are no unsupervised roads to cross.

Getting Teddy up and ready to accompany him brought its own kind of chaos: Teddy wailing because he wanted breakfast and there wasn't time to feed it to him; or often a coughing fit that would bring everything to a halt, all the time Isaac standing patiently next to the front door, tapping his book bag against his knees.

One morning, as I knelt on the hallway floor zipping Teddy into his snowsuit,

'Why don't I walk by myself? It's no trouble. It's not like I don't know the way.'

No trouble. I could print that on a T-shirt and give it to him to wear; Isaac with his quick, dark, watchful eyes, which I suspect probably see more than most.

Now, he comes down the stairs, tugging his sweatshirt into place, and I step forward to wrap my arms around him in a hug.

'You are such a star.'

Is it surprise that he is registering? He gives a quick smile.

After he has cleaned his teeth, he walks off down the path. I sit on the bottom stair with a cup of coffee on the tread beside me. Perhaps Tom is still wherever he texted from earlier. Half an hour has passed. It's more likely he will have left for a meeting and already be busy. My reply would anyway be stringy and lumpen, and a kind of withholding. I see that clearly.

Teddy has an appointment with the musculoskeletal team this morning. It's better that he sleeps; better that he is his best possible, strongest, straightest self.

The sound of a blackbird filters through from the cherry tree beyond the porch. Last week, there was a robin perilously close to the open casement. When I was a child, a great-aunt told me that a bird coming into the house is a foreteller of a death. This is why I am a woman who flaps her arms, panic-struck, to shoo away bold fledglings that alight on a sill. This is why I crane my neck, now, to make sure the blackbird is tucked in the tree and not actually inside the porch. My great-aunt's superstition is like a sticky cobweb; I would like to brush it away and feel my skin smooth and clean.

And then, there it is; a small, yawny mewl. Teddy. Awake. I scramble to my feet, the coffee untouched where it sits on the tread.

Do you wish this wasn't the end?

Join us at www.hodder.co.uk, or follow us on
Twitter @hodderbooks to be a part of our community
of people who love the very best in books and reading.

Whether you want to discover more about a book
or an author, watch trailers and interviews, have the
chance to win early limited editions, or simply browse
our expert readers' selection of the very best books,
we think you'll find what you're looking for.

And if you don't,
that's the place to tell us what's missing.

We love what we do, and we'd love you to be part of it.

www.hodder.co.uk

@hodderbooks

HodderBooks

HodderBooks